Books By
Misha McKenzie

Burke Witches
Aria's Law
Anna's Knight
Evan's Pride
Ethan's Honor

The Magic of the Heart Series
Magic Found
Magic Hidden
Magic Lost
Magic Revealed

Lost Creek Shifters
Tawny Justice

Single Titles
RavenStorm Witches

Endangered
The Lost Creek Shifters

Misha McKenzie

ICASM PRESS
SAVANNAH

Published by Icasm Publishing LLC
5710 Ogeechee Rd. Suite 200 #278, Savannah, GA 31405
www.icasmpress.com

Library of Congress Cataloging-in-Publication Data

McKenzie, Misha
Endangered / Misha McKenzie
    p. cm.

ISBN-13:978-1-942318-53-8 (Trade Print)
ISBN-13:978-1-942318-54-5 (eBook)
I. Title

Printed and bound in the United States of America

10 9 8 7 6 5 4 3 2 1

1

Bri couldn't sleep.

She rolled to her side and lay in the near pitch-dark of the room she shared with her daughter. There was just enough moonlight coming through the sheer-covered windows for her to see Min's sleeping form on the toddler bed in the corner. As she watched her little girl dream of fairies and princesses, love filled her almost to bursting.

If anyone had told her a year ago that she would find this astonishingly deep level of love for a child, she would have told them they didn't know her very well.

Never in her life had she envisioned having children. Being an only child, Bri hadn't grown up around other kids and didn't really know the first thing about them.

She apparently had that in common with her parents. Although she loved them dearly, and they loved her, they hadn't had any idea how to raise a child, so Bri had been brought up mostly under the care of nannies.

Her parents were the ultimate social sort. They'd been more interested in maintaining their rich, carefree lifestyle, jet-setting all over the world to hob-nob with names they could drop into just about every conversation they had.

Once she was four and deemed old enough to tag along, they'd carted her with them—with nanny and tutor in tow, of course. Bri disliked the constant festivities and thought it frivolous, but she'd learned to play along and act accordingly.

Her parents' love of travel was so extensive that by the time she'd reached ten years old, she'd already been to eight different countries and had had countless private instructors. And that's when they'd come back to the United States and bought a house just outside of Anaconda, Montana. To this day, she still had no idea why they'd chosen this area, so far from the hustle and bustle of the fast lane, but they had, and they hadn't moved again until after she'd graduated from high school.

Having always been taught by tutors, suddenly being thrust into public school had been a culture shock at such a young age. The students in her classes had found any reason they could to taunt and make fun of the new kid, pushing Bri further behind the persona she'd used most of her life around her parents and their friends.

And then at the age of eleven, she'd met Kaia. It wasn't until then that she was finally able to let her walls down. For the first time in her life, she'd found a friend, one who would love her for who she was and not what she could give them. She could be herself with Kaia in a way she'd never experienced before, and she hadn't realized what a relief that would be. Kaia was the first to call her Bri.

But for all the good Kaia had brought into her life, Bri still hadn't believed herself capable of loving and nurturing a child. It was a foreign concept to her and just wasn't something she'd ever been shown as a child. As she and Kaia had lain under clear blue summer skies and dreamt of their futures during their youth, kids had never been a part of Bri's grand plan. Travel, work she loved, friends—but never children of her own.

Until she'd laid eyes on Min.

The first time she'd seen that little face, it had been by chance. Bri had felt a connection right away but hadn't understood what it meant or how far-reaching it would go.

It wasn't until later, when she found that face staring back at her from the screen of her camera, that she realized just how much the little girl had affected her. She hadn't even realized she'd captured the tiny girl's image until reviewing the pictures she'd taken that day. As Bri had studied the hundreds of shots, she was stunned to find dozens of images of the same dark-eyed beauty staring back at her.

Bri had visited that country, that village, entirely on a whim. Usually, her travels were for work—a career she enjoyed and excelled at. But that trip had been something just for her—a detour from the norm—and a way to kill a few months between projects.

Being a freelance photo journalist, she had shot footage of everything from bombed out cities to the devastated faces of the people forgotten and left behind.

When her last assignment had concluded, she'd needed a change of scenery—some distance from the depressing and disturbing realities her camera had captured all too well. An idea had been floating around in the back of her mind for years, and it felt like the right time to bring it to light. This would be a project close to her own heart. She'd seen the worst of so many places. Now she wanted to see their best.

Not the palaces and finery of those countries that so many had already documented, but the simple cultures of genuine people and the beauty that surrounded them. The real life. The heart.

Before finding herself at the orphanage where she'd met Min, Bri had spent months just putzing around with no true destination in mind. She went wherever the camera lens took her, taking thousands of photos of the land, of the people, and of the happiness and community she'd discovered within them.

She'd been in Min's village only a short time when she found herself in the most breathtaking setting she'd ever seen. The park... *No*, she amended. It was so much more than that. It was a sanctuary. A place to find peace and just take a moment to breathe and think.

The village of Ban Xuang lay in the valley of several mountains, and this refuge was situated on the lower slope of one of the towering peaks. Whoever had designed it had used that steep angle and tiered it with five separate levels, each section bestowed with a wide, flat expanse of green before stepping down to the next. The short walls holding back the earth were made of smoothed white stone.

Descending down through the center of each layer was a lively stream which fell over the last tier into a rock-rimmed pond. Bri's gaze had followed the rushing water back upward to where it disappeared into the rock face, its origin beginning somewhere high up the mountain.

Large boulders had been laid as stepping stones from one bank of the tranquil pool to the other, allowing visitors a path to cross the water.

Trees, shrubs, and flowers were artfully placed, dotting the landscape all around. The vibrant greens of the foliage, the deep hues of the blooms, and the sparkling blue of the water lent a picturesque quality she'd never encountered, either in pictures or reality.

She'd spent hours there, aiming her camera in every possible direction, framing them in her mind for best results and plotting out how she'd use each shot in her project.

It was then she'd noticed the building that bordered the serene space. It was well kept, as were all the structures in this village, with two stories of white stucco enclosed by a low wooden fence.

But she still recognized it immediately.

So engrossed in the beauty through her lens, she hadn't heard the children running and playing within that fence. She gave them a brief glance but didn't really pay them much attention.

In her travels, Bri was no stranger to places such as this. Most were sad and depressing, and she'd made a point to stay clear of them whenever she was able. It broke her heart to see the somber faces of a region's youngest victims, trapped and caged within the confines of the orphanages, run either by the local church or government.

But this place, here in this setting, was like nothing she'd ever seen before. These children ran and laughed and played. The building and grounds were bright and happy and inviting. She observed them for a short while before starting to turn away.

Why that one face out of the many drew her, she didn't know. She looked much the same as all the other children. Black hair, almond-shaped dark eyes, creamy skin. But something in that child had called to Bri.

She'd fought it. She really had. But in the end, it hadn't mattered. She'd been a goner the moment her gaze had locked onto the beautiful little two-year-old.

Bri brought her thoughts back to the present. She shifted to lay flat. Folding her hands over her stomach, she stared up at the ceiling and considered.

Min had only been hers for a few months. They were still developing the bond between mother and child. Aside from the communication barrier, Min was learning to trust and depend on Bri for all of her needs—to believe that Bri would be there for her, always.

Nothing should come before that. They needed this time to forge the deep connection of familial love.

And that's why Bri had to push Kaia's handsome cousin out of her mind. She had to forget how her body had responded to just the sight of him. How it had heated and flushed, her heart stopping, only to beat again with hard, demanding thumps in her chest. How the breath had whooshed out of her, leaving her light-headed and gasping.

Under any other circumstance, she wouldn't have had a problem playing a little. A good romp in the sack, just to take the edge off. But she didn't have time for such frivolity anymore. She had a daughter now who she needed to think of first. And no gorgeous beach-bum-looking mountain lion shifter was going to get in the way of that. She refused to be her parents and let her own desires and needs overshadow those of her child.

No matter how weak and breathless he made her feel.

With a sigh, Bri threw the sheet off and rolled out of bed. She didn't bother to cover her sleep shorts and tank. Everyone was asleep, and she wouldn't be gone long. She just suddenly needed some air.

After a quick check on Min, she silently made her way out of her room and down the hall. It was late, and the house was dark and quiet. Kaia's grandmother and Jayme were sharing the spare bedroom, and the man Bri forced herself not to think about was on the couch.

Mac, while spending a lot of nights here with Kaia, had returned to his own place, taking his massive dog Moose with him. Min had fallen in love with that dog at first sight. The giant Merle Great Dane loved her just as much, and he was surprisingly gentle with her. Despite his size, he took care when he was around her not to knock her down or play too excitedly with her.

He'd become a big part of this little family they'd made.

Bri stopped in the kitchen and grabbed a bottle of water out of the fridge before taking it out onto the deck.

~~~

Erik prowled through the darkness.

He'd gone outside shortly after having met his cousin Kaia's friend, Bri Calladega. He hadn't been able to stay there—his
~~~

cat would give him no peace.

From the first scent of Bri's exotic bouquet, his inner feline had gone mad. It tore and scratched at him to be released. He wanted to be near her, to mark her with his scent, so everyone would know she belonged to him.

Erik had stood on the deck when he'd finally escaped the house, breathing in the clear night air, trying to wash her natural perfume away. But it was like her fragrance had wrapped itself around and through his sensitive nose. It had already seeped into his pores to haunt him, even when she wasn't anywhere nearby.

Rejoining the assembled group hadn't been an option with Bri still inside, and standing outside all night would only bring questions he couldn't answer.

He'd heard the sliding door open and stiffened, relaxing only when his sister had joined him at the rail.

"You okay?" Jayme asked him.

Erik was older than her by three years, and at twenty-four, Jayme was the youngest to have joined the squad—an elite group of sixteen men and women within their clan that kept the others safe and maintained order. She'd been an active member for over a year and was doing an outstanding job. She had an ingrained talent for that kind of work.

Jayme was enamored with law and police procedure. She'd already nearly chewed Mac's ears off, peppering him with questions about being the sheriff of Lost Creek. She'd even asked if she could shadow him as he worked, desperate to learn all she could about the job.

As siblings, she and Erik had looked very similar. They all did. Four boys and one girl, all with golden-blond hair and varying shades of blue eyes. Her hair was long and hung just past her shoulders in a straight sheet. Jayme's eyes were more of a soft baby blue instead of the sharp electric blue that were his.

Tall for a woman, Jayme stood at five-ten, which nearly matched his own six-foot frame.

"Yeah, I'm good. I just had to get out of there." Erik breathed in deep again, trying to dispel the hold Bri's scent had on him.

"Is it Kaia? Aunt Jackie warned you that her cat would be in heat."

"Kaia isn't the issue." He left it at that and hoped Jayme would too. But, of course, he should have known better.

"If our cousin isn't the problem, then…" She let the question trail off. "Oh…" Jayme dragged the one syllable word out to two. "It's Bri then." She gave him a sly, teasing smile. "I noticed how you two stared at each other when we first got back. You think she's hot, dontcha, big brother?"

Erik had to grin at the ribbing. "Just go back inside, brat. Tell Aunt Jackie I'll be back later. I'm going for a run."

"Seriously, all kidding aside, are you okay? You look a little strange." He glanced over at his baby sister and saw she was truly concerned.

"I'm fine. I just need to run. I'll be back in a bit."

"All right. But you know you can always talk to me."

Erik smiled at her. "I do."

As soon as Jayme had gone inside, he couldn't take it anymore and stripped where he stood, tossing his clothes into a shadowed corner.

The change seized him swiftly. Almost before it was complete, he took off into the forest.

He wished for his own home range back in Colorado where he knew every inch of forest and even had a spot he could go when he needed time alone. But he wasn't there. He was in the Lost Creek State Park.

They'd come to help Kaia—a cousin none of them had ever met. Her parents had fled from the clan before she was born. But the trouble that had driven them away had found Kaia all these years later, way out here in Montana where they'd sought refuge and a new life.

Unfortunately, both of Kaia's parents had been taken in a car accident when she'd been thirteen. Twelve years later, her older brother had also been lost when poachers had shot him while he was running in his cougar form. On her own for three years, she'd called her extended family when it looked like someone was stalking her.

And since family was family, he and a few cousins had packed up and come to finally put a stop to that threat. Her grandmother had also come, which hadn't surprised him. His Aunt Jackie was one tough lady. She'd had to be to survive the loss of her only child.

They'd all known better than to argue with her about going. They knew she wouldn't be talked out of seeing her granddaughter in person for the first time. Erik couldn't blame her for standing her ground. She'd only seen pictures that her daughter had sent through the years, and after her death even those had ceased. It wasn't until Kaia had made contact with them a few weeks before that anyone even knew where they'd been all those years.

Jackie was actually the reason he was still here when the others had gone back home after the threat had been neutralized. She'd wanted to stay a few more days to get to know Kaia, and her future grandson-in-law, Lucas McNamara. But everyone just called him Mac.

Erik had agreed to hang back with her to look out for her... and so she wouldn't have to make the twelve-hour drive back to Colorado by herself. She may be a force to be reckoned with, but she was still in her late sixties. She didn't need to put that kind of strain on herself, although he'd never say that within hearing distance of her. She'd have given him hell for it.

So, he was stuck here for the foreseeable future.

He ran and remained in the woods for hours. Only when he thought everyone would be asleep did he start to make his way back. Bri would be locked away in her room. Out of sight, out of mind, and out of scent.

Erik's cat exited the tree line and padded halfway across the lawn before he let the transformation take him. One moment, he was a large muscular mountain lion weighing close to two hundred pounds. And the next, he was a lean six-foot-tall naked man.

Being a shifter, nudity had never struck him as anything to fuss about. Living in the middle of a large clan of others just like him, seeing the human form was quite common. It wasn't anything he'd ever given much thought to.

Until he stepped up onto the deck and saw Bri reclining on a lounge chair, her topaz gaze glued to him. A bottle of water she must have raised for a drink hovered halfway to her mouth.

He knew what she was seeing. Being a part of their squad within the clan, he and his cat had to be in prime physical condition. He wasn't vain, but he still took pride in the hard sculpting of his body.

Blond hair bleached by the summer sun atop a square jaw and chiseled facial features. Bronzed skin that fit tightly over his heavily muscled chest, shoulders, and arms. Well-defined abs, lean waist, and hips, leading down to long toned legs.

Fur covered his body when his cat was out, but in this form, he was nearly hairless. Nothing on his chest, and only a light dusting on his arms and legs. Only two places on his body boasted any amount of hair.

Her eyes were resting on one of them. And it wasn't the top of his head.

Her complete attention was on his groin. Which was beginning to stir and take notice of her interest.

He ignored the errant member. Or, tried his damnedest to.

"I'm sorry. I didn't think anyone would be awake." He stifled the urge to shift his weight and cover himself. For the first time in his life, he wasn't sure what to do. She wasn't a part of the clan. Should he retrieve his clothes? Turn his back? Allow her to slink off into the house, pretending the encounter never happened?

Etiquette probably demanded he do any one of those things. But for some reason, he couldn't force his body to follow orders.

She finally tore her focus away from his hardening body. She slowly set the water bottle on the table beside her chair. "No." She cleared her throat. "It's fine. I was...ah...just getting...some...um...air."

Bri made a move to stand. And Erik, finally released from her paralyzing stare, stepped forward to open the sliding door.

And collided with her, hard body pressed to a much more supple one. Her small hands automatically went to his chest for balance, as his went to her hips to hold her steady.

Her pale blonde hair fell back away from her face as she tipped her head back to look up at him.

Erik stared into her golden-brown eyes and saw need and heat reflected back. When her tongue slid out to wet her pouty bottom lip, his gaze dropped to it. It glistened in the low light of the moon, and he couldn't resist the urge to taste her.

He took her mouth with his, and it was as if they both went up in flames. The blaze consumed them, and they were lost to it. Helpless to stop the burning.

2

Bri was on fire. And when Erik speared his tongue past her lips, she met it with equal fervor and hunger.

She had to touch him, to feel all of that smooth, hot skin. Seeing him coming across the yard and shifting back to his human form had been almost more than she could take. He was magnificent. Both cougar and man. And then he'd stepped up onto the deck, in all his mouth-watering glory. Her gaze had traveled the full length of him, from the sun-kissed tips of his blond hair to his manly bare feet.

On the return trip, her focus had stopped and held at the evidence of his manhood. She wasn't really shocked to see it growing and expanding. What surprised her was how thick and heavy it looked.

I really shouldn't be doing this. This is stupid on so many levels.

She should have just disappeared into the house as soon as she'd seen him coming. But then he'd shifted, and he'd been too damned tempting. While her mind was saying no, her body was already screaming *YES!* She wanted to be taken by him. Impaled by him. Her sex had clenched in need and short-circuited her brain.

Especially after seeing just what he was packing. She had to have it, to touch it. Feel it. Ride it.

Maybe just this once. He probably wasn't even that good at

it and thought of nothing but his own pleasure. That way she could write him off and not be bothered by him anymore.

Yeah, right.

Just from the few seconds he'd kissed her, she knew he was going to be fucking fantastic in bed.

She trailed her fingers down his exposed chest, over nipples pebbled in desire, past his flat stomach, and down. She finally came to what she'd been looking for. Craving. Wrapping her hand around his shaft, she gripped him tightly, wrenching a groan from deep in his throat. Watching his eyes go vague, she stroked him from base to tip and back.

He raised his head to draw air into his lungs. "Fuck, yeah."

Erik brought his gaze back down to hers, and she let him walk her backward. When the chair he'd found her in was at her knees, he turned and sat, pulling her down with him. As he reclined, she settled astride his hips and watched him.

He was so fucking hot. The words flitted across her mind once again. *Should I really do this?* But then she felt the steel of his erection at the juncture of her thighs, and the thought of that thick cock filling her brought a shiver of longing.

Once will be fine. It will have to be.

Never taking his hypnotic stare from hers, he slid his hand up the outside of her thigh. She knew he was watching for any indication she'd changed her mind or lost her nerve. He was waiting for her to grab his wrist and halt his movements before they went any further.

Yeah, like that's going to happen. What am I? Stupid? This was going to feel way too good to stop now. Her bottoms were already soaked just thinking about it.

He followed the crease of her hip around with his fingertips. He didn't stop until he'd pushed her pajama shorts aside and, turning his hand, found her.

Her breath caught at his first touch. A delicious wave of wanting rolled through her. It made her stomach quiver, and more wetness flooded her channel. She knew she'd be hot and slick, ready for him.

He traced the outer edges of her sex, teasing her. Except she didn't want to be teased. She wanted to be fucked. Reaching down, she laid her hand over his. Guiding his fingers to her center, she pressed them into her. It wasn't enough, but it was a start.

Her head fell back as he took her lead and thrust deep with two fingers. He curled them at the knuckles to find and stroke her sensitive core. She clutched at his shoulders and ground her hips into his hand, wanting any part of him deeper inside her.

Her body found the rhythm he set and matched it.

Erik slid his thumb up through her folds until he found her clit and pressed into it. Bri groaned. He tormented her until she couldn't stand it another second. Chest heaving, breaths panting past her lips, she bit down on the bottom one. The sting of pain tethered her to the present when her body wanted to fly.

She was losing the battle though. She was so close, but she needed his thick shaft buried deep before she erupted.

"Inside me. Now." Giving him no choice, she found his straining cock and took him in her hand. Raising up onto her knees, she positioned the head at her swollen entrance. She bathed it in her molten juices first, and then in one smooth motion, took him to the hilt.

She moaned as his breath hissed through his teeth in a gasp. She closed her eyes and swore she saw stars behind her lids.

Bri's body was stretched so tight, on the brink of being too much for her to handle. As if knowing she needed a moment, Erik's hands gripped her sides with bruising force. He took control and held her still.

She didn't know if it was her body throbbing or his, but she tentatively raised and lowered herself onto him, testing to see how much pain would follow. The pull of her inner walls over his erection was exquisite. He was so thick, there wasn't an inch of her he didn't caress. On the second thrust, the pleasure overrode everything else.

Bri looked down at his handsome face and saw that he was savagely holding onto whatever control he had left. He was giving her the time she needed to adjust to him. And it was costing him. Sweat beaded his skin, and his teeth were gritted tightly together.

Bri bent forward and sealed her mouth to his. She kissed him senseless and then pulled back. She gave him a quick smirk and swiveled her pelvis. Then she flexed her inner muscles deep inside and squeezed him as tightly as her hand had.

"Oh, fuck." Erik's eyes nearly rolled back in his head. "Do that again."

She grinned wickedly, completely relaxing her muscles before clenching down again.

After that, it was all frantic movement. Bracing her hands on his shoulders again, she set a hard and demanding pace. He met each of her downward drives with an upward thrust of his own.

Gliding his hands up her torso, Erik pushed her tank up until it bunched beneath her arms. He cupped each of her full breasts in his hands, molding and kneading them as he pinched and rolled the taut pink nipples between his thumbs and forefingers.

It drew a shuddering mewling sound from her.

He leaned up, took one into his mouth, and sucked. Hard. Her inner muscles clenched around him again.

She couldn't take any more.

She slammed down on him as the climax ripped through her. She threw her head back and closed her eyes as contractions inside of her pulsed, each wave of her orgasm squeezing him more than the last.

With a strained grunt, Erik met his own release, jetting hot streams deep inside of her.

She wanted nothing more than to lower down onto his chest and snuggle into him. She wanted his arms around her to hold her close as they both drifted off. She wanted the chance to taste him, learn the feel of him in her hands, in her mouth. And she definitely wanted a repeat of this. Many, many repeats.

This had been such a huge mistake. Now that she'd gotten a glimpse, once was never going to be enough. And to make matters worse, Bri could totally see herself falling for the guy, and that just couldn't happen. She had to go. Now. Before she did something even more stupid.

Bri ignored the way her heart stuttered. While Erik was still drifting, she rose to stand in front of him.

She looked down at him, straightening her clothes. She needed to end this, so there'd be no questions and no expectations.

Clearing her throat, Bri made it final. "Thanks. That was great. But it can't and *won't* happen again. You're not a part of my plans."

Without a backward glance, she strode into the house.

She barely made it to the bathroom before the shaking began. Hands trembling, she reached into the shower and cranked on the faucet.

"Oh God," she whispered again and again.

She stripped out of her pajamas and tossed them in the small metal trash can. She never wanted to see them again. They smelled of him, the crotch of her shorts wet with a mixture of them both.

The water was scarcely more than cold when she stepped in. As the spray rained down over her head and face, she let the tears flow.

What had she done?

She'd had the best sex of her fucking life, that's what she'd done. She could still feel him moving inside of her. Filling her, stretching her, burning her up from the inside out.

And his mouth. Holy shit, the man had some talent.

Bri wasn't shy. Far from it. She loved her body and all the ways it could give and receive pleasure. But she was also smart, and she knew when something wasn't meant to be.

Erik Reid was not meant to be hers, despite what her heart was telling her.

She scrubbed her face with her hands. So what if he'd gotten her off like nobody ever had? She wasn't a slave to her libido. She was a grown woman and a mom now, damn it! She had to think about the wellbeing of her daughter first—not her fucking hormones.

And that was exactly what she'd do. Even if it killed her.

Thankfully, he wouldn't be in Lost Creek for much longer anyway. They would be leaving in a few days and going back to Colorado. She just had to get past that, and she'd be home free. She could put him and his freakishly amazing body out of her mind and concentrate on building a life with Min.

And if he pressed her? Well, she already knew exactly what would run him off, for good. She'd been playing the role of Abrianna Elizabetta Calladega for so long, it was like breathing.

Firming her resolve, she felt better and more in control when she stepped out of the shower a few minutes later. Wrapping a towel around herself, she strode back to her room. Donning a new, clean, fresh set of pajamas, she crawled into bed and fell promptly into sleep.

~~~

Bri awoke just as she had for the last few months. With her small daughter climbing into her bed to snuggle.

"Good morning, my love." Bri brought her in close, drove
~~~

her nose into the curve between Min's shoulder and neck, and sniffed. It never failed to bring a riot of giggles.

The sound of it brought light to every dark place in Bri's life. She didn't know what she'd done before this angel had found her.

"Momma, no," Min got out between fits of laughter.

"What do you mean, Momma no? Momma is gonna eat you up." Bri made exaggerated gobbling sounds as she continued to tickle the squirming toddler. "I love Min for breakfast. She's so tasty and sweet."

"No. No eat Min. Pancakes," Min panted out breathlessly.

Bri raised her head and looked down at the beautiful little face. Her silky black hair was standing in all directions at once. Her dark-as-obsidian eyes were alight with happiness. "Pancakes? I do like pancakes." Bri considered for a moment. "Pancakes sound pretty yummy. Almost as yummy as Min."

She snarfed up more Min to the sound of her tiny cackles.

Bri finally caved and gave her diapered bottom a light tap. "Up you go. If we're going to have pancakes, we need to get out of bed."

Min scrambled up and scooted off the side. She was out the door before Bri could untangle her legs from the sheet.

By the time she put on her robe and made it to the kitchen, Min was standing on a chair beside Jackie at the counter. The older woman was letting her stir something in a big bowl.

Bri did a quick scan to see if anyone else was still asleep on the couch.

No sign of him. Bri relaxed and turned her smile back up.

"If that's pancake batter, you must have read her mind." She'd loved Jackie from the moment she'd met her the night before. Bri felt no need to don the persona she usually wore around strangers. She'd felt the same gentle soul in Jackie as she had in Kaia all those years ago. It was no wonder she hadn't needed to protect herself with these two.

Min had taken an instant shine to her too. If it had something to do with the inner cat they both possessed, she didn't know.

Jackie grinned. "Nothing so complicated. I just remember how much little ones love them." She leaned down to mock-whisper in Min's ear. "Especially, my super-duper scrumptious kitty-cat cakes."

Min beamed up at Bri, her face a mix of excitement and anticipation. "Kitty-cat cakes!"

Bri laughed. "I heard." God, she loved this little girl. "They sound amazing."

Jackie had been more than a little surprised to discover upon meeting Min that she too harbored an inner feline. But Min was so young that her cat was still sleeping and wouldn't make an appearance until she was five.

Unbeknownst to her, Bri had fallen in love with and adopted a shifter from the quaint little orphanage in Asia—a tidbit that hadn't come to light until she'd gotten Min home and introduced her to Kaia. Her best friend had taken one look and detected the slumbering cub immediately. They wouldn't know exactly what type of cat she'd be until she was old enough to shift, but until then, Bri had three more years to learn everything she could.

While they worked, Bri brewed herself a cup of coffee. She took it to the table and sat sipping it as Kaia emerged from the hall.

"Mmm, something smells really good." Kaia smiled in greeting at Bri. On her way to the coffeemaker, she glanced over Jackie's shoulder. She watched as Jackie showed Min how to pour the batter out into kitty-cat shapes.

"Wow. That's pretty cool."

Jackie leaned back and brushed a kiss on Kaia's cheek. "Good morning, dear. We're making my world-famous kitty-cat cakes."

That set Min off again, and they all laughed.

When Kaia's tea was finished, she carried it to the table and joined Bri.

She was tempted to ask about Erik but bit down on her tongue to keep the words from falling from her lips. Instead, she asked, "Is Mac stopping by to pick Jayme up this morning?"

Bri and Mac were slowly becoming friends. Not one of her inner circle in school, the only face she'd ever shown Mac was the one everyone expected of her. It was only since he and Kaia had become a couple that Bri had started to lower those shields with him. It was an unnerving process to let anyone see the real her. But she loved Kaia, and Kaia loved him, so he must be worth it.

Kaia made a negative sound as she sipped her tea. "Jayme left a while ago. She's meeting him there. Along with showing her the ropes, he wanted to get in early to make sure there aren't any repercussions from what happened."

Bri still couldn't believe the events that had occurred over the last few weeks, culminating in her best friend having to kill someone.

"You won't get in trouble, will you?" The thought nearly made Bri sick.

Kaia shook her head. "Thankfully, no one outside of the clans knew Gerald was even here. And because it was a shifter matter—and self-defense on top of that—it's being taken care of internally. Mac's more concerned about new poachers showing up from all the attention I called to myself before the whole mess with Gerald began."

Bri cocked a brow at her. "You mean when you and your cat were the ones doing the stalking and setting the traps?"

"Yes." Kaia sent her a mock glare before turning serious. "I only regret that my actions drew *more* attention to the park instead of deterring it. So, Mac is going to keep his men and the park guys on alert until we know for sure that no more poachers will be showing up for the rogue cougar."

"I still can't believe you made that one guy fall into his own trap. It had to have taken a big bite out of his," Bri glanced over at her daughter, "behind."

Bri understood why Kaia thought she had to do it. Her brother had been killed by poachers while he was in the park as a mountain lion. And because he'd died as a cat, the poachers couldn't be prosecuted more harshly for their crimes—only getting a slap on the wrist and an insignificant fine for illegal poaching. Only she, Kaia, and Mac knew the real truth.

As shifters, they needed a safe place they could hunt and exercise. If men with guns were lurking in the woods shooting anything that moved, they'd be risking their lives every time they let their cats out to stretch and play.

And just thinking about Min one day running in those same woods made Bri's blood turn cold.

"If there's a chance of more coming, shouldn't the others have stuck around a little longer?" Bri looked between Jackie and Kaia. A few of the members from the clan's special ops team had also come to town to protect Kaia from Gerald. If danger was still possible, shouldn't they have waited?

Jackie shook her head. "More cats would have only drawn more attention. Erik is out there keeping an eye on things during the day, which he'll continue to do until we leave to go back home. If no new threats arise by then, I think you'll be safe."

So that's where he'd gone. Not that she cared. She didn't want him around, and it would be far easier this way. Bri couldn't help but worry that if she were near him too much, a repeat of the night before would be inevitable. And that couldn't happen. She couldn't let him touch or kiss her again.

The only reason it had even happened in the first place was because she'd been caught unawares with the breathtaking reality of his nakedness. Barring that, she couldn't allow him to rock her fucking world again.

Bri could feel a heated flush beginning to creep up her neck. Damn her fair skin! If she didn't distract herself fast, Kaia was going to notice and wonder what the hell was going on.

"Well, I for one hope we've seen the last of hunters around here. I want the park to be as safe as possible for Min when she gets old enough to shift."

Jackie flipped some finished pancakes onto a plate and brought it to the table. Min followed close behind her, and Bri helped her up into a chair. The little girl bounced in her seat while Bri buttered and poured a small amount of syrup over one of the feline-shaped pancakes. It would be a sticky mess, but Bri let her enjoy the treat.

"Have you thought about showing Min what she'll be able to do?" Jackie went back to the stove to make more. "Little ones in the clan are exposed to adult cats from the very beginning. It's good for the babies to not be afraid, and it's also beneficial for the adults. Especially those cougars who've never had much interaction with cubs. It prepares them before they have babies of their own."

Bri glanced at Kaia. "We talked about it, but the time just hasn't been right."

"Why not right now?" Kaia set her cup of tea down.

Bri backpedaled. "Are you sure? Don't you have to get to work?" Now that the time was upon her, Bri found she was more than a little nervous about it.

Kaia smiled. "We'll keep it short this time. It'll only take a minute, and I think Min's going to love it."

"What about your cat? Will she be okay...around Min, I mean? She's never been around kids before." Bri had seen Kaia's mountain lion a few times. She was beautiful and sleek and...*big*. If something went wrong... "She's not you. Will you be able to control her?"

Kaia reached across the table to grasp Bri's hands. "My cat and I work together, and she doesn't have the same primal instincts as a wild animal would, because it's still me. Min will be perfectly safe." Kaia squeezed her hands. "Nothing is going to happen. No harm will come to your daughter. Do you trust me?"

"With my life. You know that." And because she did, she had to believe everything would be all right.

She looked down at Min. "How will we explain this so she'll understand? I don't want her to be scared."

Jackie returned and stood by Kaia. "She won't be scared. Deep down, she already knows."

"You said she was a year old when she was dropped off at the orphanage," Kaia reminded her. "If her birth mom was a shifter, she may have already seen the transformation happen. She was young, but she would remember."

"I hadn't considered that." Bri thought about the woman who had given birth to Min. She wondered, as she often did, what had happened that she wasn't able to keep her child.

"Momma. All done." Min had eaten the last of her breakfast while they'd talked. Bri pulled her thoughts back and scooped her up from her seat, pulling her into her lap.

"Min, honey. Aunt Kaia wants to show you something really special." Bri wiped at the syrup on her daughter's chin. "I'm going to be right here, so don't be nervous, okay?"

She was anxious enough for the both of them.

"How about we go into the living room? There'll be more room out there," Jackie suggested and walked that way.

Bri and Kaia rose and followed. Kaia stopped in the middle of the room and knelt down. When Bri set Min on her feet, Kaia took her tiny hands. Bri stood close by as Kaia gazed directly into Min's nearly black eyes.

"You and me and Jackie are kind of the same. We have a… friend…that we carry around with us all the time. They protect us, and help us, and love us. Yours is sleeping right now, and she'll stay asleep for a little while longer. But mine is awake, and she'd really like to meet you. Do you want to meet her?"

"Kitty!" Min grinned hugely.

Bri whooshed out the breath she'd been holding. Min could sense her fellow felines in her new shifter family.

Kaia and Jackie laughed. "Yes," Kaia told her, "that's right. She's a kitty kind of like yours. Do you want to say hi to her?"

"Pway wiff kitty."

"Okay, stand over by your Momma." Min did as she asked, but she was bouncing on her toes in excitement.

Kaia stood, and with a big smile for Bri, walked out of the room. Only moments passed when her sleek tawny cougar returned. She sat down and flicked the tip of her tail.

Min launched herself at the very large cat now sitting in Kaia's living room. Bri made a grab for her but missed.

Oh, God.

Jackie came to offer her comfort and wrapped an arm around her waist. "She's fine. She's loving this."

Bri had to admit that was true. Min was hugging and kissing the majestic lioness. And, in return, the lioness was rubbing her face all over Min, making her giggle and squirm as Kaia's long whiskers tickled her.

Min screeched in delight when a wet tongue snaked out and lapped over her face. Bri remembered trying to wipe away the sweet syrup stuck there.

They played and rolled for a while as Bri and Jackie looked on. Long before Min was ready for it to stop, Bri put an end to it. "Come on, baby girl. We need to let Aunt Kaia get to work. Her horses are waiting for her."

That started another type of celebration. "'Orsey! 'Orsey!"

Bri lifted her daughter into her arms. "Maybe later." She saw the cat pad off down the hall. "Maybe after a nap, we'll go visit the barn."

"No. No nap. 'Orsey. Kitty." Her bottom lip actually popped out in a pout. It was the cutest thing Bri had ever seen. She had to bite the inside of her cheek to keep from laughing.

Fastening the last button on her shirt, Kaia joined them, dressed again for work. "Listen to your momma, and when you come later, you and I can go for a ride. How's that?"

"Wide! Wide!"

Kaia grinned and ran her hand over Min's soft black fluff of hair. "You got it, sweet girl."

The rest of the morning was dedicated to just being with and taking care of her daughter. When she went down for her nap, Bri had a chance to catch up on some emails. After the adoption, she'd taken some time off. She didn't plan on going back until she was ready, but some of the publications she did work for were wanting an update from her. An estimate of when she'd be back.

At this point, she didn't know. And thankfully, she didn't *need* to work. She did it for the love of it. And she *would* go back. But for now, she just wanted more time to bond with her child.

In doing research on adoption, she'd found reference to cocooning. She'd never heard of it before, so she'd looked it up online. It was the practice of limiting the new child's interactions to only the immediate family, keeping the adopted child's world very small and predictable, allowing the bond between the child and parents to develop and grow without distraction.

Bri hadn't completely closed the two of them away, but she'd kept the circle small. And Min seemed to be making the adjustment to her new home and family very well.

Sending off the last email, Bri glanced over and saw Min was still sleeping. Might as well let her nap as long as possible. The afternoon would be a big one for her—going and helping at the barn always wore Min out.

Leaving her to her dreams, Bri stepped out into the hall and pulled the door almost closed. She still wanted to be able to hear if Min called out.

The house seemed still and quiet. Bri wondered if Jackie had left on an errand, or maybe she'd gone for a run in the park. Having known Kaia for so long, she knew how important it was for their felines to be able to exercise and hunt. It allowed their cats to maintain their peak shape and kept their minds healthy.

She'd learned a long time ago that if Kaia's cat wasn't allowed to stretch her legs every day, she'd get grumpy, which in turn made Kaia grouchy too.

Bri had once likened it to being around someone who was in a bitchy mood. It never failed. Spend enough time with them, and eventually, it rubbed off, making her feel bitchy too.

The way Bri understood the relationship between Kaia and her cat, they were two completely different beings sharing one space. While Kaia was in human form, she was wholly human, but could sense and feel what the cat was feeling. When Kaia shifted, and the lioness was out, she was one hundred percent feline. Kaia was there in the background, but she couldn't influence the cat to do anything she didn't want to do. She could reason with her but not force her.

And that's probably how it was going to be with Min when it came time for her to transform.

Oh, boy. The thought of it still gave her a bump to the heartrate. How was she going to raise a child that could change into a powerful predator? What if her cat form was one of the larger ones, like a lion or a leopard? The image of Min as a large cat throwing a temper tantrum was enough to make her palms sweat. She was going to have to rely on Kaia for so much as Min grew older.

They still didn't know what Min would be yet. With her being from Asia, there were any number of possibilities. Bri had spent most of the first night on the internet after finding out about Min. She'd searched for all the cats native to Asia and had been stunned by the results.

Of course, there were the big ones that everyone knew about. But it was the smaller species that had amazed her. There were so many more breeds of those, almost all of them completely new and foreign to her. There were the spotted varieties, like the Fishing Cat, Marbled Cat, and the Clouded Leopard. But there were also others that more closely resembled the common housecat, like the Jungle Cat and the Asiatic Golden Cat. And those were just a few that she'd discovered.

It kind of blew her mind.

Bri stepped out onto the deck and took in a deep breath. There was nothing she could do about any of that yet, though. She had three years to wrap her brain around it all.

Movement at the tree line drew her attention. Her eyes tracked over, and she saw Erik walking towards the house. He was fully clothed this time.

She thought of what she'd seen and done last night, and thought, "Pity."

Shit. Back the fuck up.

Bri cloaked herself behind her shields, thankful she'd taken the time to dress and do full makeup that morning. It all added to the effect. By the time he reached her perch on the deck, she was ready.

3

Erik saw her come outside from the shadows of the woods. He watched her for several minutes, thinking about the time he'd spent with her the previous night. That had been the single most satisfying encounter he'd ever had.

Memories of it had taunted him all night long. And despite the release that had shaken him to his core, his body had hardened again as images of her floated through his mind. And, much to his discomfort, had remained that way since.

His body hadn't been this far out of his control since he was a teenager. And a stiff breeze could make him...well...*stiff*.

He'd thought he could run off the worst of it, but that hadn't done a damned thing. His body still raged, and as a result, his cat was restless and ornery. Even hunting hadn't helped either of them.

She'd said it wouldn't happen again, but if he played his cards right...

He'd never had an issue when it came to women. Within the clan or out. Maybe he could talk her into an encore. They could have some fun until he left.

Plan in mind, he started out of the shadows.

And watched her change by degrees the closer he got to the house. Right before his eyes, her attitude became cold and removed. Nothing of the hot, sexy woman he'd been with the night before was in evidence. The transformation was as complete as his own when he let his cat take over.

What the hell? Was she pissed about something? *She* was the one who'd walked away—not him. And he knew for a fact she'd gotten off, so she couldn't be mad about that either.

Erik stopped at the base of the stairs and leaned on the handrail. He shot her a charming grin. "Hey."

"Hello." Her voice damned near gave him frostbite as she looked down her narrow, aristocratic nose at him.

Eyes that had burned so hot were now disdainful pools of chilly amber. She held herself rigid and formal. Untouchable. This wasn't the same woman he'd had amazing sex with only hours ago. She'd been engaging then. Demanding, giving, and sexy as fuck.

This? This was one glacial bitch. What the hell had changed?

The scathing, icy glare and the way her posture mimicked stone screamed that he wasn't good enough to breathe the same air as her. Mere hours ago, she'd been hellbent on riding his cock like he was her own personal bronco. And today, she was addressing him the way a queen would a lowly peasant.

"If you'll excuse me." Snobby, upper-crust attitude dripped from her words. "My daughter needs me." Bri made what Erik could only describe as a regal turn and then headed back into the house, dismissing him out of hand.

"Yeah, no problem. Your highness." His tone had a snap to it.

As the door slid shut behind her, Erik again wished he could get the hell out of there.

~~~

Two days later over lunch, Bri and Kaia were at the dining room table. They were on Bri's laptop going through pictures of Min that Kaia planned to put on her website. Bri had taken several dozen shots of her daughter riding horses and having
~~~

the time of her life.

Kaia planned to post a few to her website to showcase how docile a well-trained horse could be, even with the youngest and most inexperienced of riders.

When it came time to pick the one to go on the home page, they'd both agreed which of them it had to be. Min was sitting bareback astride Rayna, Kaia's palomino. Black safety helmet on her head, her little hands were holding tightly to the mare's blonde mane as she moved around the pen.

The picture Bri had shot captured girl and horse full-face. They'd been coming straight at her, mid-stride, and the expressions on both of their faces were ones of pure joy. Eyes sparkling and happy, Min and Rayna grinned into the lens.

Bri would blow it up, so their bright faces were what greeted any new visitors to the site.

They were laughing over memories of that day when Erik came in through the front door. The smile dropped off Bri's face as though she'd been slapped. She straightened her spine until she was sitting upright and rigid in her seat.

Kaia took note of the not-so-subtle movement and sent her a questioning look.

Bri knew Kaia was surprised by the shift in her demeanor. It'd been a while since Bri had felt the need to openly guard herself, and Kaia knew better than most what that looked like. But she couldn't let those shields down with the man standing before them.

It would cost her too much.

She gave Kaia a barely perceptible shake of her head. Kaia took the hint and turned to Erik.

"Hey, cousin." She smiled. "How goes the patrolling?"

Even though she kept her gaze glued to the screen in front of her, Bri could feel the weight of his stare land on her briefly before it disappeared.

Bri surreptitiously watched him while she pretended to

work on her laptop. Her heartbeat had kicked up a notch just by being near him. Her body flooded with heat, remembering what it felt like to be filled with him.

She battled both reactions down. Now was not the time to think of herself. Min had to come first. She'd promised herself it had been a one-time deal.

Maybe sometime down the road, if he came back to town and was still interested, hooking up again might be fun. But now was the time for her daughter. Her libido would just have to calm itself down, and although the sex had been amazing, she couldn't help but regret her earlier weakness.

Kaia and Erik had finished up their chat while she'd been giving herself the pep talk. When she brought her attention back, Erik was nowhere to be seen, and Kaia was leaning back in her chair studying her.

"Want to tell me what that was all about?" Kaia crossed her arms over her chest and stared at her. "What's with the ice queen showing up? I thought you liked my family."

Bri clicked on a couple of pictures and put them in a separate folder. "I do. Jackie is awesome, and Min and I both love her. Jayme seems nice. She's not around much, but I think I'd like her."

"And what about Erik? Did he do something to piss you off? I thought, after how the two of you reacted to each other that first night, things might heat up a bit between you."

Bri resisted the urge to squirm in her seat, keeping her hands busy on the keyboard. "No. Nothing is going to be heating up. He's handsome, sure, but I can't be distracted with that kind of stuff right now. Min needs me, and I have to put all of my energy into raising my daughter. My *shifter* daughter. Besides, he'll be going back to Colorado soon anyway. Even if there had been something there, what would be the point of getting it started? *None.* So, it's moot."

Bri forced a smile and clicked one more button. "I just

emailed you the three pictures we decided on. You can use them however you want, and I think they'll look great. They'll show any prospective client that visits your website that a horse trained by the amazing Kaia Reid is well-behaved enough for even a toddler to handle."

Kaia grinned just as she'd meant her to. "Well, from *your* mouth..." She glanced at the time. "I'd better get back to work. Will I see you and Min this afternoon?"

"No. Not today. I thought I'd take her into town for a late lunch and then the park. They have that great area that's just the right size for her. All the play equipment is scaled smaller. I think she'll love it."

"She certainly will. Give her a kiss for me." Kaia rose up and left to gather up what she needed to take with her.

Bri closed her computer and stood. Min was napping at the moment, but as soon as she woke up, Bri wanted to take her to that park. As she walked down the hall to check on her, she saw a shadow move in the doorway of her room.

Picking up her pace, she was surprised to see Erik standing just over the threshold. He was watching Min sleep.

"What the hell are you doing in here?" Bri demanded in a harsh whisper.

"I was coming out of the bathroom and heard a sound. I wanted to make sure she wasn't crying."

"Well, as you can see, she's clearly *not*." Bri's tone was crisp as she shoved past him, pivoted around, and put her hand on the edge of the door. She kept her gaze frigid. "Thank you, but my daughter is none of your concern."

Bri closed the door in his face. Or tried to.

Before the latch could catch, he caught it in his large hand. He held it open just enough for her to see his face.

His voice was pitched low, and the anger in it burned over her. "I don't know what the fuck your problem is with me, Princess, but you might want to watch your step."

Before she could form a response, he turned and stalked away.

Bri stayed in her room until Min woke up about twenty minutes later. She changed her diaper and cautiously opened the door. Next stop was the bathroom, which was right next door. She fixed Min's pigtails and washed her face. A little sprucing to herself, and they were ready to go.

Thankfully, she didn't see Erik as she went into the kitchen to pack a small insulated bag with what they'd need for a few hours. Cheese snacks, crackers, apple, banana, fruit snacks, drinks, and last but not least, peanut butter and honey sandwiches.

She ran back to her room to grab a jacket for Min before holding her hand out to her. "Come on, baby girl. Let's go to the park and play."

Min was so excited, Bri could barely buckle her into her car seat. Bri laughed. "Sit still, silly wiggle-worm." Bri poked Min's ribs, which made her shift around even more.

Finally, she was safely secured. Bri set the lunch bag on the floor and shut the door. Walking around her car, she yanked on the handle and happened to glance up. A large male mountain lion was watching her from the tree line.

She knew exactly who it was.

He really was impressive to behold, whether in cat form or human. Though his hair was a sun-bleached blond as a man, the fur that coated his cat was a deep golden brown. The bright blue of his eyes had darkened to a smoky, steely blue. They reminded her of the summer storms she and Kaia used to watch roll in.

She didn't realize she'd been standing there staring at him until Min called to her from the backseat.

"Momma, go!"

Bri snapped herself out of her thoughts and slid into the driver's seat. She smiled into the rearview mirror. If it was a little strained, Min would never know. "Yes. We're going. Right now."

She put the encounter with Erik out of her mind and pulled out of the driveway, determined to spend a carefree day playing with her little girl.

~~~

They got back around four. Min was exhausted from all the activity at the park and had fallen asleep in the car on the way back to the house. She didn't stay asleep though. As careful as she'd been, as soon as Bri unbuckled her and picked her up, Min's big eyes popped open.

"Hey there, sunshine. We're home." Bri grinned at her daughter and then set her on her feet so she could collect the diaper bag, cooler, and her purse.

She watched as Min took off for the front door. She waited, none too patiently, for Bri to get there to open the door for her. As soon as it was no longer barring her way, Min ran for the bedroom and her toys.

Shaking her head and laughing, Bri walked into the dining room to set her burden on the table. Jackie was in the kitchen unpacking groceries.

"As much as we appreciate it, you don't have to do that," Bri told her with a grin. "Just enjoy your time here with Kaia. You don't have to cook for us all the time."

"I know, and I have treasured every moment with my granddaughter." Jackie turned towards her. "I love going to the barn with her and helping where I can. But I also love taking care of her." Sadness tinged Jackie's eyes. "She hasn't had much of that. She's lost so much."

"She's lost more than any one person should have to. But she's also stronger than anyone I know."

"Yes, I see that too. And I'm so proud of her, both for what
~~~

she's accomplished, and who she's grown up to be." Jackie let out a big sigh. "I'm going to hate leaving her."

As much as their departure was a welcome concept in Bri's mind—only for the sake of not having to deal with Erik—she knew Kaia would be sad that her grandmother was returning to Colorado. Bri would be sad to see the women go too. She loved Jackie and Jayme. But knowing that Erik would be out of the picture would go a long way to easing Bri's anxieties. Wearing her bitch persona wasn't as comfortable as it once had been.

"And I know she's going to hate seeing you leave. When do you have to go?"

"Tomorrow morning." Jackie shook her head. "I can't believe I've been here for two weeks already. It doesn't feel like it's been that long, but I need to get back."

"Well, Min and I will be very sorry to see you go." Bri walked around the counter and hugged Jackie tight and then looked down at all the food. "What can I do to help you with this?"

They chatted and laughed as they put the food away and prepared ingredients for what Jackie would make for dinner.

And with a wonder Bri would never understand, Jackie was setting a full three-course meal on the table a couple hours later just as Kaia came in from work. Mac and Moose followed shortly after, and Jayme and Erik arrived only a few minutes behind them.

Bri excused herself to go and get Min.

Everyone talked and laughed and caught up on the day. The coming parting was discussed, and it was decided that Jackie, Jayme, and Erik would be leaving at six the following morning.

Bri said her goodbyes and left the others to enjoy their final night together. She took Min into the bathroom to bathe and get into jammies. They'd spend the remainder of the evening watching movies in her bed and playing.

If she thought about missing a certain someone, she didn't

let it show and, instead, just hugged her baby tighter.

~~~

Erik stared at the road stretched out in front of him. They'd been driving for the better part of six hours, and all of them had been lost in their own thoughts for the last few.

It was easy to guess Jackie was thinking about Kaia. No one knew when they'd be able to see each other again. Kaia had promised to visit Colorado, but it would be a while before her schedule opened up enough to take a break. Phone calls and texts would have to suffice in the meantime, but seeing her granddaughter and holding her again would just have to wait.

He knew his sister well enough to know that she was torn between her duties to the clan and pursuing the career that had always called to her soul. The group he and Jayme belonged to in the clan were much like the police force. They maintained order and protected their family from outside forces.

Jayme had followed him into their ranks and had excelled at her job, the elite faction being the closest thing she could get to what she really wanted. But she'd always craved more. The real deal—with a real badge and real authority. Having read countless crime books, Jayme saw herself in the role of detective, investigating and chasing down criminals.

And before they'd left, Mac had unknowingly dangled that dream in front of her. He'd been impressed with her skill and insight as they'd worked together to capture Kaia's stalker. And he'd told her as much, adding that if she really wanted to be a cop, to let him know. He could waive the residency requirement if she were interested in pursuing a career in law enforcement. She'd have to pass the physical and mental testing, of course, and complete the twelve-week training program at the police academy. But there shouldn't be a problem with hiring her on afterward.
~~~

So, he knew Jayme had a lot to think about. Did she remain where she was with the clan, or did she take a huge leap and move to a new city to start a new life away from everything and everyone she'd ever known?

Erik was facing his own similar dilemma.

Except he didn't have someone waiting for him. The future he was beginning to think he wanted was being denied him. Bri had pretty much shut down any further involvement between them and acted as if that night had never happened. So, why couldn't he forget her? Why had she affected him as no one else ever had? It was one fucking night, and he couldn't put the memories of her out of his mind.

Was he a masochist? No matter how callously she'd treated him, he kept waiting for her to look at him the way she had before. Why the hell was he still so hung up on her?

To make matters worse, with every mile they traveled, his cat was growing more and more temperamental and restless. He just hoped he made it home before he had to let the bastard out to run it off.

"So, what happened between you and Bri?" Jackie's question startled Erik out of his musings.

An image of being buried balls deep in her hot channel while she rode him flashed in his brain. His brows came together, and he shot Jackie a quick glance. "Nothing happened."

That she hadn't demanded.

"Then why was she so curt with you?"

"How the hell am I supposed to know?" He glared at the car in front of them. "I'm just glad to finally be going home."

Erik declined when Jayme offered to take over driving, so their silent reflections apparently over, Jackie and Jayme chatted the rest of the way. He tuned them out and tried to expel the confusing woman from his system.

At seven o'clock that evening, they drove into town. Erik had been awaiting this moment for the last week. But now that he was home, he didn't feel nearly as relieved as he thought he should have been. After pulling into Jackie's driveway, he and Jayme helped her take her bags inside and left her with a hug and kiss.

When they climbed back into the truck to drive the few blocks over to the family home, Jayme turned to face him in her seat. "Okay. Give. I know something's up."

Erik blew out a sigh. He knew his sister wouldn't let this rest. She was an expert at grilling people until they spilled it all. She'd make a great cop.

"I fucked her that first night out on the deck."

In her direct way, Jayme asked, "And what? You didn't get her off?"

He scowled her. "I got her off just fine, thank you. But two seconds after that, she gets up and leaves, and from then on, it was all straight-running-bitch from her."

His sister shrugged. "Her loss then. You don't need her, and she doesn't deserve you. Forget about her." Jayme had always had his back.

I wish I could.

Erik left Jayme at their parents' house where she still lived and then headed to his own place. The whole clan lived within a few miles of each other. While the small town in southern Colorado boasted a minor population of non-shifters, the glaring majority of its inhabitants were mountain lion shifters and related in one way or another.

With a new sense of determination taking hold of him, he resolved to throw himself into the clan. He'd keep himself so busy, he wouldn't even have time to let his mind wander. This, he thought, was how he'd forget about Bri once and for all.

~~~

The days passed and then weeks, but try as he might,
~~~

Erik had no luck getting Bri out of his mind. Every night he dreamed of her, his memories and fantasies so vivid, he wasn't even sleeping anymore. His temper was short, and his cat was nearly impossible to deal with.

He volunteered for as many patrols as he could get, booking his schedule so full he didn't have time to think. But even the familiar woods he'd run since he was a cub couldn't offer him any solace. His friends and siblings had started to avoid him, because he just wasn't good company to be around.

When Jayme was finally brave enough to face his wrath and speak to him, she confided that their parents were really worried about him. What he was doing and his reaction to this woman wasn't healthy. They'd been unable to get in touch with him for days, and he'd not returned any of their calls.

That really wasn't because he was avoiding them. He was up at the crack of dawn and gone, and only when he couldn't hold himself up any longer did he finally drag himself into bed. Besides being so sexually frustrated that he thought he might explode at any moment, he was also so physically and emotionally drained that he just didn't give a shit anymore.

"I'm concerned about you too, bro. This isn't you, Erik." She drilled him with a look. "You want my advice?"

"No," he groused, knowing his protests would fall on deaf ears anyway.

"You either need to get the fuck over her, or drag your pathetic ass back to Montana and fight for her. Is she the one you want?"

Erik bit back the urge to take her head off. He knew she was right and had almost come to the same conclusion himself. But if he were being honest with himself, there had only ever been one option.

He let out a sigh. "The Bri I knew the first night is who I want. That frigid, stuck-up bitch that came afterwards can just go straight to hell."

"Well, you'd better hurry up and get your shit figured out. This can't go on, Erik. You're a shell of the brother I used to know, and I can't stand seeing you like this anymore."

Two days later, he was loading his duffle into his car. He was just about to head out when Jayme pulled in behind him.

He walked back to her car and leaned in the window. "Hey. What are you doing here? I thought we said our goodbyes at Mom and Dad's last night."

"We did. But I'm going back to Montana too."

If it had been anyone else, her choice might have surprised him. But he knew his sister better than most.

"I'm taking Mac up on his offer. I've already enrolled in the Law Enforcement Academy there."

He was happy for her, but having two of their children leave at the same time would be a lot to take for their parents. "You've talked to Mom and Dad already?"

"Yeah. They're sad, but they understand my need to do this."

Erik nodded. They'd recognized his need to return to Montana too.

"Well, hop in and let's go."

Jayme shook her head. "I'm going to follow you. I'll need my car."

"All right then. Let's hit the road."

~~~

They arrived in Anaconda twelve hours later. They pulled into a motel and got two rooms. As Erik threw his bag on the bed, he wondered again if this were a good idea.

Was he making a mistake by coming back? It had been two months since he'd left. Would she be glad to see him, or slam the door in his face again? He purposely hadn't called Kaia to tell her of his plans. He knew Jayme had been in contact with Mac, but she'd not said anything about Erik returning also.
~~~

Now that he was here, he wasn't sure what to do next. Maybe he'd just show up and see what happened. But he'd plan it for tomorrow when he knew Kaia and Mac would both be gone. He and Bri needed to hash this out, once and for all.

4

Before the sun was even peeking over the horizon, Bri dashed out of bed and raced for the bathroom, her hand clamped firmly over her mouth.

When she flushed a few minutes later, Kaia was standing in the doorway.

"You okay?"

Bri stood and nodded. "Yeah."

Kaia came a little further into the room. "You really need to call Erik and tell him. He needs to know."

When Bri had first discovered she was pregnant a few weeks before, she'd had to come clean with Kaia. Telling her best friend she'd had sex with her cousin the first night they'd met had been a little embarrassing. For all of her temerity, jumping perfect strangers out on the back porch wasn't something she normally did.

Kaia had taken it pretty well though. She'd said she'd suspected something had happened between them but hadn't wanted to pry. She'd apparently changed her mind though, because now Kaia nagged her on a daily basis to tell Erik he was going to be a father.

"I know." Bri rinsed her mouth out. "I will. I just haven't found the best way yet."

"You just haven't found the guts yet, you mean." Kaia grinned at her in the mirror, her eyebrow quirked up.

"Yeah. That too." Bri leaned on the counter and gave voice to something she'd been worrying about. "What if he doesn't want the baby, Kai?"

The smile slid from Kaia's face as she came to her and wrapped an arm around her waist. She looked at Bri's reflection in the mirror over the sink. "Honey, of course he's going to want it. The most important thing to a shifter is family."

Bri's voice was smaller as she stared back at Kaia. "What if he doesn't want *me*?" That was the real question that haunted her. "I was so awful to him, Kai. I was the reigning Queen Bitch the whole time he was here."

A glint sparked in Kaia's grey-green eyes. "Not the *whole* time." She glanced down at Bri's still-flat stomach. "Obviously."

Bri laughed. "It was actually the best night I've ever had. In my *life*."

"See, now you're just bragging." Kaia stuck her tongue out at Bri and then laughed.

Kaia was glowing and beautiful, and Bri sent her an evil glare. "You're just as pregnant as I am. How are *you* not sick all the time? That is so not fair."

Kaia gently patted the baby nestled within her own flat tummy. "Better constitution, I guess," she said with a smirk.

"It still sucks." Bri leaned her head against Kaia's shoulder. "But I love that we're pregnant at the same time. With only a few weeks separating them, our babies will get to grow up together."

Kaia smiled warmly. "I love that too. I can't wait to see all of our kids running around and playing."

Bri straightened and took note of Kaia's robe. "Are you just coming in from a run?"

"Yup. Amazing morning."

"What about shifting while you're pregnant? Doesn't that worry you?"

"It did, but I called and talked to Jackie. And after lots of screaming and shouting for joy when I broke the news," Kaia chuckled, "she told me that it's fine for the first trimester. After that, I need to refrain from shifting for the health of me, the baby, and my cat."

"How is your cat with this development?"

"Pretty great, actually. It's almost kind of weird that she's not pushing me to shift and run every day. She knows there's a little bean in there, and she feels so happy and…maternal. She's calm and content and super mellow. Anything I want to do right now is basically fine with her, even if that means not getting to run for a while later on."

"Momma?" a sleepy voice called from the other room.

Bri and Kaia both heard it.

"I'm coming, baby," Bri called back. She turned her head and gave Kaia a kiss on the cheek. "You go get ready for work. I'll see you later. Love you."

"I love you too." Kaia hesitated at the doorway. "Are you still going to that little meadow to take pictures today? Do you need me to write down the directions?"

"I think I can remember how you said to get there." Bri gave a light laugh. "And yes, we'll be going, if I can stop throwing up long enough to get there."

"Toast and saltines. I've heard they do wonders." Kaia turned and left.

"Says the woman not at all afflicted with morning sickness," Bri shouted after her. She heard Kaia laugh and went to get Min up and ready for the day.

July in Montana was bright, warm, and beautiful, temperatures usually hovering right in the mid-eighties. Bri dressed her and Min in matching spaghetti-strap sundresses. They were white and had large colorful flowers all over them.

Bri couldn't wait to take Min to the meadow Kaia had told her about. Her best friend went there frequently while in cat form to stretch out and relax. She said it was strewn with wildflowers right now and that the setting would make for amazing pictures.

She had thousands of Min already, but she couldn't seem to stop. She wanted to document every moment of this miracle child's life. She thought of the baby she carried and felt a wave of love. For someone who never thought they'd be a mother, here she was with two. And she was loving every minute. Not the barfing so much, but everything else.

Raising two shifter cubs as a non-shifter was going to be both interesting and terrifying. But she had Kaia to learn from and lean on.

If—no, *when*—she made the call to Erik, he'd probably step up and help her out. But after the way she'd treated him, she was likely the last person he wanted to hear from—much less, raise a child with. They'd only been together that one time, and it'd been two months since then. He'd probably moved on with someone else by now.

Bri placed her hands low over her stomach. Who could have ever guessed this would happen? She'd been on the *pill*, for crying out loud. She didn't know why it hadn't worked. Maybe shifters had some kind of super-potent sperm that were immune to birth control or something. Whatever the reason, she wouldn't change a thing about the tiny life growing inside of her.

Bri took a deep breath and let it out. She was going to have to work up the nerve to tell him. It wasn't right to keep this from him for much longer. But she would explain to him that she didn't expect anything from him. That if he wanted to be a part of the child's life, she wouldn't stand in his way. Hopefully, they could co-parent amicably.

She'd just have to wait and see.

~~~
~~~

Kaia had left for work, so with Min occupied with her toys, Bri went to the kitchen to pack some snacks and drinks. She'd just added the last juice when there was a knock on the door.

Cautious, she made sure to look and see who it was before opening the door. Ordinarily a quiet place, she had a child's safety to think about now.

Peeking out the window, she drew back in shock. She couldn't believe what she was seeing.

Erik.

"Shit." Bri backed away from the door and nervously wiped her palms on the sides of her dress. What the hell was he doing here?

Probably came to see Kaia or Mac.

Okay. She could do this. She'd tell him they weren't home and he'd leave. Easy-peasy.

Fuck. No, it wasn't. She had to tell him the other news. He needed to know. She'd better suck it up and take this opportunity, since the universe was practically throwing him at her and demanding she stop being a coward.

Unconsciously, she reached up to adjust her hair and straighten her clothes. Taking a deep breath, Bri opened the door.

They stared at each other for a long beat. Heat infused her, remembering.

"What are you doing here?" Her voice wasn't as solid as she would have liked.

"I came back so we could…" His words trailed off. He was silent for a moment as he took her in and then met her gaze, studying her. Then his blue eyes narrowed and turned accusing. "You're pregnant?"

Her hand flew to her belly. "How…?" The only ones who knew were Kaia and Mac, and they wouldn't have told him.

He tracked the movement. "My cat. He can sense the difference in you." He brought his intense focus back up to her face. "Why didn't you tell me?"

"I was planning on it." Her tone should have been more clipped, but she couldn't quite reach the shields she usually pulled around her. She didn't even know why she was trying to summon them. There was no point in them anymore.

His eyes held her captive while his tone softened. "Can I come in? I came to talk to you, but I see now there's a lot more to discuss than I thought."

Letting him in would be a mistake. She knew that. She couldn't be closed up in this house with him. Even with Min there to curb anything naughty, Bri was afraid she'd make a fool of herself. Her thoughts, since finding out she was pregnant with his child, had all been about Erik. She'd missed him just being near. The mere presence of him did something to her, and she was scared she'd lose it and run right into his arms.

She needed some distance from the drugging force he seemed to have on her. "Min and I were just on our way out. She's really looking forward to going, and I'd hate to change plans now." She was trying her damnedest to keep him at arm's length. And using her two-year-old as a buffer to do it.

Yeah, great parenting skills there, Bri.

"Do you mind if I tag along? We really need to talk over a few things." His blue eyes dropped to her stomach again and back to her face. "Especially now."

Outside would be better than inside. But maybe she could set his mind to rest first. "Fine. But I'm going to tell you right off—I don't need anything from you. I have more than enough money to support myself and my kids. I'm not looking to you for any type of handout."

The blue of his irises sparked with determination. "And I'm telling *you* right off, that is my child too, and I'll support that child, and its mother. I hope we can achieve that agreeably, but either way, don't think I'm leaving you to raise that baby by yourself."

She had to give it to him for being a stand-up guy. Most would have probably cut and run when they found out they were released from duty. Not Erik, though. It just went to prove the kind of man he was.

Bri's thoughts derailed a moment as his being there really sunk in. It had been weeks since she'd seen him, and damn. He looked *good*. The dreams she'd been having about him were nowhere near as tempting as the real thing. But she needed to keep her head and find out what his plans were now that he knew.

"You can come."

"Thank you."

"I need to finish getting ready to go."

"Go ahead. I'll wait out here." He seemed to know she needed some space and turned away from the door to lean on the porch rail.

She mechanically turned and walked down the hall. When she reached the safety of her bedroom, she stopped and inhaled deeply. As she let it out, she shook herself, trying to dispel the flush that had crept over her body at just being close to him.

Ten minutes later, Bri had Min loaded into her car seat. As she shut the rear door and opened hers, she saw Erik patiently sitting in the passenger seat. Sliding behind the wheel, she swore he was taking up too much room in the car. And sucking up all of the oxygen. For some reason, Bri was having a hard time breathing with him in such close confines.

Her body was also going haywire. She felt flushed again, her heart was beating hard, and her nipples had puckered into tight little buds. Thank God he hadn't seemed to notice that through her cotton dress. Humiliating would have been an understatement.

Bri tried to put him out of her mind as she drove into the Lost Creek State Park. She followed the road around until she came to the turnoff Kaia had mentioned. She pulled to the side of the road and parked.

"From here we'll have to walk."

He nodded and silently exited the car. In the mirror, she saw him round the back and open the trunk. When he shut it again, she saw that he'd retrieved the large bag and blanket she'd put in there.

Slowly, Bri pushed her door open and slid from her seat. Since he was grabbing all of that, all she had to do was take her camera bag and get Min.

With her daughter on her hip, Bri looked for and found the landmark Kaia had described. It was a short hike through the trees, but then it opened up into a beautiful meadow. Kaia had said it would be the perfect day to come out here. And she'd been right.

When Bri stepped into the sunlight with Min in her arms, she drew in a stunned breath.

"It's gorgeous. Min, look at all the pretty flowers!"

Spread out in front of them was an area about thirty yards square. Everywhere the eye landed were bright blooms in every possible color.

Min wiggled to be let down. As she took off running, Bri got her camera out and started shooting. Normally, she could block everything out while she worked. But Erik being there had thrown her off her game. She was always aware of where he was and what he was doing.

Bri didn't even know if she'd gotten any good shots, because her mind kept jumping the tracks and steering back to him.

She was fighting so hard to ignore him that she started when he spoke.

"She's something, isn't she?" He was smiling as Min ran and jumped around. Some of the stems were as tall as she was.

On the topic of her daughter, she could agree with him. "Yes, she is. I can't believe she's going to be three next week." Bri knelt down, zoomed in, and lined up another shot. Min was bent over trying to sniff a daisy. If the little girl toppled forward in her effort, Bri wanted to catch the moment.

"Her birthday is in a few days? That's great."

"Well, the one the orphanage gave her anyway," Bri added. "She's growing up way too fast."

"Daisy!" Min cheered, pulling their attention when she'd successfully smelled the flower.

"That's incredible." Surprise and awe was clear in Erik's voice. "She knows the names of the flowers?"

Bri had to laugh in spite of trying to keep some formality between them. "Not really. Kaia had an all-white filly she was training named Daisy. So now anything that's completely white, Min calls it Daisy."

Erik chuckled. "Well. That's something too."

Bri followed Min around for a good hour, laughing at the dancing and joyous little girl while happily clicking away on her camera.

Suddenly, Min started grabbing flowers by the handful, ripping them from the ground and shredding their delicate stems. Bri was about to tell her not to, when the adorable little imp came running to her, fists full of a haphazard bouquet held out to Bri.

"Fwoers for oo, Momma."

Bri's breath hitched and tears burned her eyes. She squatted down, meeting her daughter on her own level. "That is so sweet, baby. I love them. Thank you."

The spontaneous and thoughtful gesture meant so much to Bri, and she hugged her darling girl tightly against her. She would treasure this memory forever. She vowed to take the little posies home and press them into Min's baby book with a photo and description of the day.

Min bolted out of her arms and headed straight for Erik. He'd spread out the blanket and was lounging on it watching them. At odd moments throughout the day, Bri had felt his gaze on her. And it had made her warm.

She rose to her feet, amused to see that Min still held one bedraggled flower in her other hand. Erik's face lit up at the unexpected surprise. He leaned forward and took it from her, smiling at Min. "For me? Thank you so much." Erik unbuttoned the breast pocket on his shirt and slid the crushed stem into it. The little orange bloom drooped over the edge.

Min reached out and poked Erik in the shoulder. "Kitty."

Erik's gaze flew to Bri, and she gave him a short nod as she walked over to stand close to them.

"Yes. There *is* a kitty in there. Just like," Erik returned the poke, "you have."

Min patted her chest. "Kitty sweep." Her large brown eyes held Erik's blue ones.

"Yes, it is. Your kitty is asleep. But she'll wake up very soon."

"Pway wiff kitty," Min demanded.

"She's not ready to play yet, sweetie."

Bri realized he'd misunderstood. "She means yours. Kaia has shifted for her a few times. She loves it."

"Oh." Erik looked from Bri to Min and back.

Bri only thought she'd been nervous when it was Kaia's cat. Thinking about Erik's, a much larger and more powerful male, threatened to scare her out of her mind.

She went to Min and tugged her away from Erik. "Erik's kitty is resting right now too, baby. Maybe he can play another time."

"Erk kitty. Pway." Min's tone was a little more insistent.

Yeah, he was pretty Erk-some all right, Bri thought.

"I don't mind," Erik offered easily. "Really. He's actually very good with kids. And we're far enough away from anyone who could see."

Bri's gaze darted between her daughter and the man she barely knew. Let her child play with a potentially deadly predator...or break her daughter's little heart?

Erik lived in a large colony of shifters, and according to Jackie, it was common practice for the adult cats to spend time with the clan's youngest members, starting at a very young age. Surely Erik's cougar had spent plenty of time with other kids before now?

Bri took a deep breath and tried to calm her nerves. It would probably be okay. But she narrowed her eyes at Erik all the same and pointed a menacing finger at him.

"If he makes one wrong move with her, both man and cat will regret it. You got me?"

He nodded, not at all offended by her threat. "Absolutely. And I wouldn't expect anything less. He'll be a perfect gentleman, I promise."

Erik rose and walked off into the trees on the far side of the meadow. Min tried to follow, but Bri held on to her hand.

"He'll be right back, baby girl. Let's just wait here."

Bri fought off the scene that wanted to play out in her mind of him stripping off all of his clothes.

No. You are not doing this.

Within seconds of going in, the most beautiful creature she had ever seen strolled out of the shadows. She'd only ever seen him at night or from a distance, but in broad daylight this close, he was magnificent.

He was easily two hundred pounds. With her best friend being a mountain lion shifter, she'd done research. She knew the stats, and Erik's cat tipped the scales. Broad, stocky head, long sinuous body, thick legs that led down to wide, silent paws, and a black-tipped tail swaying as he moved.

Bri was momentarily mesmerized by the way his shoulders rose and fell with each measured step he took. He really was superb. She almost forgot to be wary until he got closer, and she saw just how huge he really was. He would tower over Min.

Min, on the other hand, didn't seem to be fazed by his size at all. She was pushing at Bri's hands to let go of her. Bri looked into eyes that were a dark stormy blue, making sure they were on the same page. The enormous cougar bowed his head and then folded himself to the ground to lay on his side. The tip of his tail was flicking, but that was the only movement.

Keeping a watchful eye, Bri released Min. The little girl gave a squeal of delight and launched herself at the cat.

Bri held herself on the edge of fear, ready to snatch her daughter away the moment things took a turn. But Erik's cat was so gentle and docile with Min, it was obvious he'd done this before, letting kids, and probably cubs, climb all over him.

He seemed to be having just as much fun as Min. And Bri was shocked when she heard a loud, deep purr rumbling from the cat's chest. At some point, Bri lost her panic and knelt down on the blanket to watch them. Picking up her camera, she started to snap pictures of Min playing with the massive mountain lion.

As it neared lunch time, she called Min back. Erik rose, but instead of heading into the forest, he slowly approached her on tentative steps. Bri held her breath as he came within inches of her, and she stayed perfectly still, staring into the large feline eyes.

When his big head dipped low and nudged into her lap, Bri sucked air into her lungs. And let it out again in a whoosh as he proceeded to rub his face over her stomach, first one side and then the other. He brushed against her as a housecat would, purring softly.

With no command from her, her hand rose and was about to pet the majestic animal. But she caught herself just in time and snatched it back quickly.

Blue eyes regarded her briefly before he turned and sauntered away.

She got busy laying out their lunch and didn't look up when Erik returned.

He sat down across from her. "Sorry about that. I hope he

didn't frighten you."

"No." Bri had to clear her throat a little. "He didn't. It was fine."

They ate in silence for a bit before Erik spoke. "Are you ready to talk about this now?"

"I suppose we should." Bri wiped her hands on a napkin to give herself a little more time. She looked over at him. "I was going to tell you—I just hadn't worked up the nerve yet. I was such a…" she cast a quick look at Min munching on some cut-up grapes, "b-i-t-c-h with you, I didn't think you'd want to talk to me."

"That begs the question, why *were* you such a…b-i-t-c-h? Was it because of the…s-e-x?"

Bri had to grin at him for spelling out the words as she'd done.

"Partly," she admitted.

"Care to explain?"

Bri told him of her childhood and how she'd had to hide who she really was behind who everyone thought she should be.

"For a lot of years, Kaia was the only one who knew the real me and I could be myself around. It's only been since they got together that I let Mac in. Up until just a little while ago, he couldn't stand to be near me."

Bri hated having to admit those things about herself, proving what a shallow person she'd been. She'd pushed everyone else away to protect herself, because she hadn't been strong enough to let her true self shine through.

Since Min, though, that had all started to change. She didn't want to hide anymore, and she never wanted Min to see that fake persona. Her daughter loved her for who she was, and anyone who didn't could fuck off for all she cared.

"I heard you with the others when you thought I wasn't around," Erik revealed. "You'd talk and laugh and kid around. You were so open and friendly, so different than when I was there. I didn't understand it, but I got the hint loud and clear that it was only me you had an issue with."

"I know. I'm sorry. That night..." She paused to brace herself. "It scared me. From the moment you walked into Kaia's house and I looked into your eyes, I knew something was there. I'd never intended to act on it, but then you caught me unprepared when you walked out of the forest...n-a-k-e-d."

Bri grinned shyly as her gaze darted to Min, now stretched out on the blanket, her eyes droopy with exhaustion from the morning's activities. Erik smiled back, nodding his encouragement to continue.

"I'd never experienced what I felt with you that night, and after what we'd done...I couldn't let you get too close. I needed to concentrate on making a stable, loving home with my child, and I didn't think I could let anyone else in." Bri sighed heavily. "I didn't *want* to let anyone else in."

He watched her carefully. "And now?"

"And now, I'm just tired," she confided truthfully, sagging a little. "I'm tired of hiding behind that awful mask. I'm tired of being alone. I love this little girl with everything I have." She looked lovingly back at Min and found her fast asleep. "And she loves *me*. And that's amazing to me. In a strange way, it gives me the confidence to be myself, and to want something better for the both of us." She smiled then and brought her attention back to Erik. "And I do. I see the bond between Kaia and Mac— that shared love and commitment and honesty—and I want that too. I want it all."

"You *can* have it all."

Bri shook her head wistfully. "I don't know how. I've pushed people away for too long."

"I came back, despite the mask, Bri. I came back for *you*." The truth in his bright blue eyes warmed her. "You weren't the only one knocked off your feet by what happened." Erik scooted a little closer to her and pitched his voice low. "My world completely shattered that night, along with the rest of me. I thought I knew what I wanted—life in the clan, doing my job, keeping everyone safe. And then I walked into that house and saw you. Something hit me, dead center of my chest. You took my breath away, and my cat went bonkers. Your scent hit him, and he was already a goner."

Bri's pulse kicked as she thought back to what they'd learned of Kaia's cat. Was he telling her that his cat had chosen her? "Your cat... Does that mean we're...life-mates?

"Our animal sides don't pick our life-mates as the females do. But when they find someone they want, they can be pretty relentless. What made it so difficult was that I was in total agreement with him. But since we'd only just met and I didn't think you'd appreciate being swooped up and carted off by a complete stranger, I left. I went and tried to run it off before I did something jail-worthy."

He grinned at her. "We both know how that ended..."

He leaned in so his mouth was right against her ear. "With the best night of my fucking life." Erik's lips teased her neck as goosebumps rippled down her arms. "I couldn't stop thinking about you." His teeth grazed across her shoulder, and she groaned, her head beginning to swim. "I dreamed about you." He trailed his tongue up the cord of her neck, and she tilted her head, giving him better access to her skin. "My cat was inconsolable when we left. And so was I." His hand wove into her hair as he tipped her chin up so he could see her face. "I'd really like to make this work. I think we could have something amazing together."

His mouth took hers, and as his tongue swept inside, Bri took a leap of faith, sinking into his kiss. They already had a chemistry that not only topped the charts but melted the damned things.

As they stretched out over the blanket, Bri leaned up on one elbow and looked down into his handsome face. Her head was spinning, and her hormones were raging out of control, the need for him spiking hard and hot through her veins. "I think you might be right."

Conscious of the toddler dozing not too far away, they kissed and caressed, getting reacquainted with each other, but keeping it PG in deference to their chaperone.

Even if she *was* asleep on the job.

Content for now to just cuddle and soak in the sun, Bri and Erik spoke quietly of their families and everything else that came to mind. Seizing the moment, Bri shifted and grabbed her camera.

Rising to her knees, she snapped shots of Erik from various angles, a new plan for her future beginning to take shape in her mind.

5

It felt like a punch to the gut. She was so fucking beautiful.

Long, straight, honey-blonde hair blowing in the soft summer breeze. Amber eyes that reminded him of... *Well, shit.* They were the same color as his cougar's coat. He had pictures his mom had taken of him, and Bri's eyes were an exact match.

He knew she was the same age as Kaia, making her twenty-eight. She wasn't overly tall, but she wasn't short either. To Erik, she was the perfect height. And he already knew they fit together effortlessly.

He watched her move—the way she bent or knelt to set up the shot she wanted—practiced and professional. He'd felt a little self-conscious at first to have her taking so many pictures of him, but then he got lost just looking at her and forgot what she was doing.

Could they really work this out? It sounded like they were going to try. They'd slept together first and were getting to know each other second. But who was he to complain? They'd obviously done something right, because here they were. Even if the road had been long and painful in the process.

It scared the shit out of him that she was pregnant. He was walking into a relationship with not one, but *two* kids. He'd been around children all his life. But what did he know about raising them? Not much, if he actually stopped to think about it.

Letting his cougar play with Min had been nice. Since getting back into town and finding Bri again, his cat had been downright giddy. And he'd felt the wave of protectiveness his cat exuded for little Min. If anything or anyone ever threatened them, his cat would fight to the death for them.

And for the tiny cub that was still growing inside of Bri. The pride he'd sensed when the big male had rubbed his scent on her had been overwhelming. He'd staked his claim to both of them, daring anyone to try and take them from him.

He and Erik were on the same page when it came to that. For better or worse, this was his family now. And no one had better try to come between them.

"It's getting pretty late. We should probably get her home." Bri began to pick up the picnic debris.

Erik jumped in to help, and soon he was carrying a sleeping toddler to the car. He set her gently into her seat and watched as Bri did up the buckles, taking note for next time.

The drive back to Kaia's was a lot less stressful than the previous one. Erik reached out and grasped her hand and didn't feel at all like a dork. It was nice, actually. He'd never been a tactile person, but he liked touching her. He needed to.

She sent him a quick grin.

Arriving back at Kaia's, he carefully carried Min into the empty house and to her room. He couldn't believe how much he enjoyed the weight of her head on his shoulder and the limp, exhausted body asleep on his chest. He almost hated to lay her down. But he eventually put the little girl to bed and tucked the brightly colored blanket around her. When he rose and turned, Bri was watching him from the doorway.

"You're good at that." She smiled. "I've not managed to move her without waking her up."

"Beginner's luck. I have to say, I kinda liked it." He crossed the room to stand in front of her. He put his hands on her hips and drew her in, his lips meeting hers softly.

Only to be taken in. Taken under.

The embrace went from chaste to scorching in a heartbeat. Two months away from her was a long time after he'd had a taste. When he released her, they were both out of breath. He looked down into amber eyes that were sizzling with need. Erik took a step forward, pushing her back one, just enough to clear the door into the hallway and close it behind them.

Bending at the knees, Erik reached down and cupped her ass, lifting her into his arms. Her knees wrapped around his hips and snugged her core to his straining erection. He locked his lips to hers again, angling his head to deepen the connection. His tongue pushed past her rosy lips to plunder the depths of her mouth.

At the same time, he covered the short distance to the opposite wall. Her back came up against it with a soft thud. Her arms were entwined around his neck, her hands on the back of his head gripping his short hair tight.

Using one arm and his weight to hold her aloft, Erik ran his other hand up the outside of her thigh. When he encountered the cotton of her dress he pushed it aside. The next barrier to his goal were her panties. Tangling his fingers in the thin material at her hip, he yanked hard.

When they came loose in his hand, she gasped. He caught the sound in his mouth and took it into himself. Removing them the rest of the way, he tucked his spoils of war into his pocket.

Bared to him now, he caressed her silky-smooth ass, following the crease between her cheeks all the way down until he found what he'd been searching for. What he'd been dreaming of. Her soaked sex. She was so wet, so ready. For him.

"Touch me," Bri whispered when he skimmed his fingers over her channel.

"Oh, I plan on it." Splitting her folds, Erik ran them through the slick honey. He found her clit and pressed into it.

Bri's head fell back against the wall as her pelvis undulated. "Oh God, yeah."

He loved that she was so bold. She knew what she wanted and wasn't afraid to let him know.

It had been so long without her, his body was ready to explode. If he didn't get inside of her now, he'd lose it before they even began.

It wasn't easy in the position they were in, but Erik got his fly open. Then he pushed his pants out of the way enough to let his cock free.

It sprang forward as if searching for the heaven it knew was awaiting it.

"Now. Now. Now." Bri panted. "Fuck me, Erik, now."

With a grunt, he slammed home, rattling the frames hanging next to her.

Holy fuck, she felt amazing. Her walls were already constricting around him, milking him of everything he had. Buried to the hilt, he had to take a second to battle off the eruption threatening to consume him. When he knew he could give her what she wanted, he pulled back and thrust hard.

Her breasts were right there, but he couldn't get to them. He wanted to taste her. Suck those perfect nipples deep into his mouth. Torment her the way she'd tormented him for months. Both of his hands were clamped to her ass, holding her to him.

"Pull your dress down. I have to have your gorgeous tits."

Her hands came loose of his head and jerked at the stretchy material over her chest. She even went so far as to cup both of her glorious breasts and offer them to him. Erik took one puckered point and nibbled at it.

She mewled softly, and her sex squeezed around him.

He gave the same attention to the other and then drew her in as he'd craved. He felt her sex spasm harder around him.

Jesus. She was so fucking responsive.

His hips and mouth worked in tandem. And between the

double assault to her body, Bri shattered in his arms. He rode her through the orgasm and only let go himself when she was limp and sated.

They stood there, her pinned to the wall by his bulk, breathing heavily.

"Not a fluke," she murmured in his ear. "Not a fluke."

Erik grinned and slowly let her feet slide to the floor. He didn't release her completely until he knew she could support herself. It also gave his own body a moment to recover, his legs weak as he slid out of her.

Once she was steady, he adjusted himself, and did up his pants.

He reached up and cupped the side of her face. Brushing his thumb over her lips, he leaned down and kissed her. "Definitely not a fluke."

Raising his head, he took in her disheveled state. "Beautiful."

She gave a half-laugh. "Yeah, I'll bet." She pushed some of the wild strands of hair out of her face. "Why don't you get us something to drink while I go clean up?"

She glanced around. "Where are my panties?"

"In my pocket." Erik leered at her.

"Can I have them back?" Bri set one hand on her hip. The other was outstretched, waiting.

"No." He was enjoying this.

Bri eyed him and then smirked. "A little pervy. I like it." She laughed and adjusted her dress as she crossed to the bathroom.

~~~

They were sitting cuddled together on the couch talking, watching Min play with her babies, when Kaia came home.

She was shocked to see him. "Erik? What are you doing here?" She stopped and looked at how closely they were sitting and then grinned. "Oh, I see."
~~~

Bri felt like she needed to explain. "He showed up this morning. We talked."

"That's good to hear." Kaia nodded. "She finally told you."

"Not exactly." Erik looked at Bri and back to Kaia. "I had already decided to come before I knew. But as soon as I saw her, my cat figured it out. He could sense the change."

"And?" Kaia prompted when neither of them said anything else.

"And...we're going to try," Bri finished.

"Yay!" Kaia threw herself at Bri, landing between her and Erik, and gave her an enthusiastic hug. "I'm so glad."

"I can tell," Erik laughed, scooting out from under his cousin. "I should probably congratulate you too. Aunt Jackie and Elva were shouting it from the rooftops back home that their Kaia is having a baby."

Kaia beamed at him. "Thank you. It's very exciting. I especially love that our babies will get to grow up together." She turned back to Bri. "Come into the kitchen with me." Kaia wiggled her way off the couch. "We can girl-talk while we get dinner going."

Bri sent Erik a shrug and followed Kaia out of the room. While they had a gab-fest session, Erik kept Min entertained. When Mac, Jayme, and Moose came in, they hung out until she and Kaia had dinner on the table.

As bedtime rolled around a few hours later, Bri wasn't sure how the sleeping arrangements were going to work. She didn't feel right sharing her bed with her daughter in the same room, but Erik took matters out of her hands by saying he and Jayme had rented rooms at a nearby motel.

Mac and Kaia excused themselves to their room, Moose following slowly behind them. The poor dog had to be exhausted. Min, who was also sleeping peacefully, had played with him for hours.

Having driven her own car, Jayme said her goodbyes too,

leaving Bri and Erik sitting on the couch alone.

He pulled her into his arms and took her mouth in a kiss that had her body going fluid.

This, whatever it was beginning between them, was *so* not a fluke.

She just wished she could pinpoint how she felt about that. Bri acknowledged that she felt safer in his arms than she ever had in her life. She knew that no matter what, he would be there to protect her.

Until Kaia, she had never known a trust like that. Her parents had loved her, but they hadn't been there when she'd awoken from nightmares or been afraid of the dark. When kids had been cruel during her childhood, she'd wiped away her own tears and learned to cope, alone, with the harsh realities of life. She'd had to develop ways of protecting and soothing herself.

Her parents hadn't been equipped to raise and nurture a child. Both had come from money, and in that world, nannies were meant to be the primary caregivers. Parents didn't engage with their children until they reached an age where they could connect with them as adults.

They hadn't been bad parents; they just hadn't known any differently.

What Erik made her feel was more than she could have ever imagined, and it scared her to see how quickly she could fall for him. How easily she could come to rely on him.

He hummed and released her. "Making love to you on my cousin's couch probably isn't a good idea. Especially with them down the hall." He gave her one more kiss. "I'd better go."

"Yeah." She bit his lip and then licked where she'd used her teeth.

"Bri. You're killing me."

She grinned, leaning in close to whisper in his ear. "Dream of me."

"Why would that change now?" His blue eyes held hers. "I've

been doing that since the night I met you."

Bri's stomach did a little flip, and her body clenched. *Oh, boy.* "You'll have to tell me about them sometime."

"Maybe I'll *show* you." He smirked. "In the meantime, I'd really better go before I slide you out of those clothes and defile your best friend's sofa."

~~~

Erik was there the following day. And the one after that. And the one after that.

He took her and Min out on dates that had both mother and daughter swooning. Min was completely and irrevocably in love with him, while Bri was still trying to determine how she felt, beyond the overwhelming sexual attraction that clouded her brain and kept her from thinking straight.

Almost a week into their dating, he arranged for Kaia and Mac to take care of Min, so they could have a very adult night out at the fanciest restaurant in Anaconda.

Bri felt decadent, dressed to kill in a silvery-blue sheath of fabric that hugged her body and flowed down to brush her legs at mid-thigh. Three-inch heels accentuated her toned and tanned legs.

She wore her hair swept up off her neck and held in place by strategically placed pins. Ones that, given the slightest touch of a man's hand, would release and allow her hair to tumble down around her shoulders. She'd done her makeup with a light hand. A subtle shading on her lids and blush pink on her lips, and the result was a fresh, natural glow.

She'd not felt the need to use the full, painted mask she'd always hidden behind since Erik had returned. All aspects of her protective persona were falling away, and she couldn't be happier. She was feeling more confident and sure of herself, especially when Erik's eyes nearly crossed at his first glimpse
~~~

of her.

The drive into Anaconda was easy. They talked and, of all things, held hands over the center console. Bri thought it was nice. He seemed to crave that contact with her, and she couldn't help but admit she kind of liked it.

After parking, he opened her door for her, assisting her out with a sure hand. As they walked to the entrance, his palm warmed the small of her back through the thin material of her dress. And sent a shiver down her spine.

"How did you even get reservations here?" Bri asked as they followed the hostess to their table. "You've only been in town for a few days. This place has a waiting list a month long."

Erik slid her chair out for her to sit and leaned over her to whisper in her ear. "The owner is one of Kaia's clients. She asked for a favor, and he was only too happy to oblige."

The tickle of his breath on her neck sent chills over her skin. Bri tipped her head to the side. "Mmmm. Gotta love favors."

He planted a soft kiss below her ear before moving back around the table, his gaze fixed on her. His bright blue eyes took in every inch of her face. "You are so damned beautiful."

"Thank you." Bri smiled at him. "And you're looking mighty handsome yourself." He was dressed in crisp dark slacks that hugged his lean frame, a dove gray dress shirt open at the collar, and a deep blue and silver pinstripe suit coat. His hair was styled perfectly, and smooth cheeks told of a recent shave.

He cleaned up mouth-wateringly well.

Eyes lingered for several more beats before each picked up the menus the hostess had left.

"Since you're the local here," Erik's grinning gaze caught hers over the top of the menu, "what do you suggest?"

Bri liked that he valued her opinion. "Well, you can never go wrong with the steak—it's always cooked to perfection. The filet will melt in your mouth. But my favorite here has always been the grilled salmon. It has this creamy dill sauce that is amazing."

Erik set his menu aside. "Then salmon it is. And what cat doesn't love fish?" he joked.

The waiter arrived with soft, steaming bread and a plate full of toasted garlic with seasoned oil. They gave him their order, and Erik requested a bottle of wine that was a favorite of Bri's.

"Good choice." Bri tore a piece of bread off and dipped it in the herbed oil. "That pairs really well with the salmon." She popped the bite into her mouth and chewed, watching him. He also sampled the appetizer, never taking his eyes from her. His gaze traveled from her face to the draped neckline of the dress, and lower to her breasts.

Her nipples tightened. She could almost feel his mouth on them. But before either could say anything else, Bri heard her name being called.

"Abrianna? Abrianna Calladega. Oh my word."

The sensual mood she and Erik had been building and enjoying was shattered. Bri's whole body stiffened in response. Only those in her parents' circle called her by her full name, and she recognized the voice instantly.

Unfortunately, it belonged to a particularly nasty woman in her seventies who thought that since she had more money than God, she could treat everyone horribly and say anything she wanted, regardless of how hurtful it was.

No one ever called her on it, because between her foul attitude and expansive bank account, she could make or break a person with just a single word.

Bri sent an apologetic look to Erik and then schooled her features until every vestige of the true Bri had fallen away. In her place was the pretentious façade that Suzanna VanderGrayson-Hillyard expected to see.

Bri rose elegantly to her feet as Suzanna glided towards their table. She made a point to move past Erik, blocking Suzanna's view of him.

"Suzanna." Bri leaned in politely for the customary air-kiss and plastered a smile on her face. "How wonderful to see you."

I'd rather be rolling in horse shit.

"It has been *ages.*" Suzanna made no attempt to hide the fact that she was taking Bri's measure and finding it lacking. "Where have you been hiding yourself? Your skin looks positively dried out." Suzanna gave her a pitying look. "Aw, are you still spending all your time outdoors trying to play at that picture-taking hobby? You really should put all that away and spend some time at this marvelous spa I found in France. They'll have you looking beautiful and fresh again in no time. And who did your make-up, a blind woman? Such a shame."

You can kiss my dried out lily-white ass, you old shrew.

On the outside, Bri smiled demurely.

"I'll look into that, thank you."

Out of the corner of her eye, Bri saw Erik shift in his seat. Knowing his nature, she could guess he was about to jump to her defense, but she couldn't allow that to happen. She was used to this, and this was how the game was played.

Very subtly, Bri stepped back with her right leg, felt his foot, and leaned her weight onto it. The spike of her heel came down right on top of it. She felt him flinch under her threat, and he made no further movement.

Suzanna continued on. "How are your parents? I haven't seen them since the last time we were all in Rome."

Bri kept her expression bored. "Oh, you know my parents. They're forever flitting about, wherever the wind takes them." *Enough with the chit-chat. What do you want, you nasty old hag?* "So, what brings you to Montana, Suzanna?"

The elderly woman angled her thin nose higher in the air if possible. "I've heard there is a much sought-after horse trainer here in this nowhere, backwater place."

Holy hell, she's here to see Kaia.

"I need her for my Diamond, but I refuse to send my darling

here." The last word was said with such derision, it sounded more like she were describing the lower bowels of hell. "This woman will just have to clear her schedule for the foreseeable future and come back to my home with me."

Bri bit back a laugh. Suzanna obviously didn't know Kaia Reid at *all*.

"I've heard of her." The air of indifference was thick. "She's in pretty high demand. I didn't think she took off-site work, though."

"Oh, but of course she will." Suzanna waved dismissively. "Everyone has their price. She'll do as I say if she wants to stay in business."

Bri felt her hackles rise. *She doesn't need your moldy old money, and she sure as hell doesn't need you.*

Erik cleared his throat to speak, but Bri settled more weight on his foot again to shut him up.

"I'm sure you're right." Bri shrugged. "Well, Suzanna. It has been a pleasure. I'll be sure to tell my parents I ran into you. It was so nice to see you again."

"I'll have my girl email you the information on that spa. You'll love it."

More air kisses, and Suzanna swept away.

Bri sat, exhausted from the charade. When she looked across the table at Erik, his eyes glittered. Was it anger or mirth? She couldn't tell.

The waiter returned with their wine, and they both sat mute as he popped the cork and poured for them.

Once they were alone again, Bri beat him to the punch. "I am so sorry. But the less she noticed you, the better. She's a mean-spirited old harridan who enjoys ripping people up. I'm used to her, and I knew I could get through it with a minimal amount of bloodshed. But if she'd turned that loose on you, I would have had to rip her wig off and stuff it down her shriveled-up throat." Bri shook her head. "She normally only notices those within her same social circles, but if you had jumped in to defend me or Kaia, it would have opened the floodgates. I couldn't take that chance."

He stared at her a few more moments before his expression softened and filled with a touch of humor. "So, you drilled a hole in my foot to protect me?"

The waiter brought their food and asked if they needed anything else. Bri waited until he'd departed and took a sip of her wine, enjoying the fruity bouquet. "Yes, I did, and you should be thanking me. I deserve combat pay for that encounter."

Erik smiled, swirled the liquid around in his glass, and then looked up at Bri with serious eyes. "Could she really hurt Kaia's business?"

Bri shook her head. "Not in the long run. Suzanna may run her mouth to some of her cronies, but the ones that actually believe her aren't clients Kaia would have wanted anyway. She'll be fine." Bri grinned. "Though, I would *love* to see the look on Suzanna's face when Kaia tells her to shove it up her ass for assuming she can buy her off in the first place."

Bri set her wine glass in front of her and idly ran her finger around the rim. She uncrossed her legs and sat forward so her breasts pushed upward. "Now. How about we forget the last three minutes and continue our conversation?" She slipped her shoe off and ran her toes up his calf.

Heat flashed in his eyes. "Oh? And where were we?"

She leaned in, lowering her voice to a sensual whisper. "I'm pretty sure you were trying to decide if I'm wearing anything underneath this dress."

A small smirk lifted the corner of Erik's mouth. "I do seem to recall wondering that very thing." He paused, studying her as his gaze moved slowly down the part of her body he could see. Traveling back up to meet her eyes, his brow rose in challenge. "Are you?"

"I think that's something I'll keep to myself for a little bit longer." The easy, slightly arousing feeling was returning. "At least until dessert."

Through dinner, Bri pulled out every trick she knew to keep him right on the edge of full-on need. She found out delightedly that Erik was no slouch either when it came to fanning the flames as they ate.

Light touches, the slide of a finger over pounding pulse points. The lingering looks that had nipples puckering and panties growing damp.

Feeling excited and slightly naughty, Bri excused herself to the ladies' room where she removed her thong and tucked it into her purse. As she returned, Erik rose. Having taken care of the bill in her absence, they were more than ready to leave.

As they stopped at the door to let a couple enter, Bri made sure to back right up into Erik, letting her ass nestle against his hardened groin.

His hand found her hip and squeezed tightly in response, and when his fingers drifted slowly up and then down her curves, she knew he was searching for the telltale line of undergarments.

Finding none, he breathed close to her ear. "We need to get out of here. *Now*."

His hand stayed possessively on her all the way to the car. He walked her right to the passenger side, but instead of opening the door for her, he plastered her against it, the shadowed parking lot giving them a modicum of privacy.

He leaned into her, the length of his body pressed to hers, showing her in every detail how much he wanted her. His mouth took hers, and his tongue imitated the act their bodies wanted to complete.

When he finally released her, Bri was breathing as if she'd run a marathon. It took all of her concentration to move out of the way of the door so he could open it. Once she was seated,

Erik walked around to get behind the wheel. He winced once and then shifted his hips in the seat. Bri smiled wickedly, delighting in the knowledge he was trying to accommodate his straining arousal.

Bri's belly did a slow roll when he grasped her hand and brought it to his lips. He gently kissed each of her knuckles. He wanted her, that was obvious, but he still took time for the romance of it.

"I need you," she whispered.

He drove them straight to his hotel. Bri was trembling, and it had nothing to do with the mild night air.

As he assisted her from the car, Erik noted the shivers of anticipation and offered her his jacket.

"I'm not cold. I want you so much, I can hardly control it."

Erik had his keycard out and within seconds they were inside the dark room.

"I have to see you." He reached out and flipped the switch by the door, a soft golden glow coming to life from the lamp by the bed.

She backed out of his arms and took a couple of steps away. She glided one hand up her arm until her fingers encountered the strap of her dress. With tortured slowness, Bri slid it over the arc of her shoulder and down her arm.

When that side pooled at her elbow, she did the same on the other side. With a practiced shrug, the silky fabric slithered down her body to catch at her hips, baring her to the waist.

He came to her, his steps slow and measured as his eyes bore into hers. Raising his hands, he cupped each breast, tugging and rolling both nipples.

Bri gasped and her head fell back.

His mouth took the place of his fingers, and his hands dipped down to push the dress the rest of the way off. It puddled at her feet, and she stood naked and trembling under his touch.

Raking his teeth over her nipple when he pulled away, he

groaned. "Christ, Bri," Erik said in reverent awe as he took in the sight of her. "You're so fucking beautiful. You take my breath away."

Bri stepped out of the pool of fabric at her feet. Sliding her hands up to his shoulders, she pushed the jacket off and let it drop. She went to work on the buttons of his shirt, and when that too was peeled away, she leaned in to kiss a trail across his chest, stopping to tease the little pebbled nubs of his nipples.

"Shit." His hands buried themselves in her hair, dislodging the pins holding it in place. It tumbled free down her back.

Her fingers found the waistband of his slacks, popping the hook and releasing the zipper. Reaching into the back of his pants and over his tightly muscled ass, she pushed the layers out of her way.

He toed out of his shoes and kicked off the last of his clothes.

And then they were both naked and twined around each other, hands and mouths moving over skin, neither able to slake the need for the other.

Erik turned them and took them to the bed, easing her down onto the mattress.

Bri's breath tore from her lungs when his hand found her center. Her fingers bit into his biceps as his dipped into her hot, searching core.

Her hips surged upward, seeking, demanding more. She was mindless in her need, balancing on that thin precipice of desire for hours, and now he was destroying her last bit of control.

"I need you. I need you inside me," she panted out.

His weight shifted, his fingers leaving her, and Bri thought he'd take her and fill her at last. But he shifted off of her and turned her over onto her stomach. Stretching out above her, he kissed a path across her upper back as he trailed a hand down over the rounded globe of her ass and back into her aching sheath.

Bri groaned and ground her hips into the mattress, his

fingers pushing and curling into her wet softness until she thought she'd go crazy.

"Please. I can't...I need..."

"What exactly do you need, Bri?"

"Fuck me, Erik. I need you to fuck me, *now*."

As his hand slid away, she whimpered at the empty, bereft feeling he left behind. She arched her ass up, spreading her legs to make room for him between them. He knelt behind her and lifted her hips, pulling her towards him.

Bri rose up onto her elbows, her back arching as she opened for him. He thrust forward hard, his thick cock straining inside her.

They both gasped, hers a muffled prayer and his a raspy oath.

Erik's fingers dug into her hips as he withdrew and pistoned in again. Bri's channel clenched around him, and she reveled in every inch filling and stretching her. She flexed her inner muscles, gripping him even tighter.

"Holy *fuck*, that's amazing."

He kept the pace slow and torturous, pushing in until his pelvis met her ass before pulling out almost to the point of withdrawal. Only to make the unhurried journey back in once again.

A fine sheen of sweat coated Bri's entire body. She was burning up from the inside out. He was sending her up in flames.

She was on the verge of screaming at him to take her like he meant it, when he suddenly changed his pace. His hips pumped in deep, heavy strokes, slamming home with each thrust. The sound of skin slapping skin echoed in the room among their pants and groans.

Bri knew it wouldn't take much longer. Her body was already climbing, reaching for release.

Two more strokes, and her world exploded into a kaleidoscope of color. Her sex spasmed so violently, it tipped her into a second orgasm where nothing existed but the pleasure undulating over her in waves. Carnal, driving pleasure that took her breath and left her so near a perfect death, she didn't care if she ever resurfaced.

She was drifting, slowly coming back to herself, when she became aware of Erik's hardness still buried deep.

He hadn't come yet.

She turned her head enough to see him over her shoulder. "Erik?"

He grinned, pulling his length out over sensitive tissue and nerves. "Did you think I'd be finished with you so soon?" He pushed back in, returning to the deliberately easy pace.

Bri shuddered in response and hummed in her throat.

He stroked her inner walls a few more times, leisurely, languorously. And igniting that fire again. But before she could find his rhythm, he slid free of her.

"Roll over, baby."

Bri repositioned and smiled up at him, letting her legs fall open as his hungry gaze settled on her swollen entrance.

He stalked to her, his eyes scorching as he climbed onto her and settled his weight on his arms. He leaned down to kiss her, and Bri reached between them to guide the head of his shaft into her. Their eyes locked as he thrust into her once more.

The blue of his irises was darker, and Bri thought she caught a glimpse of his cat in them. Her desire sparked, that wild and crazed look calling to the basest of her instincts. He was on the edge of losing control, and she craved it. She wanted to shatter his world the way he was shattering hers.

Bri clamped her hands on either side of his face and pulled his mouth to hers. She bit his bottom lip before licking and sucking the pain away.

His guttural response was a deep, feral growl.

The savage sound reignited her own libido, and Bri gasped

when he reared back and thrust hard into her heated body. But she never took her focus off him.

"Let go, Erik. Take me," she panted. "Ravish me."

He set a punishing pace, his wild abandon tipping her over the edge again as he erupted deep inside of her with a harsh, carnal roar.

Sated and exhausted, they collapsed to the bed in a sweaty, heaving tangle of limbs.

Bri tucked in close to his side, her body still throbbing as their hearts beat erratically. She reveled in their closeness, the intensity of her feelings towards this amazing man almost overwhelming.

6

A couple of days later, Bri pulled into the gravel drive in front of the barn and parked. She noticed the black sedan already there but didn't think too much of it. Probably a new client here to check out Kaia's training program.

Her best friend was the greatest horse trainer she'd ever seen. In three short years, she'd built up a reputation among equestrians the world over. Bri knew for a fact that she had a waiting list a mile long of clients wanting her to work with their mounts.

Maybe she should just go and not disrupt the meeting.

If she didn't have to pee something fierce, she may have. She'd always heard pregnant women complain about having to use the bathroom all the time, and that shit was *no joke*. She wasn't even that far along yet and could only imagine what it might be like several more months down the road. Maybe she could sneak in and use the one in the barn.

She turned to look at her daughter buckled in her car seat, fast asleep.

"Aw, poor baby. So tired. Did Momma wear you out shopping?"

Erik had driven with Jayme to Helena today, about an hour and a half away. They had appointments to see some furnished apartments in the area she could rent while undergoing the twelve-week police academy course. It was another step she had to complete in order to begin her job with the Anaconda Police with Mac. They'd be back later.

While he was doing that, Bri and Min had spent the day at the mall. It was Min's third birthday, and there were a few more things Bri needed for their small celebration that evening. But then she'd gotten distracted by all the adorable outfits and matching accessories they'd had for little girls. Min had hit a growth spurt, so Bri had bought a lot of great stuff for summer and fall. And all of it was so darned *cute*.

On the trip home, Min had wanted to stop by and show Aunt Kaia all her new pretty things. But the day must have been too much for her. She was completely zonked out.

Bri's bodily needs made themselves known again. *Crap. What do I do?*

Did she dare leave Min in the car to run in and go? The restroom was right inside the door. She wouldn't be gone long, and she was parked in the shade of the large structure. The weather was mild today with a rainstorm coming in later. It was only in the low seventies. She rolled the windows down and felt a nice breeze flowing through.

Yeah, it'll be okay. I'll only be a minute.

Bri got out and closed the door gently so as not to wake Min. She jogged to the wide double doors.

She saw Kaia talking with two men. They were on the smaller side, had dark hair, and were wearing severe, well-cut business suits. But that's all she could see from the backs of their heads. When Kaia noticed her, a look of surprise and then concern flashed swiftly in her green eyes. Bri sent her a little wave, placed a finger over her lips for quiet, and pointed to the bathroom.

But before she could make it to the doorway, Kaia called out to her.

"Hey, Bri." Kaia's tone was a simple greeting, but Bri heard anxiety just beneath the surface. Those who didn't know her wouldn't have heard it, but it stopped Bri in her tracks. The urge to use the restroom was forgotten.

Something was very wrong.

Kaia turned back to the men. "Excuse me just a moment, gentlemen. I've been waiting for this delivery."

She focused on Bri again. "Can you just take that package you have home with you, and I'll pick it up there later?"

Bri saw the unease in Kaia's face. For some reason, Kaia wanted her out of there. "Yeah, sure. No problem."

She went back out the way she'd come in and got in her car. But instead of leaving, she drove around to the back of the barn. If Kaia was in trouble, Bri wasn't about to let her face it alone. She got out and approached the rear doors. She stayed to the side, out of sight, and listened.

She could hear one of the men talking.

"Yes, of course. I have stable of valuable Arabians," the first man boasted in stilted and halting English. "I want to come… meet you. See your…" he paused, clearly searching for the correct word, "facility. To know if sending animals here would be right choice."

Bri knew that accent. She'd heard it plenty while jumping around Asia. These men were from the same part of the world as Min.

Her heart skipped a beat, all the air left her lungs, and suddenly she understood Kaia's reaction. But how had they found her? It had only been a few short months since she'd adopted Min and brought her home.

Had they gone to the orphanage to look for the little girl, only to find she'd found a new home? Had they gotten Bri's name from the paperwork?

Her gut roiled. The answer was dangling just on the edge of her mind, and it carried with it a sense of dread and foreboding, but what was it? She tried to focus and think back.

It couldn't have been the paperwork. She hadn't used the

farm's address on any of those documents. She hadn't even been sure at the time that she'd end up back in Lost Creek. So why had they specifically come *here*?

Bri racked her brain. And then bile rose in her throat.

"Oh shit," she choked.

The website. They'd posted those pictures of Min on Kaia's business page just a couple of months ago.

Her stomach pitched, and her gaze flew to the sleeping child in her car.

Oh, God. This can't be happening.

Her attention was pulled back when Kaia spoke. "Well, I'm so happy you came. I'd be more than happy to explain my setup here."

Bri's vision swirled as they talked horses and regimens for a few minutes and then, seemingly out of the blue, one of the men asked Kaia, "Children for you, Ms. Reid?"

Bri had to cover her mouth with her hand to stop the gasp from giving away her presence. His grasp of the English language was sparse, but Bri understood him well enough to know he was digging for information.

"My husband and I actually just found out we're expecting our first. Do either of you have kids?"

"Yes. My associate and I. Boys." There was a slight pause. "I ask because of photo I see on your site. You have picture of Asian child. We wonder if he…adopted by you."

Bri nearly freaked, but Kaia laughed easily. "Oh, that. When I first started my business years ago, I didn't have most of what you see here now. But I still needed a way to advertise what I do, and that was just a stock photo I found online. There are websites where you can buy the pictures that other people take, and I fell in love with that one." She chucked. "I have no idea who that child really is, but come to think of it, I should probably update my site with actual facility photos and client success stories."

Nice cover, Bri thought. Wouldn't hold up if they dug, but hopefully they wouldn't.

"I see. Well, no matter." Another space of silence. "Thank you for your time. I will call with decision. Good day."

"Good day to you also."

Bri concentrated, listening for their retreating footsteps. She heard their car start up and drive off down the lane.

She ran back to her car and was standing at the rear door closest to Min when Kaia emerged from the barn.

"I thought I told you to leave!"

"I couldn't leave you alone after seeing your expression." Bri's heart was pounding like a bass drum in her chest. "Who were those men?"

Kaia scrubbed her hands over her face. "I don't have any idea. But what I *do* know is that they're shifters."

All breath left Bri. She had to bend at the waist and brace her hands on her knees, trying to calm the rising panic as she gasped for air. "They're here for Min. Oh, God. They've come to take my baby."

Kaia rubbed small circles on her back. "Come on. Just breathe. She's safe, and she's going to stay that way. *No one* will take that little girl away from you."

Bri's head finally stopped spinning enough to stand upright. She looked hopefully at Kaia. "Could their being shifters just be a coincidence? Maybe they *were* just looking for a horse trainer." She knew better, but her desperation forced her to ask.

"No, but they really do know a lot about horses, so it wouldn't surprise me if that's how they found my website and the picture of Min in the first place. But they didn't come all the way here to check out my facility. The minute they saw that picture, it all changed."

Kaia heaved a sigh. "Those two were here because of Min. As soon as I realized they were shifters, I knew they were up to something. Asking me if I'd adopted an Asian child just proved it. And you want to know something else?" Kaia didn't give Bri a chance to answer. "They have no idea who they're even looking for. They came for the child they saw on my website and automatically assumed it was a boy. That tells me they're fishing."

Kaia's eyes filled with tears and her lower lip trembled. "Oh, Bri. This is all my fault. It was my idea to post the pictures of Min online, and I am so sorry."

"Hey. It was just as much my fault. I was happy to post them. Neither of us could have known this would happen." A thought occurred to Bri. "They had to know you were a shifter too. Did they say anything?"

"No. And I got the impression they don't think much of women, shifter or not. Even knowing I was one, I doubt they saw me as much of a threat."

"Well, we both know how wrong that assumption is." Kaia, in her cougar form, had taken on an adult male that was twice her size and killed him. He'd been a mountain lion shifter too and had tried repeatedly to kidnap her. He'd already murdered several others and had shot both Mac and Kaia's grandmother.

"We have to get out of here and start coming up with a plan." Bri gazed at her sleeping child. "Mac needs to know. He'll have a better idea of what we can do to protect Min." She brought her focus back to Kaia. "No one is taking my daughter from me."

"No. They're not."

Bri suddenly felt exposed. "I need to get her home."

"Yes, go. I'll call Mac and have him meet us there."

For Bri, the drive back to Kaia's felt longer than just the five minutes it always took. She watched the road, waiting for that black car to show up in her rearview. Thankfully, she didn't see anyone and got Min inside quickly. She wasn't going to let her out of her sight until this mess was dealt with.

Kaia showed up shortly after, and Mac rolled in about fifteen minutes later. They spread out around the living room, Min playing where Bri could watch over her.

Kaia had evidently brought Mac up to speed over the phone, so Bri jumped right into it, looking up at him. "Okay. What are our options?"

"I'm not sure yet," Mac said. "We're dealing with a remote village in a country that's thousands of miles away. I have no idea what parental rights entail over there."

Kaia opened her mouth to argue, but Mac stopped her. "But that doesn't mean I'm not going to find out. It's just going to take some time."

He turned to Bri. "Exactly how much do you know about Min and her situation?"

She took a deep breath. "Unfortunately, not much. I was in Laos working on a project. I'd flown into the capital and just picked a direction at random. I headed north and wove my way through the country over the next few weeks. Eventually, I happened upon Ban Xuang. That's where the orphanage was where I found Min."

"What did they tell you about her?" Mac prompted, taking a small notepad out of the breast pocket of his uniform shirt.

Bri thought back to her initial meetings with the organizers of the facility. "She'd been found on their doorstep when she was guesstimated to be a year old. No note, no nothing. And no one ever came looking for her. She'd been there about a year when I came along."

"What about the adoption process?" Mac sat forward.

"Like I told Kaia, I greased every wheel and called in favors to expedite it." Her eyes widened. "You don't think they'll use that against me, do you?"

"Everything was still done by the book though, right?" Mac clarified. "All papers duly authorized and filed?"

"Yes. I followed every step. I just used my family's clout to speed up the process."

"Then you should have nothing to worry about." Despite Mac's assurances, Bri was still worried the adoption could be overruled. If the father showed up, would the governing bodies of Min's home country demand Bri give her daughter back? Did blood relatives take precedence over legal adoptions, in favor of having the child be raised by their own families? There were countless stories of courts in the US siding with biological fathers after the fact. Would Laos be the same?

"Bri," Kaia broke into her horrifying thoughts, "have you received any official notices or emails from Laos?"

"No, why?"

"What address is on the adoption paperwork?"

"The one to my apartment in California. I use it as a base when I'm not in the States."

Kaia continued to question her. "Are your mail and deliveries still being sent there?"

"No. I made sure all of my correspondence would be forwarded here when we moved in. Where are you going with this?"

"I think I know." Mac glanced at Kaia and gave her a slight nod.

"Most people," Kaia started, "who feel they have a claim to something, will go to the authorities. They let the law deal with getting it back, because the law is typically more successful, and their decisions can't be disputed as easily. But if you haven't received any emails or letters from the adoption agency or orphanage in Laos, it seems these guys skipped that step. Instead of following the remedies already in place in their own country, they decided to follow where the website led them."

"And that," Mac finished, "tells us they probably have no legal rights to Min that would hold up in court. That's why they used the training facility as cover for their visit."

Bri's mind was racing, "They came here, not even knowing if the child in that picture was a boy or a girl."

Kaia picked up the explanation again. "They obviously don't know her, and I doubt they'd ever laid eyes on her before seeing the photos on my site."

"So, how would they have recognized…?" And then it hit Bri and her heart stopped. "Her birthmark. It's clear as day in that image." She remembered cropping the photo and noting how well it showed up. "It has to be a family trait."

Mac nodded. "I'm thinking you're right. That's the only thing that makes sense—the only way they could have possibly recognized her."

Kaia watched Min play for a few moments and then brought her attention back, eyes narrowed. "But now that I think about it, neither of those men had it. If one of them is her father, the trait skipped them. Or…it came from her birth mother."

Bri's gaze swung to Mac. "If one of them *is* her father, would that mean he'd have a legal right to pursue custody?"

He held up a hand. "Like I said before, I don't know what the laws are in Laos when it comes to paternity. But if you want my guess, I'd say they don't have a leg to stand on legally, or they would have taken that route. Since they didn't, I can interpret that a couple of different ways." Mac counted out on his fingers. "First, Min is either blood-related to one of them, but they have no sufficient legal recourse. Or second, neither of them are family, but instead, maybe members of the clan Min would have belonged to."

"We'd speculated that her parents may have broken away from the group," Kaia reminded Bri. "Maybe Min's birth mom took her away to protect her. In just the short time I was with them, I got a really bad vibe from both of those men. They are not good people."

"How do we stop them?" Maybe if she had something to do, Bri wouldn't feel so helpless. If she had some task to assign to her brain, it wouldn't jump to the worst possible outcome. "Can we find out which clan they belong to? Track them down and dig up information on them? Find out exactly who we're dealing with?"

"I think Erik or Jayme would be the ones to ask about that," Mac suggested. "I'm at a loss when it has anything to do with the shifter clans."

"Mac's right." Kaia clasped Bri's hand in hers. "When Jayme and Erik get back—" Her words were cut off by the appearance of her cousins.

Bri felt a wave of relief knowing Erik was there now. She prided herself on being a strong, capable woman, but sometimes she needed someone stronger to lean on.

He took one look at her stricken face and knew something was wrong. He came to her and gathered her close. "What's happened?"

His arms felt right around her. They made her feel safe. "Two men came to Kaia's work today. They're shifters from Asia, and we think they're here for Min." Bri felt a hardness settle over Erik. She glanced up at his face and saw that he'd just gone into full-on warrior mode.

He looked down to where Min was playing on the floor. His grip on Bri tightened. "They'll have to go through me first."

"And me." Jayme had gravitated towards Min when she'd heard the news and now stood hovering over her protectively.

Mac recounted what they knew, and all the things they didn't.

"I can look into that," Jayme offered. "I've got some connections I can tap." She switched her gaze to Kaia. "Do you think they gave you their real names?"

"Only one way to find out." Kaia left briefly. When she came back, she was holding a laptop. She handed the computer to Mac and then reached into her back pocket. Her fingers emerged holding two business cards. She studied them as she sat down next to him.

Once it was booted up, Kaia told him the names. "Rasa Chai

and Yuu Feng."

"Wow," Bri muttered. "Someone had a lot to live up to."

"What do you mean, sweetie?" Kaia asked.

"Oh." Bri looked up. She hadn't realized she'd spoken out loud. "I did some research on Lao names while I was waiting for my paperwork to come through on Min's adoption. I didn't know if I'd change her name or not, but if I did, I wanted something with special meaning. I looked at so many lists and most had girls' and boys' names, as well as their meanings. Rasa, if I remember correctly, means King. Chai translates to victory."

"That *is* a lot to live up to." Kaia smiled at Bri. "Did you pick Min? What does it mean?"

"I didn't, as it turns out. When I saw that it means clever and quick, I decided to leave it."

Kaia laughed. "Oh, she is definitely both of those." She squeezed Bri's hand. "And so are we. We won't let anything happen to her."

Mac typed and clicked away on the laptop. "According to this, Rasa Chai is from Thangon, Laos. It lies a couple hundred miles outside of the capital of Vientiane."

"Which is where I flew into. As I traveled north, I passed right through there. If Min's mother was running from Rasa or someone else in the clan and headed north, sooner or later, she'd run into Ban Xuang. Just like I did."

Everyone took that in for a second.

"What else does it say about him?" Kaia brought the conversation back on track.

"He's in the horse world. He's got a website here featuring horses he owns and breeds." Mac glanced at Kaia. "You were right on that note—he had to have been searching trainers when he came across Min's picture."

"Can I borrow that?" Jayme indicated to the computer. "I'll email a friend of mine and see what I can find out about the region and the local clans there."

While Jayme set to work, Erik leaned into Bri. "If anyone can find the information we need, it's Jayme. She's a master of the internet."

7

All the wheels had been set in motion. With nothing more to do but worry, Bri took Min and readied her for bed. She tried to keep a light heart while her daughter splashed and played in the bath water, but it was hard. She couldn't even make herself leave her side after putting her to bed. While the others worked in the living room, she only made it as far as her own bed. She sat with her back against the headboard watching over the child that had become her whole life.

When a quiet knock sounded, she called to come in.

It was Erik. He brought a plate with a sandwich and chips on it. "You didn't eat much at dinner." He joined her on the bed and set the plate on her lap.

Bri didn't think she'd be able to eat around the lump of fear lodged in her throat. But she picked at it to make him feel better.

"Jayme will get to the bottom of this, Bri. She's brilliant on a computer. If she weren't such a stickler for the law, she'd so be a hacker." Erik bumped her shoulder with his and smiled over at her.

Bri tried to return it but knew she hadn't been successful.

"She has friends all over the place," he tried to reassure her. "Most on the good side, but there are some on the dark side too. She has an extensive network within different clans around the world. It's always been a pet project of hers to learn everything she could about other species of shifters. She's spent years writing and emailing dozens of clans. She has quite the circle of friends." Erik rubbed her hand in comfort. "Between all that, we'll know more soon."

Bri had thought about what she could do as she'd gazed over at her daughter. "I have some contacts of my own I'm going to employ, starting with the orphanage and the adoption agency. I have to know that Min is mine legally. I'll be damned if they'll use some loophole to take her away from me."

Even knowing she'd followed every step to the letter of the law to adopt Min, doubt still crept into Bri's mind. She let her head fall to the side to rest on his shoulder. "But what if they can? What if those men—"

"Hey." Erik stopped her by reaching across and grasping her chin in his hand. He made sure she had nowhere else to look but into his eyes. "No one has a claim on that child but you. She's right where she's supposed to be. She's a shifter and will be raised with shifters who love her."

"She's not a mountain lion, though."

His hand dropped away, and his face went hard. "I don't give a flying fuck if she's a wolf or even a crocodile. She's a part of this family, and she'll fucking stay that way."

Erik's conviction made some of Bri's nerves settle. But she had to grin at his choice. "Wolf, huh? So, the cat/dog conflict reaches even the shifter level?"

His features relaxed when he saw she was teasing him. He bent to kiss the top of her head. "Yes, it does. It can get ugly… so very ugly." He closed his eyes and shook his head, his face a mask of devastation.

Bri laughed at his overly dramatic performance and couldn't help but appreciate his efforts, just to make her smile. She fell another step closer to being in love with this incredible man.

"But I won't go into that now." He pointed to the turkey on white. "Now, how about you eat some of that? My kid in there is hungry."

"He is, is he? Well, we can't have that." Bri lifted half to her mouth and took a bite. It was pretty good and went down easier than expected.

"He?" Erik asked, something sparking in his blue eyes.

"Oh, I don't really know that yet. It's just easier than saying he-or-she every time."

"I guess that makes sense."

Bri ended up being hungrier than she thought. She finished off the entire sandwich and chips while they sat and talked. Setting the plate on the bedside table, she turned back to Erik and snuggled into his side.

"Will you stay for a while and just hold me?"

"All night, if you want me to."

~~~

They were still wrapped in each other's arms when she awoke. Her room was bathed in darkness as Bri yawned and stretched, rubbing up against Erik's large sleeping form. They were both still fully clothed, and his arms remained tight around her. He'd held her all night. Just as he'd said he would.

She tipped her head back to gaze at him.

How had she gotten here? Lying in bed with a gorgeous man she was falling for, more every day. Pregnant and with her two-year-old daughter sleeping nearby.

Less than a year ago, she'd been alone, bunking in a sweltering hut in some God-forsaken forest, traveling the world taking pictures with only herself to think about. She couldn't believe how much had changed in such a relatively short time.

Bri was brought out of her thoughts by a tapping sound on the other side of her door.

Erik's eyes shot open, and he was across the room in a blink. He opened the door to his sister.
~~~

"I've got something, and I didn't think it could wait."

Jayme showed signs of having been at the computer all night. Her eyes were tired and red, and her long blonde hair had been pulled haphazardly into a messy bun. She too was still wearing the clothes she'd had on the previous day. Bri couldn't believe she'd stayed through the night, not even returning to her hotel to continue her search.

She pushed herself out of bed to join them. A glance at Min revealed she was still sleeping. "Come on." Bri motioned Erik and Jayme out of the room. "I'll make us some coffee, and you can tell us what you found."

Except Bri had to make a side trip to the bathroom for her morning vomit session. It seemed as soon as she became vertical, her body revolted.

As she exited the bathroom, she glanced over at Kaia's bedroom door. They'd want to know what Jayme had found too. But she hated to wake them until she knew what Erik's sister had discovered.

She turned and continued down the hall to join Erik and Jayme.

Since they'd beat her to Kaia's single-cup brewing machine, each had made their own coffee. Jayme and Erik sat with theirs at the table in the dining area that connected to the kitchen. Bri noticed there was a third mug waiting for her.

She sat and sipped gratefully. The tea soothed her stomach.

Fortified, she looked at Jayme. "Okay. Let's hear it."

Jayme nodded and then met her gaze. "It's not good."

Bri's heart sank.

"It took a while to get anyone to talk to me. My sources were reluctant to admit they knew anything about what I was asking. But, it seems that area of Laos is home to a clan of Indochinese Tigers, and what they're doing is being kept hidden from the other tiger clans throughout Asia, for fear that it would reach the ruling clan for that area."

Min's heritage hit Bri square in the gut. Her daughter could be a tiger. *Holy shit! A fucking tiger!*

Jayme went on, oblivious to Bri's astonishment over the news. "With the decline of their numbers due to illegal poaching and a rapidly shrinking natural habitat, it has become…common practice…for members of the leading families in that clan—the affluent families—to…" Her voice trailed off and she hesitated, her eyes darting quickly to Bri and Erik before she cleared her throat and took a deep breath. "To purchase young shifter females from families who can least afford to turn down the money. They take them with the express purpose of turning them into breeders.

"Female shifters in that region have become very scarce, but also very highly prized. But because those running the breeding program will allow nothing less than full-blooded female shifters to participate, these dominant families consider it to be within their rights to take whatever they want, with or without the impoverished families' consent."

"Jesus." Bri felt sick, and this time not from the pregnancy. "So, not only are they buying babies from destitute couples, but they're also stealing babies from the ones who won't agree to the deal?" Bri's stomach roiled in protest.

Erik took her hand in his and squeezed her fingers in solace. When she turned to look at him, his eyes were grim and showed he was just as affected by this news as she was.

They saw Jayme drop her gaze to the cup in front of her.

Bri's spirits plummeted even further.

"Sis?" Erik prompted her. "Just tell us."

She let out a wavering sigh and looked at her brother. "As we've always been taught, if the human side of a shifter is under extreme duress or in a life-threatening situation, the animal side has been known to take over without warning to protect them both."

Jayme swallowed audibly. "But these men…have a drug

they use to suppress the tigress...so they can rape these girls without threat of injury from their cats. And if the girls themselves put up too much of a fight, they're drugged too, to make them more compliant...more *receptive*."

Jayme's voice was raw with emotion. "They are subjected to this reprehensible treatment over and over, all in the demented interest of building their clan numbers up again."

"Those bastards." Bri's hand went to her stomach. "And those poor girls." She looked at Erik and then to Jayme. "Do you think that's what happened to Min's birth mother?" Bri's brows furrowed. "Wait. But then how did Min end up at that orphanage?"

Jayme took a sip of her coffee as Bri tipped up her own mug. If Erik's sister were feeling anything like she was at the moment, she knew the drink was more to calm the chill running through her veins than because of thirst.

Jayme set down her cup and continued. "Through a friend of a friend, who happens to be a member of that very clan, I found out that some of the girls try to run away. They're housed apart from the rest of the clan. They're bred, go through their entire pregnancy, and give birth without ever leaving that building. Sons are desired as future warriors for the clan, so they're taken away and given to the families of the men who'd impregnated them. The girls though, are more valuable to the clan as a whole. They're usually raised in that place and put into the breeding program as soon as they have their first cycle. She said these practices are known throughout the clan, but because everyone is scared of these higher-ranking families, no one can do anything about it."

Tears silently rained down Bri's face.

Jayme went on, somber. "Understandably, some can't take it. Some try to flee, and some choose death. The ones that run usually get caught again and are brought back. But according to the friend, there have been a few who have gotten away."

Jayme paused to let that sink in and then exhaled deeply. Her voice was reluctant when she added, "There's more."

Fuck! How much worse can this get?

Bri had to take a moment to gather herself. She was nowhere near ready to hear the rest, but she had to. She nodded numbly to tell Jayme to go on.

"I've spent all night going back and forth with my friend, who in turn has been messaging with the clan member who's sharing this information with us. The contact from inside works in the clan's nursery school. When I asked specifically if any of the captive women had a birthmark in her eye, the friend said there was no way to know. The breeders are never allowed visitors, and they're kept locked inside their chambers, so no one knows what the birth moms look like. But, after some probing, we found out there are two more children at the school, both boys, that also have birthmarks in their eyes. One is four and the other is five years old."

"Including Min, that's three babies in three years." Bri felt such sadness for the poor mother subjected to that kind of treatment and loss. "Raped and forced to become pregnant repeatedly. Only to have your children taken from you."

"I also learned that Rasa Chai is the heir-apparent to this tiger clan. His father led for several years until his death. Normally, another male leader would have been chosen to take his place, but evidently, Rasa's mother had been the true heir, using her husband as a puppet of sorts to rule over the clan. Upon his death, she stepped out of the shadows and took over. No one has had the nerve to oppose her. She's a tyrant and rules by fear, and she's also the one who implemented the practice of breeding these young girls."

Bri felt the bile rising. She couldn't listen to any more. Jumping up, she raced for the bathroom. She was retching when she felt someone brush the hair away from her face. Erik knelt and stayed with her until the sickness ran itself out.

"Oh, God, Erik." Bri leaned into him and pressed her face into the solid beating of his heart. "How can they treat people like that, some of them only children themselves? And Min. Her mom had to be so scared when she gave birth to a daughter, knowing she'd be subjected to the same fate."

His hand stroked her back. "But Min is here now, and no one will ever hurt her. Or they'll answer to all of us."

Bri thought of what she'd learned about the clan. "They're *tigers*, Erik. How can you fight that?"

"You let me worry about that."

Could nothing be done to stop what those monsters were doing?

Suddenly, something Jayme had said popped into her mind. "Jayme mentioned a ruling clan. What does that mean?"

"Every species of shifter has a governing group that oversees them. I don't know nearly as much as Jayme does about all the different clans, but the ones in the Far East are some of the largest in the world, mostly because of dense populations, but also because it's home to the most species of cats.

"Throughout Asia, there are a number of tiger shifter clans, representing most genuses of tigers. To keep all those clans working properly and obeying the rules, they all report to the one ruling clan that's located in central China. Since most mountain lion shifters are native to the U.S., our own governing clan is in Arizona."

Motion in the doorway drew their attention.

Bri looked up to see Kaia there. "Oh, honey. Sick again? Do you want me to..." She trailed off, taking a good look at Bri. She was sure her face was red and blotchy from crying and throwing up.

"Are you all right?" Kaia rushed in. "Is it the baby?"

Bri hurried to assure Kaia before trying to gather herself. "No, no. The baby is fine. Jayme dug up some information on that clan." Her voice choked off in a hoarse whisper. "It's horrible, Kai." Bri shook, thinking about it again. "So horrible."

Kaia spun on her heel and went to get the news firsthand.

"You feeling better now?" Erik swept her hair back, concern dimming the bright blue of his eyes. "Can I get you anything?"

"No. I'll just finish my tea, and I should be okay. The thought of those girls got to me."

"As it would anyone." He helped her to her feet.

"Thank you."

"Come on. Let's go find a way to put these fuckers down."

Mac had also joined the discussion. And as he and Kaia got caught up, Bri sipped her tea, swallowing her fear and letting anger rise up. Being overly emotional right now wouldn't protect her child. She needed to have a plan in place for when those bastards came for her. Because they would. Their callous indifference to the rape and captivity of the clan's youngest members, coupled with the fact that they'd traveled all this way over a picture they'd seen online, meant they weren't the type to give up that easily.

And she had something they felt belonged to them. They would try to take it back at any cost.

Bri's resolve firmed as fire and defiance spiked through her system.

They wouldn't get to Min unless it was over Bri's dead body.

8

They spent a little more time talking over coffee. Mac was going to do what he could through legal channels to find and surveil Rasa Chai and his associate while they were here in Montana. Erik and Jayme were sticking close to Bri and Min, just in case those men decided to make a grab for the little girl.

And Erik would be ready when they did. He wanted to rip their fucking throats out for all the pain and suffering they'd caused to so many of their own kind, and for causing Bri so much distress and upheaval.

Seeing her upset to the point of actually getting ill had torn something in him. This was a time that she should be happy and basking in the joys of pregnancy and motherhood—not being scared to death that pedophiles were coming to enslave her daughter.

Hearing what Jayme had said had triggered a hate in Erik so volatile that he'd had a hard time tamping down his cat. But he had, because Bri needed him. Right now, she needed his strength and certainty that no one would ever hurt her child.

So that's what he would give her. He'd be that rock for her to lean on. But he'd also be making damned sure that Bri and their baby came through this untouched.

With that in mind, he and his sister were sharing the guard duties. Until Jayme left for Helena, that is.

She'd already offered to postpone her start date at the police academy to stay and help protect Min. But Erik had insisted otherwise. Becoming a cop was something she'd been looking forward to for so long. She'd already gone through all the testing and was on track to begin classes next week. They'd even lucked out and found her a place to live not too far from the campus. It wasn't much, but it would suit her well for the next three months.

After that, she'd be coming back here to Anaconda to work with Mac as a full-fledged officer of the law.

Erik was proud of his little sister and didn't want anything to get in the way of her dream. He and Kaia could protect Bri and Min on their own.

Indochinese Tigers, while still large compared to his cougar, were the smallest of the species. The male usually topped out at around four hundred pounds—twice his own cat's size, but Erik wasn't too worried about that. His cougar was in peak physical condition and knew a thing or two about fighting.

The members of their elite group were held to a strict training regimen back in their clan. Designed to put the cougars through their paces, the programs were ultimately geared towards agility, stamina, and strength—basically a hardcore feline obstacle course with varying circuits focused on maximizing their physical prowess.

The highest in their ranks set rigorous goals, timing their progress and always pushing them to go harder, faster. They squared off against each other regularly, trying out new techniques to keep them fresh, wary, and on their toes in an instant. And they didn't pull any punches, or claws, as the case may be. They ran and jumped and climbed and hunted on a daily basis, always pushing their limits to go above and beyond. When it came to the protection of clan members, they were a serious threat to anyone who dared.

And that was only cat's play. In their human forms, they worked out just as rigorously, perfecting their physique and endurance—anything that might give their cougars an edge against an opponent.

So even Erik knew he was a force to be reckoned with, and he wasn't scared of anything.

Even some fucking, lame-ass tigers.

Erik was the first to see Min emerge sleepily from the hall. She dragged one of her dolls with one hand and rubbed her eye with the other.

Bri was chatting with Kaia in the kitchen, so he went to the little dark-haired beauty and knelt down in front of her.

"Well, good morning, sweetie." He pointed to the doll dangling from her fist. "Who's this? Does she have a name?"

"Baby," she told him as she hugged the doll to her chest.

Erik had to grin. "And she's such a pretty baby. Just like you."

"Erk. Kitty." Min smiled up at him.

"Maybe later, pumpkin. How about we get some breakfast first? I bet your momma has something special for you."

Erik slid his hands under her tiny arms and lifted her to perch on his forearm.

"I think someone is hungry." He turned to the women in the kitchen and saw Bri's eyes light up.

"Hey, my love." Bri rushed over to them. "Good morning."

Erik thought she'd swoop in and take Min, but she only reached up to smooth the hair from her face. He was kind of glad she hadn't. The weight of the itty bit of a girl felt soothing against him. He'd held kids before, but not any who had become so important to him. And knowing that she could be in danger had his protective side surging.

"What's your fancy today?" Bri smiled up to Min. "Anything you want, since we got distracted and missed out on your birthday yesterday. Do you want cereal, pancakes, waffles, cinnamon toast?"

Min's diapered behind bounced up and down on Erik's arm.

"Kitty cakes!"

Bri beamed and turned to Kaia. "I don't know, Kai. Think we can do your grandmother's recipe justice?"

"I think we need to try, because there is a sweet girl here who needs to eat some."

"Kitty cakes! Kitty cakes!"

Now Bri did take her. "Let's go get you cleaned up, and then you can come help Aunt Kaia and Momma make them."

Erik could hear the excited toddler chatter all the way down the hall. He had no clue what Min was saying, but Bri responded to all of it, comprehending or not.

Mac came up beside him and caught him staring off in the direction they'd gone. "I remember that look," Mac teased him. "It means you're done for."

Erik swiveled his head around to arch a brow at Mac. "I was a goner the moment I saw her."

Mac laughed and slapped him on the back. "Well, at least you don't deny it. Come on. Let's get the table cleared off and have some breakfast."

He, Mac, and Jayme put away all the papers pertaining to Laos and set the computer aside. Even though she wouldn't understand it, Min didn't need to be exposed to any of that filth.

The next hour passed in stark contrast to the previous. They talked and laughed over Min's antics, dropping chunks of pancake to Moose who'd taken up residence near her chair. He'd quickly become her best friend.

The others razzed him about Min calling him Erk. He grinned and dismissed the ribbing, rather fond of the name, and wondered idly how he'd feel if Min ever called him Daddy. His heart did a funny thing that told him he might like that even more.

For now, though, he had to get his head back in the game. He had other work to do to keep that little girl and her mother safe.

Shortly after breakfast was cleaned up, Kaia and Mac got ready to leave for their respective jobs. Mac said he'd get started on locating their visitors as soon as he got to the office. He'd begin by checking out each of the local motels and finding out if any lodgers from out of the country had arrived recently.

"Come on, Moose," he called. "I'll take you home before I head to the office. Duncan can come over to play with you today."

Erik had heard of Duncan. He was the son of Mac's neighbor. He'd come in when Mac wasn't home to take care of Moose and keep him company.

"You can leave him here if you want," Bri offered. "He and Min can hang out."

"Are you sure?" Mac asked.

"Absolutely."

"Okay, then." Mac nodded and then looked down at his dog. "You take care of these girls and keep an eye on things."

Moose made several vocalizations back to Mac.

"Glad you got it covered." Mac and Kaia turned to go. And Moose took up his position next to Min's chair again. This time, it was clearly a guarding stance.

Erik, like Moose, planned to stick to his girls like glue. If they left the house, they would not be out of his sight.

Bri excused herself to go and get herself and Min dressed for the day, Moose following close behind. When they returned, she had a backpack-style bag thrown over one shoulder.

"So, what's on the agenda for today?" Erik asked.

"Not a whole lot." Bri set the bag on the table and began to inventory the contents, replacing items when needed. When he caught a glimpse of diapers and toys, Erik realized it was Min's bag. "I told Kaia I'd do the grocery shopping today, even though she tried to fight me on it." Finished, she zipped it closed with a quick motion.

Honey-colored eyes met his, and in them he saw

determination and a momma bear ready to fight for her cub. "I won't hide. They're coming, no matter if I stay here or go about my business as usual. But when they do, I'll be ready. *We'll* be ready."

"Yes, we will be." By the way her brow raised, Erik knew he'd surprised her. "Expected me to put you under house arrest, didn't you? Believe me, I thought about it. But whatever they're going to do has already been set in motion. We just have to stay vigilant and prepared. And that's why Jayme and I will be with you. Everywhere you go."

"Okay. Good." Bri gave a short nod. The discussion was over as far as she was concerned. "After shopping, I have some computer work I need to do here at the house. I want to get in touch with my contacts in Laos and verify that all paperwork pertaining to Min's adoption was filled out and filed properly. I'm not giving these men a legal leg to stand on if they decide to go that route. She's mine, and she's staying that way."

"You're damned right she is." Erik leaned in and kissed her.

Jayme was waiting for them in the living room. She'd been working on Kaia's computer all morning, trying to find anything else she could on the clan Min had most likely been born into.

Under Erik and Jayme's watchful eyes, they loaded up into Bri's car. Shopping went smoothly. Erik didn't think Rasa and Yuu would have had time enough to find out where Kaia lived yet to stake it out. They should be safe to move until then. But Erik still didn't breathe a calm breath until they were locked inside the house again a few hours later.

To give Bri the time she needed on her task, Erik kept Min entertained. He knew her normal naptime was approaching soon, so he found something for them to do in the bedroom. As the time drew near, he had her choose a story. They crawled up into Bri's bed to read it, Moose taking up sentry on the floor next to them.

Sometime later, in a light doze, Erik's exceptional hearing

caught the door opening. He opened his eyes to find Bri approaching the side of the mattress. She was smiling softly down at them.

"Now, that's a sight," she murmured.

He looked down at the small body stretched out over his. Min's head was resting right beneath his chin, and he could feel the slight weight of her tiny feet mid-thigh. His large hand was spread over her narrow back, keeping her secure.

He placed a soft kiss on the top of her head. "She fell asleep like this," he whispered to Bri. "And I didn't know how to move her without waking her."

Under Moose's supervision, Bri gently crawled up onto the bed with them. Erik extended his free arm, and she curled into him. Her blonde hair fell over his shoulder, and he kissed her on the forehead.

"Did you find anything out from the people in Laos?"

"Hmm...later." Bri snuggled into his side farther and gave a deep sigh.

Erik lay there with the two women he was coming to love using him as a pillow.

And there was no place he'd rather be. They were both safe and sheltered in his arms.

~~~

Bri couldn't believe she'd actually slept. She hadn't meant to. Erik and Min had looked so cute all cuddled in together, she'd had to get in on it too. And suddenly she'd been so tired. As soon as she felt the weight and warmth of him near, she'd dropped out. She'd never been much of a napper, but she guessed she could blame the pregnancy for that.

There were probably any number of things she could have been doing to utilize her time more wisely, but she wouldn't change a thing about the time she'd spent there with them.
~~~

Min stirred from her perch atop Erik's chest, rubbing her nose into his shirt. She always did that when she woke up, and Bri found it adorable. She'd rub her face into whatever she'd been using as a pillow, and then her little hand would scrub at her eyes as she struggled to wake.

She was slow to do that, but once she had, it was an all-out sprint. Until she fell asleep again. Bri was learning all of Min's little quirks and habits. She loved that so much. She'd missed the first two years of Min's life and all the firsts that had come with them. But she would be there to see every single one of her daughter's milestones from here on out.

Bri smiled at the miniature little human, in awe of how perfect she was. "Hey, beautiful." She reached up and tried to tame some of Min's silky black hair. "Did you have a good nap?"

Min pushed up to her elbows and gazed down at Erik. He'd woken at her first movement and was smiling up at her.

"Erk."

"Hi, sweetie." His hand skimmed up and down her tiny back.

Min scrambled up to sit astride Erik's stomach. Bri knew what was coming next. Did she warn him or just let it happen? She grinned but kept her mouth shut as Min began to hop up and down on Erik's stomach like she was riding one of Kaia's horses.

He gave a grunt as the air was forced from his diaphragm. "Easy there, cowgirl." He poked his fingers into her ribs and drew squealing giggles from her.

Her daughter was breathless and smiling when Erik relented his tickling torture. She recovered quickly though, leaning forward to cup a small hand on each side of Erik's face. Min's dark eyes held his blue ones. Bri had to wonder what her daughter thought was so serious all of a sudden.

"Erk. Kitty. Pway."

Usually he would give her anything she wanted, so when Erik didn't agree right away, Bri glanced up to his face. It was clear he was struggling with a decision, trying to find a way to say no without breaking Min's little heart.

Min and Erik's cat played together almost every day, and not once had he ever declined her request. Bri had come to trust his cougar unconditionally with her daughter, so Erik's hesitancy now could only mean one thing—he was worried about their safety. Bri thought quickly, trying to find a compromise where both Min and Erik could get what they wanted before the meltdown happened.

"What if," she interjected before Erik could speak, "instead of going outside, your cat and Min just played in the living room for a bit while I make us all something to eat? Jayme's here. She can keep an eye on things while you're...busy."

She could see the way his mind weighed every possibility. In the end though, she figured he just couldn't hold out against those big brown eyes staring down at him. Bri never could, so why would he be any different?

Erik gave in and grinned at the little imp. "I guess a few minutes couldn't hurt."

"Pway! Pway!"

He sat up, lifting Min's wiggling form off of him. As soon as she was on her feet, she ran to the door.

"Hey," Bri called to her, rolling out of bed. "Hold up a second, love."

Min stopped and looked back to Bri. She was all but vibrating in anticipation. Bri gave Erik a long, appraising once-over before changing what she'd been about to say. She knelt in front of her child.

"Go find Jayme. Stay with her until Momma gets there."

Min nodded vigorously and scooted off down the hall with the dog close on her heels.

Bri closed the door behind them, clicked the lock, turned, and leaned back against the wooden panel. She eyed Erik up and down.

His blue eyes instantly heated. "We don't have time for that, Bri."

"I know. Pity." Bri stalked towards him. "I just thought I'd help you get out of those clothes."

Bri set her words into action. She grabbed the hem of his t-shirt and pulled it up and over his head.

"Mmm." She ran her hands over his chest. "Nice." She leaned in and spread kisses over the taut skin she'd revealed, stopping to give each nipple her attention.

He groaned deeply, his hands going to her hips. "You are intoxicating."

While her mouth was busy, her hands went to work on his jeans. She had them open and pushed down over his hips in seconds.

He obligingly stepped out of them.

His body was hard as stone when she took him in her hand. They didn't have time for what he was probably expecting, but maybe they did have time for a little something else. Bri smirked up at him and then lowered to her knees in front of him. Keeping her gaze locked to his, she ran her tongue up the underside of his shaft.

"Oh, Christ, Bri." His hips flexed helplessly, and his hand came to the back of her head.

She couldn't play the way she wanted with them being under the gun, but she could at least give him this quick release.

Gripping the base of his cock tight, she licked her lips and slid them over the head, swirling her tongue around the sensitive skin there.

Erik jerked and grunted. His hips thrust forward, searching for more.

She took him deep without warning, and his hand fisted in her hair. A growl resonated in his chest.

"Oh fuck, Bri. Where the hell did you learn how to do that?"

Between lips, tongue, and hands, Bri swiftly took him over

the edge. When she rose to stand before him, she grinned at the dazed look on his face.

"You owe me," she said with a wicked sparkle in her eye.

"I sure as hell do." He kissed her. "And I'll pay up, have no doubt of that."

"I hope so." Bri patted his chest and gave him one more scorching kiss. "I'll leave you to your shifting then."

Her last view of him before pulling the door almost closed was of him standing statue-still in all his glory. He really was a masterpiece.

She had to take a couple of calming breaths before making her way to where Min was chattering away to Jayme. When Jayme saw her, she looked up laughing.

"Do you know what she's saying?"

"Ninety percent, no." Bri chuckled. "But the ten I do, usually helps me to decipher the rest. She's excited right now. She's getting to play with Erik's cat for a few minutes."

Jayme grinned as the feline in question came sauntering out of the hall. "I never thought I'd see this," she teased her brother. "Big tough mountain lion playing with a little girl." She pulled her phone out and held it up to snap a few pictures. "Wait until the guys back home see *this*."

The massive male growled at her and showed his teeth, clearly not impressed with her sense of humor. Jayme only laughed harder.

Bri worried that his sounds of protest might frighten Min, but that was not at all the case. She walked right up to him and gave him a hug, wrapping her small, thin arms around his neck. With one more glare at Jayme for taking yet another picture, the cat gave his attention to the toddler.

Bri marveled at the sight. Outside, he was obviously a very large cat. Inside, walking down the hall and now strolling around her living room, he looked even bigger, like the walls were shrinking around him. But when Min's tiny body wrapped so lovingly about the muscular cougar, he looked positively monstrous.

Such a huge, brawny creature…at the absolute mercy of an energetic three-year-old. The vision brought tears to her eyes, and she snapped a few pictures herself.

For the next half hour, they rolled and tumbled across the living room while Bri fixed a light meal. At one point, she looked in to see Min on the cat's back, getting the ride of her life. He slowly prowled around the room to her delighted giggles.

Soon though, Bri had the snacks set out, and it was time to call a halt to the fun. Min put up a small fight, but a large head nudged her in the behind towards the bathroom to wash up. Once she was done and on her way to the dining room, he stalked off down the hall.

Only a few minutes later, Erik emerged fully clothed. The three adults and Min sat and munched on crackers, cheese, shaved deli meat, and fruit. Bri couldn't cook for shit, but she could set an hors d'oeuvres tray like nobody's business.

"Are you looking forward to getting your classes started?" Bri asked Jayme.

"I am." Jayme smiled. "I followed in Erik's footsteps and joined his team, knowing it was the closest I could get to the real thing, and hoping it would be enough. But it wasn't, and I needed something more. You can't even imagine how excited I am to be doing this."

"Why here? Why didn't you just join the police force in Colorado closer to home?"

"I thought about it. And probably would have eventually, if I hadn't come here and met Kaia and Mac. I was surprised to find I liked the idea of branching out on my own. I love my family, and I love my clan, but I think I needed to get away to do this. Being the baby of the family, and the only girl to boot, is a lot to deal with."

"Hey now," Erik complained good-naturedly, "I don't think

we made your life too awful. The four of us looked out for you and made you tough."

Jayme shot him an incredulous glare and then turned to Bri. "My four *loving* older brothers tortured me relentlessly."

"Pffft. Whatever. We made you *stronger*."

"You guys took my dolls and pulled their heads off before using them as chew toys," she said in mock-disgust.

Erik sent a *do-you-believe-this-bullshit* look to Bri before turning back to his sister. "You were a tomboy. You didn't need any of those girly dolls anyway."

Bri bit back a laugh at the younger woman's ire as Erik popped back retorts as fast as Jayme could air her grievances.

Jayme doubled down. "Mom had to keep my hair short for years, because you asshats would drag me around by the ponytail all the time and tie it in knots."

He sat back and crossed his arms over his chest. Humor lit the electric blue of his eyes. "It was better that way. It didn't get caught on branches or sticks. And no one else could pull it to hurt you."

Jayme looked outraged. "Are you actually trying to say you did me some kind of *favor*?" She leaned forward in her seat, tilted her head a little, and gave her brother a hard stare. "You jerkwads scared off every guy who worked up the nerve to approach me."

He only grinned, not at all repentant for that particular offense.

Which pissed Jayme off even more, as she let loose a growl at him.

Bri had to disguise her chuckle behind a cough. She'd better step in before this escalated any further. She'd seen Kaia and Jace go at it more times than she could count and knew it could get out of hand quickly. Lifting both of her arms, she spread them wide like she was holding them back. "Okay, okay. Let's dial it back, guys."

Erik remained as he was, and Jayme sat scowling at him. "Bully."

"Brat," Erik shot back.

Jayme stuck her tongue out at her brother and he laughed.

Behind all the frustration of siblings razzing one another, it was as clear as day that despite Jayme's list of injustices, she loved her brothers dearly, and they her. Bri, being an only child, had never gotten to experience the companionship and contention of having a sibling. The closest she'd ever gotten was Kaia, and she'd become the sister Bri had never had.

Bri looked over at Min enjoying the byplay between the two and thought of the child she carried. Life would certainly be interesting.

9

Late that night, Erik and Jayme roamed Lost Creek, the state park that butted up behind his cousin's property. With Mac, Kaia, and Moose on site with Bri and Min, he'd felt safe enough leaving them so his cat and Jayme's could do a little reconnaissance.

At dinner, Mac had filled them in on what he'd found during his search for their visitors from Laos. The two men were staying at a motel on the outskirts of Anaconda. They'd chosen one that backed up to dense woods, taking two rooms on the ground floor.

As shifters, they would need space to let their cats out to run and hunt. And that particular motel offered the best option.

Mac couldn't assign his men—deputies who knew nothing of shifters—to run surveillance on them. There was no way to know if this clan was as careful about keeping their secret as the more local mountain lion shifters were. If one of them transformed and the wrong person saw it, he'd have a lot of questions to answer. Ones he'd rather avoid.

He'd do what he could on his own, but constant observation during the day was going to be difficult.

The night was another matter altogether. Erik and his sister would be staking out the motel after the sun went down. They'd take up positions in the woods and wait for the Laos tigers to show their hand.

They'd debated whether or not he and Jayme should split up, one patrolling days and the other stalking nights, but with two tigers in town, they decided it was better to have two-on-two if the bigger cats went into the park at night.

Mac had taken out a map and shown him and Jayme where the motel was located.

"Shit," Erik muttered when he saw where Mac pointed.

"Yeah. I caught that too," Mac agreed. "It may be thirty miles away from here by road, but a straight shot through the park puts it at a hell of a lot less."

"And that's an easy route for a big cat too," Jayme added, looking around the table at them all. "I have to ask… Do they know where we are? Or was that location just dumb luck?"

Erik had a sinking feeling. "If they didn't before, they will soon."

Mac sighed. "I say we assume they know where Kaia lives already and prepare accordingly."

Erik turned to see how Bri was taking the news. She was scared, understandably, but keeping it together and putting on a brave face. She was strong and determined, and she'd put her faith in him to protect Min. He was the first line of defense for her daughter, and Erik refused to let her down.

Shortly after that, the meeting had broken up. Jayme had excused herself to shift first and then waited for him just inside the tree line. Bri had followed him out onto the deck, and he took her into his arms to kiss her.

"Be careful," she told him when he released her.

"Count on it." Erik smiled at her, turned, and jogged out to join Jayme.

Each carrying a small pack around their necks with a cell phone, their cats kept up a quick pace. They neared their destination as the moon was cresting the sky. The last half-mile or so, they slowed. He didn't want to tip off their targets in case they were out there, watching.

They'd covered about three quarters of that distance when Erik heard something coming towards them through the trees. He stopped and chuffed a signal to Jayme.

His warning had been unnecessary; she'd heard it too.

Making a choice quickly, they took to the trees. The one he'd picked was an easy fifteen-foot vertical jump. About thirty feet away, Jayme was also perched on a wide branch. This would give them an advantage over the newcomers.

As Erik knew all too well from his training, predators rarely kept an eye to the sky. That was a habit of prey, and the bigger the cat, the more arrogant they were.

They sat silently and waited. Whoever or whatever approached was taking care not to make much noise. Erik's large blue eyes scanned the forest floor, on guard for anything.

Through the shadows, two tigers materialized. They moved slowly, stealthily. Erik held perfectly still, crouched low to the thick limb, just as he knew Jayme was. They watched as the two animals padded oblivious beneath them.

Were they only out for a simple stroll? Or were they right now preparing for an ambush?

Having found Kaia at her place of business, it wouldn't take much more effort to find out where she lived. If they stalked her house long enough, eventually they would get lucky and spy the little girl. They could keep her inside and out of sight, but nothing was foolproof, and keeping Min locked up wasn't fair to her either.

So Erik had to ensure they didn't make it that far. If they looked like they were headed in Min's direction, he'd just have to dissuade them.

As the intruders skulked out of sight, Erik dropped silently to the ground. Jayme followed, and together they trailed behind, careful not to give away their presence.

The two tigers ahead were of comparable size. Both had a larger and stockier build than his cougar, their bodies broader and heads blockier. He'd expected that, but it was good to see them in person and size them up. The more he knew about his opponents, the better.

They wandered for hours, Erik and Jayme keeping to the shadows as they prowled from a distance, stalking their quarry. It didn't seem as if they had any destination in mind. They ran leisurely and hunted small game almost lazily. Erik studied and absorbed everything they did, from the way they moved to how they captured their prey—sometimes individually and sometimes as a team. Every bit of information would assist him when the time for watching came to an end.

Once the two tigers were tucked back into their motel rooms, Erik and Jayme shifted back to human form, so they could discuss the situation.

Jayme jerked her head back in the direction of Kaia's house. "You head back to Bri. I'll stay and keep an eye on them for the rest of the night. There's not much left of it anyway, and I don't expect them to venture out again. I'll let you know if anything changes though."

"Okay. Call me."

Jayme nodded.

Both took their feline forms again. Jayme jumped up onto the low branch of a tree overlooking the motel, and Erik sprinted off, stopping only when he found the pile of his clothes in the woods behind Kaia's house.

When he snuck back in through the sliding door, Mac emerged out of the darkness of the living room, his ever-faithful dog at his side. He was fully dressed, and his service weapon was in his hand next to his thigh.

"Anything?"

"You had a couple of tigers in the park for a while, but they kept to the other side and never made it out this way. They've already turned in, but if this pattern continues, they should be sleeping for at least part of the day and running at night.

We'll stay on them and track their movements. We'll know the minute they decide to make a move in this direction."

Mac nodded. "Kaia bunked in with Bri and Min," he told Erik. "You can wake her and kick her out."

Erik shook his head. "Nah. Let them sleep. I'll take the spare room."

"All right." Mac rubbed his eyes with his free hand and yawned. "I'm going to bed for a couple of hours before I have to get to work. It's going to be a long-ass day."

"See you later." Erik walked to the door of the extra bedroom, grasped the knob, and at the last minute, looked over his shoulder at Bri's closed door. He needed to see them and check on his girls. Turning, he went to her door and quietly opened it.

Bri and Kaia were both in the bed. He took a step towards them, and Kaia's eyes flew open. She looked directly at him, and he saw the predator in her eyes. Until recognition finally dawned.

She eased out from under the covers and came to him.

"Everything okay?" Her voice was barely there.

Erik nodded.

"I'll go to my own bed then. You can take over here."

She was gone, and Erik was left standing there, his gaze resting on tiny Min as she slept peacefully, splayed out like a bursting star across her mattress. He couldn't help but smile at her sweet innocence as he turned to watch Bri sleep.

He knew he probably wouldn't doze off, but he could at least lay with her and feel the heat and softness of her body.

Erik stripped down to his boxers and slid in next to her. He rolled to his side and pulled her against his chest. He heard her sigh and relax into his hold. Even in slumber, she knew him and that she was safe.

He did end up drifting off sometime later, but as she started to stir, he woke and kissed the top of her head.

"Good morning."

Bri turned in his arms until she faced him. "When did you get here?"

"A few hours ago. I came in to check on you and Min, and Kaia woke up."

"Were you able to find those men?"

"Yeah. But other than doing a little hunting, there was no suspicious activity. We'll keep them under surveillance."

She burrowed into him. "I hate knowing you're out there like that."

"It's what I do. I keep my clan and my family safe."

"I know. But they're *tigers*, Erik."

"It doesn't matter *what* they are. If they mess with the people I care about, I won't hesitate to take them out."

~~~

Another day passed with nothing more than a jaunt in the night.

Erik and the others had just sat down to breakfast when Kaia came in. She was holding her phone in front of her.

"You won't believe this. Those bast—" she glanced at Min happily munching on her toast, "*men* emailed me that they want to come out to the farm again and talk more about bringing their horses in."

"Why would they do that?" Bri asked skeptically.

"Because they still think Kaia's the one who brought the Asian kid from the photo to America. And they want it back." Erik held Bri's gaze for a moment before turning to Mac. "It could be a diversion. One meets with Kaia, and the other hangs back to come here to search for any sign of...what they're looking for."

Mac took a moment to contemplate Erik's theory and then nodded. "You could be right. Which means we'll have to split up to cover both locations. I don't like it, but we can't leave them
~~~

any openings."

"I'm assuming you'll be going with Kaia today?" Erik understood, because he'd damned sure be staying close to Bri as long as these fuckers were near the area.

"Yes," Mac stated unequivocally.

"Are we sure that's a good idea?" Kaia asked. "We already know Rasa dismisses women completely. If you're there hanging over my shoulder, he'll be more guarded. If I'm by myself, maybe he'll let something slip."

"You're *not* going alone." Mac's voice was hard, and it was clear there were no alternatives. "They don't have to see me, but I'll be close."

"Jayme should be back from her last rounds shortly. She can be there with Kaia too," Erik added. "If we're wrong and both of them do show up there, we'd all feel better knowing you have more backup. Plus, it'll let them know Kaia isn't the only shifter in town, in case they decide to get squirrely."

"She hasn't slept, Erik." Bri turned to him. "She has to be exhausted."

"She'll be all right for a while yet. We've done this before."

"I still think sending everyone with *me* is a mistake." Kaia pressed her point. "What if the email is a smokescreen, just to get me out of the house? What if I'm at the barn waiting with all this protection, and they both show up here instead? Bri, the baby, and Min need all the cover they can get."

Erik gave her argument some thought, but it didn't feel right. "I don't see it playing out that way. If someone doesn't meet with you, there's a chance you'd come home too early. My bets are on one keeping you busy at the barn, so the other can come search here."

"And the big, badass enforcer can handle a tiger twice his size, all on his own?" Kaia tipped her head to the side, arching a brow at him.

"Yes." Erik said confidently. "This is exactly what I'm

trained for. I've spent years preparing for scenarios such as this. If I can't hold my own against one tiger, I don't deserve my position."

Erik paused, waiting for further argument. When none was voiced, Erik went on. "Bri and Min will stay here out of sight, and I'll cover the house. I think we keep this friendly. If we show any anxiety about them being here snooping around, they'll pick up on it and know we're hiding something."

"Sounds good," Mac agreed.

When Jayme came in, Erik briefed her on the plan. A few minutes later, Kaia left for work with Jayme riding with her. Mac followed behind in his car.

Erik closed and locked the door once they were gone, and then did a circuit of the house to make sure all windows and doors were secure. The email had stated they'd like to meet Kaia at nine. It was closing in on eight-fifteen now, so if something were going to happen, it would be soon.

In an effort to keep Min quietly entertained, they were going to tuck her, Bri, and the dog away in the bedroom to watch movies. The curtains were also drawn shut, with no crack for anyone to see in, should he get that close to the house.

Erik got them settled, gave them both a kiss, and then slowly closed the door. He prowled from window to window, watching and waiting. He got the text from Mac saying they had a car approaching, but no sign yet if there were one man or two in the vehicle.

A second text came soon after. *One.*

So that meant the other shifter could be there at any moment. Would he come from the front, or the back? Erik was banking on the woods. It afforded the most cover, and unless they had another car, this guy was going to be on foot.

Erik weighed the odds and concentrated on the shadows cast by the forest. And sure enough, something moved within the deeper shades of gray.

And almost as soon as the motion registered, Erik's cougar went wild, growling and clawing to take over. He sensed the threat to his mate and cubs and wanted to rush the intruder and rip him to shreds. It took all of Erik's control to hold the big cat at bay.

A full-on attack wasn't the right way to go just yet, though it would certainly make him and his cat happy. For now, he needed to see exactly what these little bitches were up to.

And if the tiger decided to come out and play... then Erik would be only too happy to oblige.

He held his position just to the side of the sliding door as the man in the woods emerged and looked around.

Having never seen either man, Erik didn't know if this was Rasa Chai or Yuu Feng. Whoever he was, he was compact— short and well-built. His close-trimmed hair was as black as his loose-fitting pants, thin-soled shoes, and t-shirt. Erik rolled his eyes. Add a black mask to the mix, and he'd look just like a damned ninja. He wondered vaguely if that were his intent.

The man strode across the yard like he owned it, not bothering to hide his presence at all.

Cocky bastard. You probably think it's empty, don't you? Or maybe only attended by a young, naive babysitter keeping watch over the child you want to steal? Not today, asshole.

When he was just about to take the last step up onto the deck, Erik pulled the door open.

The guy was so completely taken aback, Erik was almost amazed his tiger didn't make a surprise appearance to protect him. Erik grinned inside.

"Hey, there." He closed the door behind him and crossed the deck with an easy gait. He was careful to keep his expression welcoming and nonchalant—just the good-ol-boy-next-door. "Are you lost? Did you get turned around in the park?"

Erik knew the tiger could sense he was a shifter too. *Yeah, motherfucker—another one. This job won't be as easy as you thought.*

The Lao man recovered quickly from being caught in the wrong place at the wrong time and grabbed on to the line Erik had tossed him. "Yes. Lost," he said haltingly. "You live here?"

"Yeah." Erik smiled straightforwardly. "My sister and I just recently moved in with my cousin. She had an early meeting this morning, so my sister went to help her out. I'm finally able to enjoy a quiet day to myself. You know how women can get."

Calculation simmered in the deep brown of his eyes. "So, you are alone here?"

"Sure am." *Keep digging, douchebag. You won't find anything.*

"Could I maybe…go in to call…friend? My phone…battery dead."

"Sorry, man." Erik shook his head regretfully. "My cousin doesn't have a landline here anymore. We only use cell phones nowadays." He dug his own out of his pocket and offered it to him. "You can use mine though."

"No." His gaze never stopped moving. He took in everything about the house—every window, every door. "That is okay. I will…just go."

"Are you sure? Can I give you a lift somewhere?"

"No. I can…find my way back. Friend will be waiting."

"All right then. Be careful out there. You never know what could be lurking in the woods."

"Yes. Yes, of course." His eyes scanned the back of the house again, looking for any clue that might prove Erik was lying about being alone, or that a child might also live there. "Thank you for your help."

"No problem. Nice meeting you." Erik gave him a short wave.

Without another word, the shifter turned and retraced his steps back to the trees. Erik wanted to follow, but he wouldn't dare risk leaving Bri and Min alone.

He disappeared back into the house but kept a wary eye on the retreating figure. Erik stayed vigilant long after the man had gone, just on the off-chance he doubled back again.

He spun around when he heard a sound behind him. It was Bri.

"What are you doing? I told you to stay out of sight." He glanced behind her. "Where's Min?"

"I *am* out of sight, and Min fell asleep watching her movie. Her knight in spotted armor is watching over her. I heard you come back in a while ago, but I just now got away. What did he say?"

Erik pulled the curtain firmly over the door and sat down at the table. Bri sank into a chair across from him.

"Not much. He picked up the line I dropped him about being lost and ran with it. He was definitely here to search, though. He was shocked when I walked out and greeted him. I don't think he expected anyone to be here, but that didn't stop him from casing the place right in front of me."

"So, we didn't learn anything."

"Actually, we did, though it's not good news. We know they're not giving up. We know they believe the kid they're looking for is here. And they won't stop until they find her. We both heard what Jayme found. Males are sought after by the families, but females are just as important, if not more so. They need as many shifters as they can get to repopulate their ranks. Even though they're still clueless about Min, they want the child, regardless of gender."

"How do we get them off her scent?"

"The only way men like this know. With violence."

Bri was silent for a moment, and he studied her face, wondering what she was thinking.

"I want to say fuck these guys and dare them to make a move. And if it were only me, I would. But it's *not* just me. It's my innocent daughter, and the baby we made together. I have to do everything in my power to protect them. So, what if we just keep Min hidden until they lose interest? I could take her away, to my parents', BFE, anywhere but here."

Erik understood her flight response. But none of that would make a difference. "No matter how careful we are, they're going to find her, Bri."

She paled. "Then what do we do?"

"We make it crystal clear that this child is off-limits to them. That we'll take on anyone who comes at us." He paused and took a deep breath. "Look. After today, they'll know there are three shifters here. I'm sure they did their research after meeting Kaia and know that the largest wild cat in America is the cougar. And being tigers, they probably don't consider that much of a threat. But, that's where they'll make their mistake—in underestimating us."

"Should we call in more of the clan? At this point, the bigger the army between the tigers and Min, the better I'd feel."

Erik had thought about calling in more cougars, but he'd ultimately decided against it. "I'm afraid if we present them a show of force like that, they'll go to ground and wait it out. My clan-mates would come in a heartbeat, but they wouldn't be able to stay indefinitely. Eventually, they'd have to return to Colorado, to their jobs and their families. The Lao tigers are cowards at the core. They're not going to make any move while a contingent of mountain lions are here. I believe they'd just cool their heels and come at us once everyone was gone which would drag this on much longer than it needs to be."

Bri rubbed her hands up through her hair. "God, I hate this. I just want this to be over, so my daughter can be *safe*."

Erik reached across the table, grasped her hand, and pulled her to her feet. He guided her around the table and down onto his lap. Both legs dangled off one side, and she laid her head on his shoulder.

Erik wrapped his arms around her and squeezed, trying to lend her his strength and confidence. "I know, baby. The faster this is ended, the sooner we can start making memories as a family. It's not going to be easy, but I think we need to continue as we've been doing. They're confident right now, and they're bound to make a mistake. And when they do, I'll be there to send them straight to hell.

Erik smoothed a hand over her hair. "I will do everything in my power to make sure nothing happens to that sweet girl in there, or you and our baby. You have my promise on that."

10

When Mac dropped Jayme off an hour later, Bri was getting Min a bowl of cut-up strawberries and grapes.

"You want some?"

Jayme slumped into a chair at the table. "No. I'm off to get some sleep as soon as I compare notes with Erik."

Having heard his sister come in, he walked in carrying Min. He set her in her seat and then lowered into the one next to her.

Bri placed the bowl of fruit in front of her daughter. "Now, remember. No grapes for Moose. They'll make him sick, and you don't want that, do you?"

"No gapes fuh Moose." Min repeated. "Sawbewwies fuh Moose?"

Bri laughed, sitting on the other side of her daughter to make sure no little green chunks found their way to the floor. "Yes, strawberries are okay for Moose."

With Min finally settled, Bri turned to look at Jayme. "So, what happened at the barn?"

"Rasa was the perfect gentleman. He discussed horse training with Kaia and nothing more. She's right in that he doesn't think much of women. He didn't pay me any attention whatsoever, even knowing I was a shifter too. Mac stayed out of sight, but close enough to jump in if the guy tried anything. But there was nothing hinky about it. He played it straight."

"So, he was only there to keep Kaia away from the house while his beta searched it for evidence," Erik stated matter-of-factly.

"Pretty much," Jayme agreed. "What did Feng do?"

Erik replayed their encounter.

"They're obviously not taking our word for it." Jayme tiredly tucked strands of her long blonde hair behind her ears. Her light blue eyes were dull with fatigue. "They'll keep trying to get into the house."

"I know." Erik looked down at Min and ruffled her hair. "But they'll find that isn't as easy as they thought."

Jayme was drifting in her seat. "Go get some sleep, sis," he told her. "We'll be back in the woods tonight."

She nodded and walked off down the hall to the spare room.

"What are we going to do?" Bri watched him over the top of Min's head.

"If they make another move on Min here, I'll be ready to stop them."

"How?"

"That will be up to them."

~~~

Erik and Jayme were patrolling the acreage between Kaia's house and the tiger's temporary lair. Judging by the position of the moon, Erik knew it was after three in the morning. A time when any normal, law-abiding human would be tucked into their bed, sound asleep.

But not these fuckers. Erik watched from above as the two tigers bounded over a fallen tree and ran in the direction of Kaia's. He fell into step behind them, knowing that Jayme was up ahead and would block their path.

She gave a loud scream that stopped them in their tracks. They both flattened their ears and hissed in return at her
~~~

intrusion.

Erik stalked up behind them, curled his lip back to bare his large fang teeth, and screamed a cry of his own. The cats startled and spun to face the additional threat before splitting their attention between the two cougars growling and pacing toward them. Erik and Jayme worked in sync to make sure neither of them was able to break free and run.

Taking a chance, Erik shifted, dismissing his nudity as a minor inconvenience. "One of you want to man-up, so we can talk? We're all reasonable shifters here. We can share this forest for as long as you're in town, with a little bit of due respect."

He kept a careful eye on both tigers, watching for any indication that one was going to strike. Erik could transform in the space of a heartbeat, and at this distance, he would have plenty of time to set his cat free again before they reached him.

As the silence stretched on and he got no reaction from either feline, he began to pull his cougar to him, when the tiger on the left became a man. Erik assumed it must be Rasa Chai, since he'd never seen this man before. It certainly wasn't the same one who'd made the visit out to Kaia's just earlier that day.

"We know you hide a child of our clan!" Rasa's hands fisted at his sides.

Erik noted that his speech cadence was a lot more fluid than Bri and Kaia had described. No more searching for elusive English words—the lying bastard spoke it fluently.

Erik was done playing games. These dickheads needed to know exactly how this was going to play out.

"The only child here was adopted legally, according to the governments of both Laos and the United States," Erik's voice was hard as stone, "and is of no interest to you or your *clan*. You need to leave. Go back home, and be glad I'm letting you walk out of here."

Erik took a step forward and raised an accusing finger.

"We've done our research on you, and we know all about the foul and inhuman practices of your clan. Pursue this—make even one more move against us—and I'll make damned sure the ruling clans in your country know exactly what you're doing."

Black eyes narrowed, and rage moved over Rasa's face. Erik got the feeling this was a man accustomed to getting what he wanted. And those who refused probably didn't live very long. As the son of the leader, he'd be second in command and wield the most power underneath her.

"You have no right to speak to me that way. I am tiger, and demand you give me the child."

"See, that's never going to happen." Erik kept his voice smooth and light now, knowing his nonchalance was as offensive as his refusal, if not more so. "You and your buddy had better tuck your tails and run along home like good little kitties. And don't you *ever* let me catch your striped asses anywhere near here again."

Erik never took his eyes off the man before him. He knew Jayme was locked on the other one.

He caught the flash in the dark eyes moments before the coward shifted, and Erik's cougar was ready. He leapt forward and tackled the tiger to the ground. As Jayme engaged with the second, Erik went tooth-to-tooth with the four-hundred-pound cat.

He used his speed and agility to dodge the massive paws that swiped out at his face and neck. Before the bulky cat could regroup, Erik raked his claws down the banded hide, drawing blood.

The tiger roared his fury and charged.

Leading with anger was never smart in any encounter. Rasa's rage may lend to his strength, but Erik had steely control and unwavering discipline, which made him all the more dangerous.

While the tiger struck out wildly and with no particular strategy that he could tell, Erik timed his attacks, waiting for the bigger cat to launch before countering when his opponent was most vulnerable.

Erik's cougar was quick and nimble, easily able to sidestep or duck to avoid the worst hits, while still conserving his energy to do the most damage. His years of training and practice gave him an advantage that his adversary did not possess.

They went at each other with everything they had. Erik landed blow after blow, the wounds he inflicted leaving gashes of red soaking the orange and black fur. Rasa got in a couple of lucky strikes, leaving deep gouges across Erik's stomach.

But the tiger was tiring fast, the feline not accustomed to the tactics of a regimented soldier. His reflexes were slow and sloppy, which meant the royal patriarch relied on others to do his dirty work for him. He was fat and lazy, more interested in raping young girls than fighting his own battles or keeping his cat in shape.

Rasa's sides were heaving, and he was losing ground, which made him even angrier. His cat growled his frustration, his desperate attempts to take the cougar down failing and futile.

Erik spared a glance to his sister and saw that she was holding her own against the other cat. There was blood on both of them, but her movements didn't indicate any serious injuries.

Rasa, in an effort to take advantage of Erik's inattention, made a foolish and uncontrolled move. Erik avoided it easily, and before Rasa could ward him off, Erik had his fangs clamped over the tiger's jugular. The upturned legs flailed, claws extended as he tried in vain to meet his mark. He fought until Erik put more pressure on his airway, cutting off precious oxygen.

Rasa finally went still. He lay panting and struggling to breathe, but not nearly as resigned as Erik would have liked.

This ignorant motherfucker didn't know when to quit, his body still radiating tension rather than just surrendering in defeat. His arrogance evidently knew no limits.

Erik noticed that the forest had suddenly gone silent. He glanced over and saw Jayme and the other tiger watching him. Seeing his clan leader beaten and held on the edge of death, Feng didn't know what to do next. He had to be the beta to Rasa's alpha—used to taking orders from his superior and never thinking on his own.

Turning his attention back to Rasa, Erik brought his teeth together another fraction of an inch and growled into the dense mass of fur in his mouth. Rasa didn't move but hissed out his displeasure.

Erik thought for a moment that he'd hold on to his bravado and try to fight Erik off, but instead, the tiger receded and transformed back into a man.

Erik adjusted his bite as the thick jowls shrank to the vulnerable neck of the naked man lying docile underneath him. The taste of blood was hot and metallic in Erik's mouth, and his cat was demanding to finish him off. To remove the threat to his cubs once and for all and be done with it.

Talking him down and explaining his reasons, Erik was finally able to convince him to release the man. The disgruntled cougar reluctantly backed off and let Erik take over.

The clan leader scuttled away, his hand to his neck as he tested the wound Erik's cat had left there. He studied the blood on his fingers.

Rasa's jaw set, and he looked like he was about to let his mouth overload his ass.

"Don't be fucking stupid. *Leave*, while you still can." Erik hovered over him, his jaw clenched and his voice cold as steel. "Come at us again, and your clan will be down two more tigers. From what I understand, that's a loss you can't afford."

Erik nodded to his sister that they were done here. He

shifted back to mountain lion, and together they left, stopping only when they were out of sight. They took up positions to watch what the tigers would do.

The second man shifted and tried to help Rasa up, but the alpha swatted at him bad-naturedly and barked an order at him in their native language. They exchanged words for a few minutes, shifted back to tigers, and went back in the direction of their motel.

Erik and Jayme returned to Kaia's. Just as had happened the other night, Mac met them as they came in.

Mac's eyes scanned all the blood. "You guys all right?"

"We're good. We just need to clean up."

Erik took a few minutes to fill Mac in on his conversation with the tiger while Jayme excused herself to the bathroom to start washing off. After going over every detail and answering all of Mac's questions, the sheriff was satisfied and retired to his room with Kaia.

His sister helped him rinse all the blood off and doctored his wounds, taping a large bandage over the gashes on his torso. The injury would heal quickly, the gauze only a barrier to keep any seeping from staining Bri's sheets.

So as not to scare Bri or Min when they woke up, Erik wore a t-shirt over the dressing across his stomach. He was sore, but he wouldn't miss out on the opportunity to feel Bri curling up next to him. Carefully, lying with her, he pulled her into his arms.

Erik didn't sleep that night. He kept all of his senses open for any clues to the tigers' whereabouts. Try as he might, he just couldn't seem to dismiss the nagging feeling that this was only the beginning.

<div align="center">~~~</div>

The next few days passed quietly, but Bri didn't make

the mistake of letting her guard down. She didn't want her daughter out in the open, so she was careful to keep Min inside and away from any of the doors or windows.

They were hoping this lag in action meant the tigers were preparing to leave. Until they got confirmation that the men had left the country, however, she wasn't easing up.

As of that morning, they were still in town, holed up at that same motel. She wished she knew what they were doing. Mac was taking time out of his workdays to keep an eye on them, while Erik and Jayme spent each night in the woods.

After today though, Erik would be doing the night patrols by himself. Jayme had left for Helena a few hours before, and classes would begin tomorrow and last for the next twelve weeks. Helena was an hour and a half away. Not far, but she wouldn't be able to make the trip back often, as most of her time would be taken up with her studies.

Erik was so proud of her and wouldn't listen to one word about her staying. He'd remained in the woods all morning, giving Jayme the time she needed to finish packing and get on the road. Pursuing her career was too important to her, and he'd be damned if he were the one standing in her way.

Bri understood, but she was a little worried about Erik running the forest solo. They'd both come home with some pretty gnarly looking wounds the last time. And that was when the fight had been evenly matched. Thinking about him out there alone against two tigers made her stomach twist in knots.

She needed her daughter safe, but not at the expense of the man she was coming to love. Each night she held her breath, not daring to relax until he was back with her the next morning.

He'd explained why he didn't want to call any of his clanmates in, and she understood, but she was still nervous. Besides not wanting to drag this out, a battalion of cougars might lead to an influx of tigers, and they hardly needed a shifter war being waged in the Lost Creek State Park.

She watched for him now, standing at the back door, eyes scanning the tree line for his sleek form among the trees.

When she saw him finally walking across the yard, she let out a sigh of relief. She'd just opened the door for him, waiting for him to walk into her arms, when she saw two cats emerge out of the shadows.

"Erik." His name was only a breath.

He perceived the warning in her tone and spun quickly around. Seeing the tigers, he pushed her further into the house.

"Get inside and lock yourselves in your room."

Bri hesitated, earning a glare from Erik. "Get inside. Now."

Tears burned her eyes, but she ran. As soon as she slammed the bedroom door behind her, Kaia was on her feet. To make the enforced house arrest a little easier, she'd been spending time with Min in the mornings before leaving for the barn.

"What is it?"

Bri's voice shook. "They're here, and Erik's all alone."

With Jayme an hour and a half away and Mac in Anaconda—too far to get here in time—they were on their own.

Kaia knew her well and reached out to grasp Bri's hands. "Please don't tell me you're thinking of going out there. Those are tigers, Bri. Let Erik handle this. He'll be better off knowing you guys are safe without having to worry about you."

It's two against one, damn it! She had to *do* something. She couldn't just sit back and wait for them to kill him.

She stared deep into her grayish-green eyes and prayed she'd understand. "I can't. I have to try. I love him, Kai."

Kaia nodded, and with a squeeze of reassurance, released her hands.

Suddenly, it hit Bri what she needed. She ran to her closet. Up high on the shelf, tucked behind an empty suitcase, was a locked metal box. Inside that container was the pistol Bri had carried with her for years. As a woman traveling mostly on her own, she'd acquired it as a way to defend herself.

She'd never had to use it but had practiced with it until she could hit her target from any distance.

When she turned from retrieving it, Kaia's eyes widened in disbelief.

"Where did you…You know what, never mind."

Bri looked from her best friend to her child and back. "If they get past us, you're the last line of defense. I hate asking you to risk—"

"Stop right there." Kaia held up her hand to halt Bri's words. "You don't have to ask. It's my risk to take, and I'll do it to protect this sweet child." Kaia pointed a finger at Bri. "You just make sure you don't get hurt out there either. You have your own bundle to think about too."

"I *am* thinking about it. That man out there is this baby's father, and we can't lose him."

With the weapon behind her back, Bri went to where Min was sitting on her bed reading books. She placed a kiss on top of her head. "Momma will be right back. Aunt Kaia and Moose are going to stay here with you for a minute. I love you."

Bri straightened, took a deep breath, and marched to the door. After disengaging the lock, she stepped out. Just before closing the door again, she gave Kaia one last look. "Don't let anything happen to her."

"Be careful."

"I will." Bri quietly shut the door.

Just as she'd been taught, she checked the magazine. Thumbing the release, the mag dropped into her left hand. A quick glance told her it was full. This particular model had a double stack mag which allowed her to carry eleven rounds plus the one in the chamber. Twelve 9mm bullets against two large tigers.

She liked those odds.

Ramming the magazine back home, Bri flipped the safety off and hurried to the dining room. Through the sliding glass door, she could see Erik's cougar engaged in battle with one of them in the middle of Kaia's back yard. As she watched, the other was preparing to join in and double-team him.

She gripped the handle and slid the door open hard. Taking her gun in a two-handed grip, she walked out onto the deck. The tiger that had been poised to strike turned at the interruption and saw her.

She held the sight steady on him. "Try it, asshole."

He gave a furious roar but halted his attack. In her head, Bri knew she should shoot him anyway. And she wanted to, so badly. He was here to take her little girl from her and sentence her to a life of servitude and forced breeding. He deserved to die for that alone. Not to mention what he was doing to countless others who hadn't been fortunate enough to get away.

But in her heart, she knew she wouldn't be able to. Not like this. Not without giving them a chance to be reasonable. Erik had issued an ultimatum when he'd encountered them in the woods, but Bri needed to see for herself if only evil resided behind their eyes. She had to know that killing them was the only alternative.

Gun still trained on the second cat, she cast a fast glance to Erik. He and the first Lao tiger were biting and clawing savagely, her arrival masked by the roars and screams of the two warring beasts. Both had sustained rips and gashes along their sides, the goal to rend skin and muscle from bone.

The tiger looked so much bigger than Erik. But Erik was holding his own, his smaller size giving him an advantage over the bulkier cat. But how long could he last?

"Hey!" she shouted over the growling and hissing.

Still, neither heard her. Both were zeroed in on their opponent to the exclusion of everything else.

Shifting the barrel of her pistol a fraction of an inch to the left, Bri pulled the trigger. The bullet plowed into the ground inches from fur and paws, gaining the attention of both combatants.

"You two need to get the fuck out of my yard." She came down the three steps to stand in the grass, never taking her aim off the intruders. When the cat engaged in battle with Erik took a step in her direction, Bri fired off another round. This one took a tuft of orange fur off his leg. He growled his outrage but didn't take another step.

"The next one will go through you, so don't tempt me." Bri got on with the message she wanted delivered. "You tell your mother that baby is *mine*." The men still didn't know Min was a girl, and she'd only become that much more desirable if they knew.

"And I will protect *my child* until my dying breath." Bri thought of the man who was right now hurt and bleeding on their behalf, and the woman inside who would lay down her life for Min.

Bri was on a roll, and apparently Erik thought so too. He'd slowly been backing away from the tigers during her tirade, which was all the better.

"And one more thing while I have your full attention. What you dickless wonders are doing to your own clanspeople is disgusting! You breed your women and girls like dogs—all in the name of your clan. Yeah, we know about that. Your bullshit *entitlement* issues don't entitle you to a goddamned thing, you nasty pricks. Keep it up, and your leading clan is going to know about it too. You're pathetic, and you ought to be ashamed of yourselves."

Bri tilted her head and added one more thing. "Now get your ugly, striped asses out of my yard and leave us the hell alone!"

When they didn't move as fast as she thought they should, Bri let loose three rapid-fire shots right at the ground by their feet. "Don't test me, motherfucker. I said *go*."

The Lao tiger roared, but knowing he had no other choice, began to back away.

She held the gun aimed at them until they were lost in

the shadows of the woods. She lowered it as Erik's cougar approached. When he was standing on the deck next to her, he shifted.

His whole side was covered in blood. It ran in rivulets from his torso and down his leg. His breathing was labored, but thankfully, his voice was steady and hard.

"We'll get into you *not* staying safely inside with Min in a minute." His blue eyes drilled into hers. "You do know they're not going to leave. They're too overconfident to realize they're outmanned and outgunned. They'll be back."

Bri let out a breath and inclined her head. "I do." She brought her gaze up to his. "But I had to do it, Erik. I had to see if there was any decency in them at all. I had to see with my own eyes that they were so purely vile." Bri shrugged. "If they come back, there'll be nothing more I can do. And if they make that mistake, I'll shoot them myself." Her voice cracked.

Erik took her into his arms. "Aw hell, baby."

Bri soaked up his strength for a moment until she remembered his injuries. "Let's get you inside. I need to look at your wounds."

As they walked into the house, Bri instructed Erik to sit while she gathered what she needed.

Having heard their voices, Kaia emerged from the hall. She scrutinized Bri head to toe. "Thank God. I heard the shots." She looked at Erik. "You okay?"

He nodded. "I'm good. Just some scratches. Looks worse than it is."

Before Bri could even ask, Kaia added, "Min's in the bedroom playing with her toys. She got scared when the gunshots went off, but I told her everything was okay and that her momma was scaring off some pests." She took in Erik's injuries. "You might want to get that cleaned up before she comes out here."

Erik glanced down at himself. "You've got a point." He headed off in the direction of the bathroom.

Bri watched as Erik disappeared down the hallway. She turned back to her best friend. "Thank you for understanding why I had to go out there. I wouldn't have been able to live with myself if I hadn't at least tried."

Kaia waved her off. "I would have done the same thing if it had been Mac out there."

They walked into each other's arms and hugged tightly. Bri whispered into Kaia's ear, "And thank you for loving and guarding my daughter."

"Always."

Bri stepped back. "I'd better go help Erik bandage up."

Kaia smirked at her. "No worries. I'll keep Min occupied, just in case you guys get a little...*distracted* in the process."

11

Bri was still smiling when she walked into the bathroom and closed and locked the door behind her. She laid her gun on the counter and pulled out the first aid supplies. She was getting what she'd need organized when Erik stepped out of the shower.

Bri got her first good look at his wounds.

"Oh, Erik." They definitely weren't the nothing he'd implied. There were puncture marks along his neck and shoulders, and deep furrows running around his side, along his hip, and down his thigh. For anyone else, an ER visit would have been mandatory. For a shifter, butterfly bandages would close the gouges well enough until they completely healed in a couple of days.

Even knowing that, the sight of him still hurt her. Blood oozed sluggishly from several of the gashes.

She laid a gentle hand near the grooves that followed the line of his ribs. The tips of her fingers traced each jagged edge.

His hand came up to rest on top of hers. "I'll be okay."

Her gaze rose slowly to his. "I know. But that doesn't make these any easier to look at." She paused and tried to find the words she needed to say. "What you're doing for me and my little girl…"

Bri paused, changing what she'd been about to say. "That night we had sex—barely before we knew each other's names—I swore to myself that I didn't need you in my life."

As she spoke, Bri began to tend to Erik's wounds. He remained still and silent, only lifting his arm to give her better access to his torso. She dabbed away some blood and applied a row of butterfly strips. She kept her eyes on her task, careful not to make eye contact.

"Sure, you were hot and sexy and tempted me in a way no one ever had. But I didn't think I was in a place where I could pursue that. I had a newly adopted child that required all of my time and attention."

She moved on to the next furrow, pulled it together with her fingers, and taped it.

"That night scared the shit out of me. I took a shower afterwards, shaking and sobbing over the sheer immensity of it. The way you made me feel was so overwhelming…Never in my life had anyone ever affected me so completely in such a short amount of time. Or *any* amount of time, for that matter."

Bri dropped her attention to his thigh. She had yet to look up into his extraordinary face to see his reaction to her words. She was a little embarrassed to be laying herself open like this. But he was putting his life on the line for her and her daughter, and she at least owed him that much. He'd suffered greatly for it already.

"So, I pushed you away. Or rather, I *drove* you away. Except the universe obviously had other plans. I was on the pill the night you and I got together. I travel a lot, and things can happen, but I don't take chances like that." She nodded towards the gun. "I protect myself in more ways than one."

She placed the last bandage and took her time smoothing it out.

"I don't know why it didn't work." Bri gathered up the mess and tossed it into the same trashcan her pajamas had ended up in that first night.

Taking a bracing breath, she straightened and finally looked him in the face. He didn't move a muscle as his eyes searched hers, and his expression gave away nothing. It worried her a little, but she pushed on.

"But I'm glad it didn't. And I'm glad you fought for us and the life we could have together. If you hadn't...I would have never known I could feel this way."

He finally spoke, and his voice was gravelly. "What way?"

He was so handsome standing there, completely naked, bruised, and bandaged, yet still tall and strong. Imposing. The literal lion at the gate.

Bri had no doubt that he would continue to fill that role for her and their children until the day he drew his last breath. Never again would she have to face the dark alone or fear someone meaning to do her harm.

She placed her hands flat on his chest and felt the rapid and erratic thumping of his heart. He wasn't as unaffected as he seemed. The irregular cadence matched her own and gave her the courage to finish.

"That I could love you as wholly and deeply as I do. My life never would have been complete without you in it."

His hands came up slowly and wrapped around each side of her neck. His bright blue gaze took in every aspect of her face and finally came to settle on her eyes.

"I've been hiding a pretty big secret of my own since that night." His thumbs grazed over her lower lip. "Since the moment I saw you, really. I knew it then, but I tried to ignore it."

"What secret?" Bri's own voice was whisper soft.

"I love you, Bri. And I can't live without you."

Bri smiled as tears welled in her eyes.

Erik pulled her closer and covered her mouth with his. Conscious of his injuries, Bri wrapped her arms around him and sank into the kiss. Her body instantly heated, and desire unfurled low in her core. Her nipples puckered and ached to be touched.

She felt the hardness of his erection pressing against her and desperately wanted him inside of her, filling and stretching her, surrendering to him as she went up in flames.

Before she lost her mind and forgot how beaten up he was, Bri pulled out of the embrace. Sleeping in a room with a toddler didn't afford them much time alone, so not taking advantage of it now was damned near impossible. But she did it.

She had to remember he'd just fought a tiger twice his size.

"We can't do this," she sighed as he tried to bring her back to him. "I just fixed you up, and you're not ready for that kind of physical activity. We don't want you bleeding all over the place again. Besides, Kaia needs to get to work, and our daughter is waiting for us."

He stilled, studying her. "*Our?*"

"That's what you want, isn't it?" She grinned up at him.

"You have no idea how much." His blue eyes shimmered, and he kissed her gently. "Thank you for sharing her with me."

"There's no one else I'd rather have in her life." She gave his hand a squeeze and sent him a brilliant smile. "I'll get you some clothes and check on Min."

She was just about to open the door when he grasped her arm and tugged her back. He kissed her quick and hard. "I love you."

Bri smiled. "I love you too."

~~~

After putting Min to bed later that evening, Erik, Bri, Mac, and Kaia sat around the dinner table and discussed what their options were for dealing with Rasa and Yuu.

There was something niggling at Erik. Nights on patrol were long, giving him plenty of time to think. He looked up and pinned Mac with a hard stare. "God forbid this should ever
~~~

happen, but let's say they somehow manage to get their paws on Min. What's their plan then, and where do they go from there?"

"Back to Laos," Bri answered automatically. "Back to their clan."

"Yeah. But how do they get her there?" Erik asked the group. "Do we assume they're smart enough to already have the forged documents they'd need to smuggle a kid out of the country? Even if they had her listed as a boy, that wouldn't pose much of an issue. Just change her clothes, and boom."

"If not them, then Rasa's mother would have thought of supplying him with the papers." Mac leaned in. "From what we've learned, she's the brains."

Erik nodded and scratched his chin. "So, he's got the kid and he's ready to fly. Does he try flying commercial? There's a lot of scrutiny involved with that—heightened security checkpoints, long lines, hours of waiting. He's got a scared kid in tow, one who's probably been listed as missing already, and an Amber Alert would have been issued. We know where he's going. We can point authorities right to him."

Mac groaned. "Fuck. You're exactly right. He's got to have a private plane somewhere. Son of a bitch! I should have thought to check how they even got here." He grabbed his phone to presumably get someone on that when he noticed the time. "Shit. It's too late to reach anyone tonight. As soon as I get to the office in the morning, I'll start digging into that. I'll know what they have and where it is in no time."

They went over ideas for a few minutes longer before finally pairing off to go to bed. Erik and Bri closed the door to her bedroom behind them. He turned and went to check on Min, just to reassure himself she was tucked in and safe.

The blanket had fallen off the side of the bed from her rolling and moving, and she was sleeping peacefully on her side facing him. He picked it up and covered her with it, squatting down just to look at her.

She was so beautiful. And he loved her so much already. Just like with her mother, he'd fallen hard the first time he'd ever seen her, drawn in by those big dark eyes and impish features. She looked so delicate, but he knew she'd have a core of strength like few others.

That little tigress sleeping inside of her now would one day emerge and be something to reckon with. She'd be magnificent. And if everything went as he hoped, she'd grow up calling him Daddy. He'd make sure she never had anything to fear and show her that she could be anything she wanted to be. And more.

This tiny little girl would mature into one hell of a powerful woman.

"Is she okay?" Bri came to him and laid a hand on his shoulder.

He rose, turned, and pulled her into his arms. "She's perfect."

Bri looked lovingly down at her daughter. "I've always thought so."

They moved as one to the side of the large queen-sized bed. Undressing quietly, they slipped under the bedding and into each other's arms.

"I want to take my girls out for the day. Go do something fun."

Bri's body tensed. "Erik, we can't. It's not safe yet."

"They know the child they want is here. That secret is out, and I think if we enlist the help of our friend with the badge, we should be able to get out of here for a few hours with no tiger the wiser."

She bit her lip in the darkness, her tone still wary. "I'd rather not have them know she's a girl." She raised up on her elbow and looked down at him. Her blonde hair fell forward over her shoulder, and her amber eyes shone in the low light. "I'm afraid if they know, she'll become even more of a target."

"I think we can get around that. I'm sure she has some gender-neutral clothing she can wear. I just think you both need to get out of this house. I know she's been asking for a long time about going to Kaia's barn or to the park."

"You're still injured from the go-round with them this morning. I just don't think this is a good idea right now."

Erik mirrored her position and looked at her straight on. "I'll be healed enough by tomorrow to make this happen, and I have a plan. I'm not leaving your side. I promise I'll keep you both safe." He leaned in and kissed her, whispering against her lips. "Let's go have some fun, and to hell with anyone else. My girls need a day out on the town."

He played his ace. "You can take your camera. We can go back to that meadow and have another picnic." He nuzzled her neck. "I really like how the last one turned out."

She melted into him for a second before putting a hand to his chest and pushing him back.

"First of all," she scowled at him, "that's playing dirty. You know I have a weakness for taking pictures, especially of Min. Second," she heaved out an exasperated breath, "we do both need to escape these walls. But it scares me, Erik. I can't lose her. I *won't*." She paused, and he could see she was tempted by his idea. "We can go. But know that I'll be packing more than just my camera."

He knew immediately what she meant, and he didn't have a problem with that.

"Pistol-packing momma. I like it." Erik leaned his weight into her, pushing her onto her back. He slid down her body, kissing as he went.

Just before disappearing out of sight, he lifted his head to meet her gaze. "You're going to want to be very quiet." He smirked and dipped his head to her lower belly.

He heard her quick intake of breath as he ran his tongue along the top edge of her panties. Curling his fingers around the elastic band, he removed them and pushed them aside. Settling back in place, Erik slid her thighs wide.

Being a shifter, his senses were heightened—even in human form—beyond that of a normal person, although they didn't even compare to those of his cat. But with that extra awareness, he could see her spread out for him perfectly. And she was already glistening for him. Bri was a very sexual woman. He loved that about her. She took what she wanted but also gave it back unselfishly. She was sexy and confident, beautiful and strong.

She was everything he could have wanted.

Running the fingers of one hand through her silky folds, Erik dipped into her slippery center. Sliding back out, he thumbed her clit and her body jerked, but she remained resolutely mute. Bri wasn't the silent type, always vocal about what she liked and wanted. Erik smiled wickedly to himself, determined to see how far he could push her.

Leaning in, he flattened his tongue and lapped from her core to the top of the sensitive bud. It rent a violent shiver from her, and as he drew back, he could barely hear her cursing on an exhale of air.

"Fuck. Fuck. Fuck."

Erik grinned like a fiend and bent to her again. When he sucked that little button into his mouth, she writhed. Her hands found the blanket on either side of her, and when the fabric moved over him, he knew she was bunching it tight in both fists.

He thrust two fingers into her heat and moved them in and out as he continued to feast on her. Using lips, tongue, and fingers, Erik licked and flicked, her hips urgently seeking to be closer. She undulated and rose to meet his mouth.

And still she made no sound. Erik's cock was so hard it was painful, throbbing and demanding to be buried deep in the wanton creature before him.

Just when Erik thought he wouldn't be able to take another moment without her, Bri's sheath constricted around him. Wave after wave of pleasure stole her breath until she was panting and shaking.

He gentled his touch, caressing her softly through the aftershocks.

When she finally stilled, he crawled his way back up her long, slim body. As he emerged, she grasped his face in her hands and pulled him to her, angling her head and kissing him deeply. He knew she could taste herself on his lips and he groaned, the thought so fucking hot his balls ached.

His steel shaft lay against her stomach, and he couldn't wait any longer. He needed her. Reaching down, he was about to drive into her when she suddenly rolled, switching their positions.

"Now it's your turn to keep quiet," she whispered.

As she slithered down to find his throbbing cock, Erik cursed in his mind.

Oh, fuck. He wasn't sure if he had the discipline she did.

As her lips wrapped around him and took him in, his eyes squeezed shut. And then she did some little swirl and lick with her tongue that had stars exploding behind his lids.

He had to bite back a particularly ripe oath.

Her mouth tortured him for several more minutes, her palms cupping and squeezing his balls to add to the intensity. Her hand went to the base of his shaft and gripped so tight he gasped. Holding the tension, she devoured him whole. With so much pressure wrapped around his cock, he became so much more sensitive to her touch.

She grazed her teeth up and down his length, raking the sharp edges against his taut skin. Raising her head so that only the head of his cock was in her mouth, she flicked at the underside.

Before he could recover from the burst of sensation, she

swallowed him to the hilt. Sucking hard, she began to pump him with her hand and mouth, setting a rigorous pace. He knew he wouldn't last long. He could feel the base of his spine tingling. It traveled through his body and concentrated in his balls.

Unbidden, his hips thrust upward, his cock hit the back of her throat, and he erupted.

He gradually became aware of Bri kissing her way back up his body. She didn't stop until she was tucked in next to him. Somehow, Erik got his arms around her and held her close.

"You. Are. Amazing." His voice was non-existent. He was spent and barely holding on to consciousness. No one had ever made him feel this way.

Only her. For the rest of his life, he only wanted to be with Bri.

~~~

As Bri went through Min's clothes the next morning looking for something not-too-girlish, she started to get nervous.

Even with what Erik had planned—to have Mac show up to the hotel to question the Lao men, distracting them and assuring Erik, Bri, and Min could slip away from the house— was it smart to take her out like this? What if something went wrong? She'd be vulnerable in the open. Here inside the house, Min was safe. Out there, anything could happen.

They *were* both going a little stir-crazy. She took a breath and chose to believe in Erik. If anyone could protect Min, it was him. He'd already proven how far he would go to keep her safe.

Kaia came in as she was having second and third thoughts. "Where are you guys going today?"

Bri ran her hand through her hair. "I don't know. Erik has it all planned out."

Kaia knew she was scared about taking Min out in public.
~~~

"You're in good hands. Mac's ready to do his part, and Erik would never let anything happen to either of you."

"I know." Bri held the red shorts and plain white t-shirt in her hands. "In my heart, I know he wouldn't have suggested it if he didn't think it was safe. But in my head, I can't keep from worrying about those men finding out she's a girl."

"I think I have something that will help with that." Kaia pulled something gray and small out of her back pocket. She ran her fingers around the bill and over the top of the cap.

"Jace used to wear this when he played t-ball. From pictures, I would guess he was about four at the time. It sat on his shelf beside the trophy for years. After he died, I didn't have the heart to get rid of it."

"Oh, Kaia." Bri took it and straightened it out, the image of the tiny cap blurring in front of her eyes. It would fit Min perfectly and hide her chin-length black hair and delicate features. She stared down at it before looking back up to her best friend.

She blinked back tears as she leaned in and gave Kaia a hug. "Thank you for this. It'll definitely help." Bri made an effort to shake off the feelings of sorrow and dread. She smiled, even though she didn't really feel it. "We're going to have fun today and not worry about anything else."

Kaia smiled, her own eyes shimmering with moisture. "Exactly." She paused and winked. "But don't forget your gun."

Bri laughed and actually felt better. "I won't."

"I gotta run. You guys should stop by the barn later. A stray cat had a litter of kittens under Helen's porch. The momma hasn't been seen in a few days, so Helen has been bottle-feeding the babies. Min would love them."

"She sure would. I'll run it past Erik."

"Cool." Kaia gave her arm a reassuring squeeze and then turned to leave. "Be brave."

At the same time, Erik came in with a towel-wrapped,

giggling Min. He'd offered to bathe her this morning, and Bri had been all too willing to let him. He was so soaked, it was hard to tell which of them had actually had the bath.

She laughed. "Did you fall in?"

"No. This kid seems to think she's a breaching whale frolicking in the tub. She had water sloshing all *over* the place." He drove a finger into Min's side, and the teeny girl dissolved into giggles. "It's even dripping off the ceiling," he said in a mock growl.

"Erk aww wet." Min beamed at Bri.

"I can see that. You did quite a number on him, didn't you?" She went and took the girl-burrito from Erik. "Come on. Let's get you dressed, so we can go bye-bye."

She laid Min on her bed and began to dry her off.

Min looked up at her. "Going?"

"I don't know. You'll have to ask Erik."

Min twisted her head around until she could see him. "Going?"

"That's a surprise. You'll just have to wait and see."

"Well, then." Bri secured the second tape on the diaper, held Min's hands, and pulled her up until she was standing on the bed. "We'd better hurry, so we can find out."

Ten minutes later, Bri surveyed her daughter, trying to view her with a critical eye. Wispy black hair tucked into the ball cap, white tee, red shorts, white socks, and tiny white Converse tennis shoes.

She still saw a girl, but anyone who didn't know her would see a little boy. *Hopefully.*

That first step out of the house with Min, Bri felt exposed. She glanced at Erik, and he gave her an encouraging smile.

"This'll work. Trust me."

"I do. It's those other fuckers I don't trust."

"They'll have other things to worry about besides us today." He was grinning at her, but she saw the awareness in his eyes. He may seem relaxed and out for a fun day, but he was conscious of everything around them. "You just enjoy yourself today. That's your only job."

Bri promised herself she would.

Having already gotten the all-clear from Mac, they piled into the car, and Erik drove them to the zoo.

They spent hours and hours looking at all of the animals, watching the different shows, and eating everything under the sun until Bri thought she might be sick.

Min had the time of her life. And so did Bri. Other than a school field trip when she was young, she'd never been to a zoo. She lost herself in the amazement just as much as Min did. They laughed at the antics of the monkeys, stood flabbergasted at the sheer size of the elephants, and cringed when Erik insisted they go into the reptile house.

They were standing outside of the mountain lion enclosure, watching a big male sunning himself on an outcropping of rock. "Can you...communicate with him?" Bri asked in a low voice.

Erik laughed. "Nope." Min was perched on his wide shoulders, pointing at the big cat, babbling. "Not even in animal form. It doesn't work that way."

Bri turned back to the captive cougar. "He's beautiful. But not as much as yours."

Erik leaned down to nibble on her ear. "I'm glad you like him. He's pretty crazy about you too."

From there they walked to the bears.

"Uh-oh," Erik said with a grin. "I think someone lost the battle."

Bri glanced up to see Min slumped over Erik's head, asleep. They'd brought her stroller, but she'd insisted Erik hold her up high, where she could see everything. Bri cleaned their purchases out of her seat and helped disentangle Min from Erik's back.

Bri laid her in the reclined seat and pulled the sunshade

over her.

"What do you say we find someplace to rest a bit too?" Erik brushed a kiss over her cheek.

"Sounds good. I could use a cold drink and some shade."

They found what they were looking for not too far away from a lemonade cart. Bri sat on the bench and leaned into Erik's side as they sat and watched all the people go by.

"Any sign of trouble?" she asked him, casually looking around.

"None at all. We've had a clear day." His hand rubbed up and down her arm. "Having a good time?"

Bri leaned her head back and gazed up at him. "The best. Thank you for this. I needed it more than I thought." She dropped her eyes to Min, resting peacefully in her stroller. "She needed it worse than I did. She's too young to understand what's happening, but she still knows something is wrong. I hate *that* most of all. She's had enough trauma in her three short years of life. She doesn't need any more. That's my one wish for her—to have the best possible life I can give her."

"And she will," Erik promised, kissing the top of her head. "We'll get through this, and we can get on with our lives."

"Which will be where, exactly?" The thought had been weighing heavily on Bri's mind as she and Erik had grown closer. "My life is here. Yours is in Colorado."

"See, that's where you're wrong. My life is wherever you and our children are. If that means I move here, then that's what I'll do." He smiled easily. "We can start our own satellite clan of shifters here in Montana. But, I refuse to live with my cousin and Mac forever. I think we need to start looking for a place of our own. We'll be married soon and have a baby coming shortly after that. We'll need more room."

Her heart stuttered. And then the idea settled. She filled with warmth as an image of their lives together bloomed. "Married?"

He nodded decisively. "Yup."

Bri snuggled into his side a little more, content and relaxed. "Don't assume you won't have to ask me properly. I won't put up with any half-assed marriage proposal."

His arm tightened around her shoulder and he chuckled. "I wouldn't dream of it."

They didn't get home until after dark. They never made it to the farm, but that was okay. Min was happy but exhausted, regaling Kaia and Mac with her adventures over dinner, while Bri and Erik helped them to understand most of it.

"Oh my goodness!" Kaia responded to Min. "It sounds like you had quite a day! Did you see the monkeys? Those were always my favorite. The way they swing around and play."

That set Min off on another long babble-fest that even Bri had a hard time catching.

Bri pulled her camera out and showed them a few of the pictures she'd taken on the viewing screen.

"I can't wait to get some of these printed off to put in her book."

"Her book?" Erik asked.

"Yeah. I'm making her a scrapbook of everything we've done since the day I got her. "By the time she's a teenager, she'll have dozens of them." Bri laughed. "I am forever taking pictures of her. I have a whole series I took while we were still in Ban Xuang."

That brought to mind the park she'd found.

"I would love to go back someday." She looked over at Erik. "You wouldn't believe the beauty of Min's country. The orphanage where I adopted Min is at the base of the mountains, and right beside it is the most spectacular park I have ever seen. So tranquil and so beautiful. I'll show you some of the pictures, but they don't do it justice."

"I can't imagine that. Your photography is stunning," Erik surprised her by saying.

"You've seen my work?"

"I Googled you," he said unabashedly. "And Kaia gave me a few sites to check out. Like I said, what you do is incredible."

At the word Google, Bri's heart skipped a beat. It wouldn't have been difficult for him to learn just how wealthy she was. No, not just wealthy—fucking *loaded*. What her family had made the rich look like paupers. She freely admitted they were wealthy, but just how wealthy was where she ran into problems. Would that change the way he looked at her?

"You Googled me?"

"Yup." He lounged back in his seat, his eyes level with hers. "That's quite a family you've got there. Goes back a long ways. And all of them rolling in it. Deep."

"Yes, they are." Bri felt herself sitting up straighter. Her voice was crisper. "So am I."

"Yeah. That's usually how it works." His expression wasn't giving anything away. He still looked relaxed and comfortable. "You know what I was thinking we need to do?"

"What's that?" Her shields were sliding firmly into place, ready to hear what he thought they should do with all that money, now that they were getting married. Travel, cars, cabin cruisers, vacation homes—supporting him so he could pursue a life-long dream of puppeteering or some shit. She'd heard it all.

Yeah. Like that was still going to happen if he thought he could sponge off her.

"We should have a show in a gallery here in Anaconda." He leaned in, taking her hand in his. "Show off some of your photography. Everyone needs to see what you can do with a camera, babe. That series you did in Turkey was gut-wrenching."

Bri just stared at him, stunned into silence. She swung her gaze to Kaia who was just sitting there, grinning at her like a loon. "I think that's an incredible idea. I can't believe we didn't think of it sooner."

"You, umm," Bri had to clear her throat and shift her thinking, "you want me to have a showing for my work?"

"Yeah." She could see the love and pride in his eyes. "I want the whole world to see the artist that you are."

"But..." Bri finally understood what the word flummoxed meant. "You don't care?"

"About what? Your money? Hell, no. That's all you. It has nothing to do with me." Those bright blue eyes narrowed a bit. "And it'll really piss me off if you honestly thought it would make a difference to me. You were born into that, Bri. Why should that change the way I see you? I love you. Does me being a shifter affect how you feel about me?"

"No. Of course not." Bri felt chastened, embarrassed she'd even suspected him of being so shallow.

"Good. Now let's move on."

It was clear Erik was done talking about it.

~~~

A couple of hours later as they lay in bed, Bri couldn't settle. She felt there was more she needed to say to him. The dark would help with what she had to do.

"I'm sorry...about earlier. It was a knee-jerk reaction."

"Don't worry about it," he said into her hair as she nuzzled his neck.

"I do, though. It's been a recurring theme all my life. As soon as someone finds out about me, they start thinking of ways to help me spend the money."

"Hence, the stuck-up-ice-queen routine," he added.

"Partly."

"I hate to break it to you, babe, but I've known you were out-of-this-world rich for quite some time now. It wasn't hard to connect the dots. And...Kaia gave me a come-to-Jesus-meeting after I got back from Colorado. She confronted me and said
~~~

that if I wasn't here for you after she kicked my ass, I could turn it around and go right back home."

"She said that?" Bri couldn't help but laugh. She should have known Kaia would try to shelter her from heartache.

"She did. Scared the shit out of me too."

Bri laughed. "She did not."

"She did. She's scary. You know her—you know how protective she is over those she loves."

Bri lay quiet for a moment. "So, it really doesn't bother you? That I have more than enough to support us?"

"There, we'll have an issue." His voice turned firm. "I told you before, and I'll tell you again—I take care of what's mine. You take what you have and put it away for our kids. *You* won't be supporting this family. I will."

And a weight lifted from her chest. She tilted her face up to look at him in the darkness. "How would you feel about me at least pitching in on the big-ticket items like houses, cars, vacations, or college tuition?"

Erik was silent as he thought that over. "I think we can work something out."

Bri snuggled into his side and drifted off to sleep, feeling loved and completely at peace.

12

The sound of glass breaking woke Erik some time later. He was up and out of bed in seconds. Min, startled awake, began to cry, and Bri rushed to comfort her. She picked her up into her arms and then joined Erik.

"What's happening?"

"I think our Lao tigers are getting bolder." He looked down at Bri. Her amber eyes were wide, her arms tight around a whimpering Min.

Erik needed to find these assholes and put the fear of God into them. But he couldn't leave Bri and Min unprotected. For the first time in his life, he was being pulled in two directions.

"Come on." He grasped her arm and guided her towards the bedroom door.

They were met in the hall by Kaia and Mac coming out of their room. Moose was at Mac's side, growling low in his throat.

"What the hell do they think they're doing?" Mac demanded as smoke began to fill the hall. "There's a kid in here, for Christ's sake!"

"They're probably getting desperate," Erik said through gritted teeth. "This job wasn't as easy as they thought it would be. I bet Momma Chai is getting pretty damned pissed about it taking this long."

"Well, we can't just stand here and wait for them to either come in or burn us out." Kaia was livid. She looked up at him with a grim smile. "What do you say the two of us go hunting?"

Erik hesitated but Mac stepped in.

"You and Kaia go. I'll stay here with Bri and the baby. We're both armed, but don't let those idiots get past you. I'd rather not have to face-off against a tiger. I got lucky and survived a cougar attack, but I don't want to push my luck. Plus, someone has to make sure they're not trying to burn the house down."

Erik took Bri into his arms and kissed her, then dropped a peck on Min's head. "I'll be right back."

"You'd better." She cupped her hand to his face.

He and Kaia each stepped back into their respective bedrooms to strip and shift.

Erik's cat returned just before Kaia's came stalking out of her room.

Mac was alone and watched each of the cougars. "I put Bri, Min, and the dog in the bathroom and told her to put a wet towel under the door to keep the smoke out." Mac coughed as the heavy gray mist grew thicker. "I haven't seen any flames, so I think this is just a smoke bomb. They probably hoped to drive us out of the house in a panic. They'll be out there waiting, ready to jump us."

Evidently, Mac had gotten used to having one-sided conversations.

He coughed again and looked at each of the mountain lions standing before him. "I know you guys know what you're doing, but if I might make a suggestion, go out through the attic. There's a small window on each end. You'll have to shift to open them, but then you can jump up to the roof. There's not much of a moon tonight, so that'll help, and it should give you guys a chance to case the place and get the drop on them."

Erik thought that was an excellent idea. His cat nodded and looked to Kaia. She was in total agreement.

The three of them moved to the end of the hall where there was a hatch in the ceiling. Mac pulled the folding wooden steps down, and Erik and Kaia bounded up them with ease. Once they were up, Mac let the ladder fold back into place.

Erik surveyed the attic and then shifted back to human form. Kaia followed his lead and was soon standing next to him. "I think it makes more sense to go out the same window. Doing this naked is going to suck, so I'll help you out and up."

Kaia nodded as he went to slide the pane up on one of the windows.

It took some doing, but he and Kaia were soon lying on the still-warm asphalt shingles looking out over the lawn.

"Any sign of them?" she asked in a toneless whisper.

"Not yet." He glanced to the side and held her stare. "Ready for this?"

He knew she was good in a fight. He'd watched her take down a male cougar that outweighed her by at least a hundred pounds. But this was another matter entirely. These cats each weighed four hundred pounds, minimum. Compared to her one hundred, that was a huge difference. He knew she was game, but he was worried about her.

And she knew it. "I'm not stupid enough to think this will be easy. They're massive next to my lioness, but the alternative is unthinkable. They *can't* get to Min."

Erik nodded. "If he hasn't shifted yet and you can catch him before he does, all the better. But if he does go tiger, stay just out of his reach. Use your small size and speed to your advantage. These guys are lazy and out of shape, but they're mean as hell and fight dirty. Remember that."

She nodded. "I will."

"All right. Let's do this."

Within a blink, two mountain lions occupied the roof of Kaia's house. They stayed low and scanned for the attackers. Erik spotted the first in the driveway. A shadow darted between the cars. By body shape, he knew it was Yuu Feng. Since he wanted Rasa for himself, he drew Kaia's attention and pointed her in the direction of where the man was waiting.

They hadn't transformed yet, probably waiting to see what the occupants of the house did. And trying to kidnap a child from their parents without arms would just be stupid.

Kaia leapt off the roof on the far end and landed soundlessly. She was doing just as he would have wanted, staying to the heavier shadows and stalking her prey until she was in a position to take him down. Hopefully, before he had a chance to shift. That would make it a lot easier on her.

Erik blocked his cousin out of his mind and went back to searching for Rasa.

If one was watching the front of the house, it only made sense that Rasa would be guarding the rear. With that in mind, Erik scanned the perimeter to find the threat.

It didn't take long. Erik rolled his eyes. Rasa would never pass for even a mediocre soldier. He was out there, twitching and fidgeting around in impatience after so long with no movement from inside.

Prey acquired, Erik dropped to the ground.

He hung back, concealed in darkness. Rasa was hiding just within the darker woods. To get to him, Erik would have to cross the large open expanse of Kaia's lawn. The moon may not be giving off much light, but he would still be seen if he tried to approach. His options were limited.

Erik decided to test Rasa's mettle. Erik had already bested him twice; would he dare face him again?

Stepping out of the shadows, the sleek cougar strode to the middle of the yard and sat down.

His opponent emerged full of bravado but held at the border of the yard.

The cougar's copper head tilted to the side. *Well, what's it going to be, asshole? Wanna go again?*

Rasa only stared at him for several minutes, not daring to make a move.

Finally, frustration over his own cowardice won out and Rasa yelled, "I will kill you all and take the child!"

Erik's cat, unconcerned, lowered to lay on his belly.

Rasa raised his hand to his mouth and gave a loud, short whistle. Within moments, the other man came running around the side of the house with Kaia's cat hot on his heels. He made it about halfway across the backyard when she took a giant leap and tackled him from behind. They landed on the ground with a thud and tumbled hard over the soft grass.

He howled when Kaia's cat raked her long claws down his back. When she bit down on his shoulder and upper arm with a violent shake, a feral scream of pain ripped from his throat.

Given some time, the Lao man would heal from the wounds. But the message itself would linger. *Come at us again, and we will fuck you up.*

Erik's big male switched his gaze to Rasa, curious to see if the alpha would step in and come to his clanmate's rescue. Hatred burned hot and bright in his dark eyes, but he remained defiantly still and did nothing.

The lioness slashed and tore at her prey until Erik's cat growled low, telling her he'd had enough. She immediately ceased and left the man lying mangled and bloody in the grass, the tawny cougar sauntering over to join Erik's as she flopped to her side and began to groom herself.

Erik still stared Rasa down, not at all surprised that the yellow-bellied pussy refused to breach the protection of the forest to help his beta to his feet. The man struggled to gain his balance, but Rasa completely ignored him, leaving him to stumble and lurch the rest of the way over Kaia's lawn and into the shadows of the woods.

Even as the injured man labored to continue on, Rasa remained at the tree line to glare at Erik's cat for a few more beats. Finally, in a huff of disgust, he too slinked away.

When the sound of their retreating feet could no longer be

heard, Erik and Kaia returned to the house. Standing on the deck, they shifted and stepped inside.

The smoke had mostly cleared out already.

Mac came from the hall with Kaia's robe and a pair of sweats for Erik.

Once clothed, Erik went straight for the bathroom to collect Bri and Min. Knowing she was armed, he knocked first. "Bri, baby, it's me."

The door was thrust open and there she stood, momma bear protecting her cub. He glanced behind her to see Min sitting in the dry bathtub playing with her toys. She looked to be having fun.

Bri handed him her pistol and went back for Min. "What happened?"

"Let's sit and go over it. Mac will want to be filled in too."

They took a moment to get Min settled back into bed and then joined Kaia and Mac who were gathered in the dining room.

Erik hadn't thought he saw any blood on Kaia but checked on her anyway. "You okay?"

She nodded. "Yeah. Not a scratch."

"What happened?" Mac prompted.

Kaia took a breath and started. "I was stalking my guy and was about to engage him when we heard Rasa yell out. Then the whistle came, and he took off running. I gave chase and when we rounded the house, I saw you," she looked at Erik, "sitting there in the yard. I wondered what you were up to, but then my cat was on top of him. Let's just say she sent a very clear message."

Erik picked it up. "With her guy up front, it only made sense that Rasa had to be out back somewhere. When I saw him hiding in the woods, I knew there was no way for me to make it across the yard without being seen." Erik gave a shrug. "I figured I'd see just how big Rasa's balls were." He shuddered. "Not very, as it turns out. Faced with a confrontation, he just sat back and watched as Kaia's cat ripped his partner to shreds."

The disgust he felt filled his voice. "The fucker did nothing to save him. Kaia could have killed Feng right in front of his eyes, and he still would have sat there with his dick in his hands. He stood by and let the whole thing happen, and when it was over, he wouldn't even go to him and help him. He's nothing but a fucking coward."

"Is that normal?" Bri asked. "I mean, I know tigers are supposed to be solitary animals, but I honestly expected them to be a bit more…aggressive."

"They usually are. But everyone is so afraid of his family, he's never had to actually *fight* for what he wants. He shows a little muscle, threatens some violence, and gets his way. I think what we have here is someone who's ridden on the tail of mommy's reputation for so long, he's never met anyone who's stood up to him before. He has no idea how to actually follow through when his opponent isn't afraid of him."

Erik paused. "Don't get me wrong—he's still dangerous. Maybe more so, because when his bluff doesn't pay off, he becomes enraged and strikes out like a spoiled child would."

He sighed. "Only *this* spoiled child is a full-grown, four-hundred-pound Indochinese Tiger."

13

Bri was about at the end of her rope. Since the attempt to smoke them out four days prior, Rasa and Yuu had cleared out of the motel and had taken up residence in the woods behind Kaia's house, prowling and growling and making it known that they were watching and waiting.

Every single night.

They didn't do anything. They were just…there. All the goddamned time.

Bri was nearly ready to scream in frustration. The tigers had to know they were never going to leave Min unprotected. What was the point of their little display, and why didn't they just give up? They needed to go back to Laos and leave them the hell alone.

"I'm ending this tonight," Erik told them over dinner. "One way or another."

"I'll go with you," Kaia added. "Apparently those guys didn't learn their lesson the last time."

Two hours later, Bri was standing with Erik at the back door. "Please be careful. I have a bad feeling about this."

Erik wrapped his arms around her waist and pulled her in close to his body, kissing her soundly. "I'll be fine. These assholes are all show."

"Yeah, assholes you've bested three times now. If he's the type of man you think he is, he's probably got a raging hard-on for you. I'm just afraid he'll do something drastic to try to save face in front of his clanmate and even the score."

"I promise I'll be careful. And Kaia will be with me to watch my back." He reached up and tucked a strand of hair behind her ear. "I love you. I'll be back by morning."

"You'd better be." Bri cupped his face in her hands and brought his head down to meet hers. She kissed him long and deep.

Kaia emerged from the hall wearing her bathrobe. "You ready?"

He nodded. "Let's do this."

Bri watched them walk out the door. She knew she wouldn't be getting much sleep until they were both back, safe and sound. Her gut roiled and she bordered on nauseous, but it wasn't the pregnancy. Something wasn't right.

She went through her normal nighttime routine with Min. Once her little girl was tucked in and on her way to dreamland, Bri walked back to the kitchen and got a cup of tea. She carried it to the dining room table and made herself comfortable to wait.

Mac found her a few minutes later. "This may take a while. Why don't you try to get some sleep?"

Bri looked up at him. "I can't. I can't settle for some reason. I have a bad feeling."

That caught his attention, and Mac sat down with her. "What kind of bad feeling?"

"I don't know." Bri rubbed her forehead. "I can't pin it down. I'm just uneasy about them being gone tonight."

"Erik was trained for this. And Kaia is no slouch. They know what they're doing," he reminded her needlessly.

"I know. Like I said, I can't explain it." She took a slow sip of her tea.

Mac rose, walked to the coffee machine, and brewed his own cup. He brought it back to the table. "How about I wait with you?"

They spoke a little but mostly sat in their own thoughts. The longer Erik and Kaia were gone, the more her anxiety level rose. What was happening out there? Why was tonight different than every other night he'd gone to patrol? He'd always come back. She had to believe he'd come back safely tonight too.

At just after two a.m., Bri and Mac heard something outside, kind of like a thump or a thud. Their gazes met in panic, and then they were up and moving. Bri beat Mac to the sliding door, only because she'd already been on that side of the table.

Bri jerked it open and saw Kaia's cat lying on the steps of the deck. There was blood coating several places on her body.

Bri gasped as she and Mac rushed to her. "Oh, God. Kai."

"She's breathing." Mac was checking her vitals, running his hands over her fur, looking for wounds. "We need to get her inside."

Bri scoured the back yard seeing nothing. "Where's Erik?"

Mac lifted the female cougar into his arms. "I don't know. Let's get her inside and find out what the hell happened."

Bri helped Mac get Kaia's cat to the couch. Once she was settled, Bri ran to the kitchen to wet a towel. When she returned, Mac was trying to rouse the unconscious cougar.

"Hey, baby. It's time to wake up." He rubbed the side of her muzzle.

While he kept talking to her, Bri wiped at the blood on her tawny fur. She didn't see any life-threatening injuries. Most were just scratches and scrapes. So why was Kaia out cold?

She found the reason on her hip, and her heart skipped a beat. A small, round wound. "Mac, she was tranq'd."

Had Erik been drugged too? Where was he? The two men had to have been behind it. But why?

As soon as the question entered her mind, Bri knew the answer. Because Erik and Kaia were the only things standing between the tigers and Min. With both cougars indisposed, the path would be clear for them to take her. Two normal humans were no match for shifters.

Was Erik hurt? Was he lying dead out there somewhere?

Oh God, Bri silently wailed.

"That's it." Mac's excited tone broke into her thoughts. "Come on, baby. Wake up now."

The cat came around slowly. As soon as enough brain function returned, she started to transform. Soon Kaia was lying on the couch looking up at them. Bri rushed to cover her with a blanket.

Bri couldn't hold back the question. "Kaia? Where's Erik?"

Kaia struggled to sit up, clutching the cover to her. "It was an ambush. We were chasing the tigers, and we were attacked from behind. Rasa must have found someone to help him. Before we knew what was happening, they were shooting darts at us. The first missed me, but the second found its mark. I was able to get it out quickly, but enough of the drug went into my system that it was hard getting back here."

She looked at Bri, and there were tears in her eyes. "They took him. I saw him go down. The men—strangers I've never seen before—they put him in a small cage and carried him away." Her gaze went from Bri to Mac. "If he's left in that cage, he won't be able to shift back. It was too small. It barely fit his cougar, but it definitely won't fit a man of Erik's size."

Bri's hands trembled where they rested over their baby.

Kaia grasped Bri hands in hers. "We'll find him. I know where we were attacked. I'll start there and track where they went."

"You're not going out there alone," Mac told her in no uncertain terms.

"I have to. Bri and Min *can't* stay here without protection," Kaia shot back. "This is the whole reason they pulled this particular stunt. The tigers will take advantage and come for them. Someone has to be here."

"Fuck!" Mac pushed up to his feet, paced, and thought, and then spun back to them. "All right. I'll get some of my men out here. I obviously can't tell them the entire truth, but enough so they'll know someone is stalking Bri and Min and means to do them harm."

Mac went off to make his calls.

Bri turned to Kaia. "I have to go with you. I have to know he's okay."

Kaia twisted her body around until she was facing Bri. "No. You need to stay here with your daughter. She needs you. I'll find Erik," Kaia promised. "I'll bring him back to you."

"Kaia..." The words blocked up in her throat. Her fear wouldn't let her finish the sentence.

She wrapped Bri in a hug. "I know. I love him too. We'll get him back."

"They're too prideful, and Erik's beaten them too many times. They'll kill him, just out of spite."

Kaia shook her shoulders lightly. "Bri. Look at me. They won't. I am *going* to find him."

Mac came back. "I've got four men coming within the hour. Two will take up stations out front, and two will be on the back of the house. We'll have you covered, Bri. No one is going to get in here."

The next hour passed in a rush of activity, even though the minutes continued to drag by for Bri. She watched it all, as if through a fog, as Kaia went over maps while Mac packed a backpack with everything he thought they'd need. Bri saw guns and ammo being loaded in, as well as water, a first aid kit, and a powerful flashlight.

It scared her out of her mind to know that Erik would probably need the medical supplies more than anything else. Caged and defenseless with no way to fight back, those fucking tigers would torture him mercilessly. But how bad would he be by the time Mac and Kaia found him?

As they prepared to leave, Bri prayed.

The officers assigned to stay with her seemed nice enough, but there were no words of comfort they could offer to make the time until Erik was rescued pass any easier. Until Kaia and Mac brought him home, there was nothing for her to do except wait.

~~~

Erik's mind was pulled back from the blackness of unconsciousness as his cougar gradually came around.

When the cat's mind had cleared enough, he tried to rise to all fours. And was instantly barred from further movement. He was in a cage, the hard metal so closely encasing him, he couldn't even flex his muscles from his crouched position.

What the hell?

The cougar tried and failed to bust through the walls holding him. He ended up panting and tired and still locked up tight.

Given the close confines of the enclosure, he knew shifting wasn't an option.

The cat tried and failed again to break his bonds.

"Trying to escape is useless." Rasa was sitting in a chair across the room. His triumphant tone reeked of his victory.

His cougar flattened his ears and screamed his fury at Rasa.

The foreigner only smirked, lounging back in his seat.

Having a pissing contest wouldn't help Erik figure out where he was or how he'd gotten there. So, he tuned him out and tried to assess the situation. He remembered chasing the tigers, beginning to zero in on them and picturing what he would do when he finally got his paws on them.

And then he'd felt the punch of something hitting him in the side. When his legs buckled underneath him, he knew they were in trouble. He thought he'd heard Kaia's cat scream, but he couldn't be sure.
~~~

Had she been captured as well? They'd obviously been shot with a heavy sedative. Did that mean Kaia was being held here too? She wasn't in the room with him, but that didn't mean she wasn't being kept somewhere else.

Panic roiled in his gut as realization sunk in. With both him and Kaia captured, what did that mean for Bri and Min? Was Feng making a move on them right this minute? Or was it too late and he already had? Erik had no clue how long he'd been out of it. The woman he loved could be dead or dying, and the daughter he'd only just met could have been ripped from his life.

Erik and his cat screamed as the painful thought lanced through them.

No. He couldn't lose it. He had to keep his shit together, so he could think and plan. He'd have to bide his time—wait for the perfect moment to attack and kill these motherfuckers, find Kaia, and get back to Bri and Min.

Rasa rose and sauntered over to the side of his cage. Erik saw that he held a long metal stick of some kind in his hand. As the end of it came near him, Erik got a good look at it.

Oh, fuck.

The tip of it made contact with his cat's hide, and a jolt of electricity seared though him. It felt like it was burning a path along all of his nerve endings.

Even when Rasa backed off laughing, pain still rippled through the cat's entire body. He lay in the confined space, breathing heavily, trying to fight off the lingering effects of the drug and the torment of being electrocuted.

Rasa hit him again, his face alight with glee as he watched him convulse and writhe.

This went on and on through the night and all the following day. When the cat could no longer react from exhaustion and it became boring for his captor, he proceeded to jab a blade through the bars and into his cat's body. All the cuts were shallow. They weren't meant to kill him—the purpose was solely to prove that he was completely at Rasa Chai's mercy.

Of which Rasa had none.

His once-proud cougar was cowering in agony, and there was nothing Erik could do about it. He considered transforming, despite the cramped quarters, just to spare his poor feline any further torment. But there was no way it could be done without several broken bones.

He was well and truly trapped.

As evening approached, Rasa came and squatted down next to the cage. "This should go to show you, as Darwin said, only the fittest survive. I've beaten you. You are nothing. And as fun as it's been to prove that to you, there is still so much more to be done."

Malice darkened his features. "I think I'll go get that hot cock-tease of yours and let my tiger fuck the little bitch. He's really going to enjoy getting to sink his teeth into that tight piece of ass." He sneered, baring his teeth. "He's never had a blonde before. I'll bet they really are more fun."

The cougar growled and hissed, his protests falling on deaf ears.

Rasa revealed a syringe filled with a milky-white substance. "Maybe I'll keep you around long enough to let you watch." Rasa smirked and aimed the tip at Erik's cat's hip.

He roused enough to try to avoid it, but there was nowhere to go. The thin silver needle pierced his hind end, and his head began to swim instantly. Before he knew it, darkness was enveloping him.

~~~

Mac and Kaia had been gone for hours, and Bri had yet to sit down. She walked the floor in the darkness, pacing from the kitchen to the living room and back. She'd retrieved her pistol
~~~

when her friends had left. Even with the guards outside, she wasn't leaving anything to chance.

This would be the perfect time for those fuckers to come for Min. Erik was captured, the other cougar out looking for him. They would think the child they wanted was left protected only by weak humans.

She'd show them weak.

All the lights in the house were off, but the moon outside hung brightly in the sky, lighting the surrounding yard. She would have the advantage if anyone approached, her eyes already adjusted to the much-darker interior.

On one of her circuits, Bri noticed that the patrolmen stationed in the back were gone. She'd watched them for several hours and knew their routine. Their absence meant something was wrong.

She immediately went to the room she shared with Min. She'd already worked out what she'd do if they ever showed up here. And now she put that plan into action. She gently scooped up her sleeping child, blankets and all, and ran for the bathroom.

Bri laid her in the tub within the cocoon the blankets had made around her. Thankfully, for once, she was able to move Min without her waking up. It wouldn't last if Bri had to fire her gun, but this room was the safest and easiest to defend. Unlike the rest of the house, the bathroom had only one small window over the toilet, and it was nowhere near big enough for a tiger, or man, to fit through.

Locking and closing the door softly, Bri went to the end of the hallway and sat with her back against the wall. The master bedroom door was about five feet in front of her on the right, her own door that same distance on the left. And the door securing Min from danger was past that.

From this position, she could see anyone coming down the hall to search. If they attempted to gain access through one of the bedrooms, she'd hear them first and they'd walk right out in front of her.

With ears attuned to any sound, Bri heard a click and then the sliding door as it opened.

Shit. He must have jimmied the lock. The inner sanctum of her home had been breached. Calmly, she thumbed off the safety of her gun.

The dining room where the door was, was down the hall and on the left. She waited in the darkened hall, wondering which would come around the corner.

Man or beast?

He had to have been human to open the door, but was he still? Or had he shifted into his tiger form?

She wouldn't know until he emerged only a few yards away.

Her pistol was in a two-handed grip, resting on her upraised knees. Her aim was steady, fueled by determination and a desperate need to defend her daughter.

She would not miss her target. She was ready to kill if it meant protecting Min from the likes of Rasa and his clan.

Bri took a deep breath, let it out slowly, and sighted down the barrel.

She heard no footsteps, but the shadow cast from the moonlight on the floor moved closer to the opening of the hall. He was still a man. Bri tightened her grip and flexed her finger. She'd been taught to lay it along the side of the weapon until she was ready to shoot.

She was ready. Sliding her right index finger down, she wrapped it around the cold metal trigger.

Sitting low the way she was, housed in deeper darkness, Bri hoped he wouldn't see her right away, giving her a chance to shoot before he could come at her. She knew it only took a moment for them to shift.

When he stepped into the opening, Bri saw that it was Yuu. Familiar with shifter anatomy, Bri knew the wounds Kaia had inflicted were already in the process of healing. Probably not completely, but evidently enough to attempt a kidnapping.

As he took his first step towards her, Bri squeezed the trigger.

He must have sensed something at the last second, because he started to dart back the way he'd come.

Her shot still found its mark, though. Not center mass as she'd intended, but she'd seen the blood bloom high on his shoulder before he ducked out of the way.

Bri got to her feet and, leading with her gun, stalked forward. As she passed the bathroom door, she heard Min whimpering. The loud report in the narrow space nearly deafened Bri, startling Min awake.

"Shhh, baby. Momma will be right there."

She walked carefully to the corner and stopped. Just as she was about to risk a glance to see if he were still there, the front door was kicked in and the other policemen came storming in.

Bri immediately lowered her weapon and said in a rush, "He was here. I shot him, but I think he ran out the back."

One officer swept the place and cleared it, and the other followed a blood trail out through the sliding door. The intruder was obviously gone.

The one to clear the house came back to Bri. "Are you okay, ma'am? Was it your stalker?"

Bri nodded, flipping the safety back on and tucking it into the rear of her jeans. "Yes. I think he might have done something to your friends, though. I didn't see them out back in their usual spot, and that's how I knew something was wrong. I got my daughter to a safe place, and that's when I saw him. I shot him as he was coming at me."

He nodded, and as he went to find his colleagues, Bri hurried to collect a crying Min, keeping her gun ready at the small of her back, just in case.

The patrolman found his coworkers on the side of the house.

They'd been knocked out, the knots on the back of their heads evidence of a likely concussion, but they'd recover. Bri was just relieved that the Lao tiger hadn't killed them.

She hoped and prayed she could say the same about Erik.

~~~

A few hours later, Bri and Min were snuggled on the couch. The injured men had been sent to be examined by doctors, more were in their place, and reports had been taken about the incident.

Min had conked out again once everything settled down. Bri was exhausted, but she still couldn't sleep.

The sun was up, and yet there was still no sign of Mac or Kaia or Erik.

Oh, Erik. What are those bastards doing to you?

~~~

When Erik began to drift towards consciousness again, he was lying naked on a cold concrete floor. He was weak, and his head ached like there was a jackhammer drilling into the side of it. He took a moment upon waking to hold it between his hands, fighting off the nausea that threatened to make his broken body wretch.

His head finally cleared, and he was able to stand. His legs felt loose and wobbly underneath him, but he stiffened them. He refused to show any sign of frailty.

How had he gotten out of the cage and shifted back to human? Erik looked around the room. It was the same one as before, only the small cage was gone and he was alone. Remembering the suffering his cougar had endured, Erik tried to reach for him to check on him.

But it was like hitting a brick wall.

There was nothing there.

His cat was gone.

What. The. Fuck?

He recalled nothing after getting the shot of what must have been a sedative. What could Rasa have given—

Suddenly he knew. The drug the tiger clan gave to the girls that fought too hard. Somehow it suppressed their feline, making them easier to control. That's what that bastard had in the syringe. It must have knocked him and his cat out.

The next question was what had they done to him after that?

He checked himself over, looking for any indication of new injuries. But his body was just as mangled as his cat's had been the last time he'd seen it.

Erik reached for the cougar again, trying to coax him to come back or wake up—he didn't actually know how the drug affected the animal side—but still the emptiness remained.

He felt lost without him, an expanse of vacuum where his best friend used to be. Since he was five years old, that cougar had been his other half, and he'd never been without him.

He started to worry that the powerful male might be gone for good. But then he remembered what Jayme had said about the girls. The clan did this to them over and over. So that meant at some point, their tigers must come back.

And his cougar would too.

He had to hold on to that belief, or he'd fucking lose it. He was a mountain lion shifter, damn it! He wouldn't know how to live without his burly feline at his side.

Prowling the sparse room, Erik found nothing that would help him escape. It was about ten feet by ten feet. The walls were concrete block, and there was one small window up high on the wall. The door was metal and didn't have a knob on the inside. Just smooth cold steel.

They were obviously holding him in some kind of basement. He wondered again where Kaia was. Was she, right now, in a similar room to this? A similar situation? Had they suppressed her cat as well?

"Kaia?" He tried calling, but there was no response.

The lock on the other side of the door clanged as it was released. Erik held his ground until he saw Rasa's tiger stalk in. He padded around the perimeter of the room, never taking those dark eyes off of Erik.

The big orange and black male growled deep in his chest and suddenly swiped out at Erik.

Involuntarily, he backed up a step but caught himself before he could take another.

"What's the matter, Rasa? Is this the only way you can beat me? By taking my cougar away so your tiger can face an unarmed man? That's the *only* way you'll ever beat me, you fucking dickless coward."

Erik knew he was digging his own grave. He couldn't take on a full-grown tiger and win without his cat. But there was no way in hell he was going down without a fight. He braced himself and met the attack head-on when Rasa leapt at him.

Erik soon discovered that Rasa was only there to further wear him down—inflict the most possible damage without actually landing a killing blow.

The tiger only left when Erik lay bleeding profusely and barely alive. There were rake marks and puncture wounds all over him, and the pain was almost more than he could bear.

When the darkness settled in around him some time later, he welcomed the reprieve.

~~~

Erik didn't know how much time had gone by when he surfaced again. As he fought past the pull that wanted to swallow him again, he got to his hands and knees. Breathing the lightheadedness away, Erik gained his feet, trying not to
~~~

slip in the pool of his own blood coating the floor. He had to hold on to the wall to remain upright, but he managed it.

It was then he saw the bucket just inside the door.

Moving cautiously, he saw that it was half-filled with water. He scooped up a handful and sniffed it. He didn't detect any chemical odors, but that didn't mean much.

Knowing Rasa wanted to keep him alive long enough to torture him again, Erik sipped the water in his palm. Finding it cool and fresh, he drank his fill and then sloshed more of it over his head and chest.

Red-tinged water dripped down his body, stinging as it ran over all the many bites and scratches the tiger had left on him.

The burn roused him further, and with new determination, Erik limped around the room. He had to find a way out of there. He'd fight to his last breath, but given the condition of his body, he wasn't sure how much more damage he could sustain. He needed to get back to Bri and their daughter. He needed to return to the woman he loved, the woman he planned on spending the rest of his life with. He just hoped they were still there to go back *to*.

His life was *not* going to end here, at the hands of a cocksucker like Rasa Chai.

When the door opened again, Rasa was back. Erik watched him closely, mentally trying to prepare for round two.

His body, already ravaged from the last time, couldn't withstand the second assault for very long. He fell to the floor, the well of unconsciousness taking him under once again.

14

His mind was awash with images and sounds he couldn't understand. He could have sworn he heard Kaia, roaring and screaming. And of all things, Mac. But when he pried his eyes open, he was still lying on the cold, bare floor, no further threat looming over him.

Realizing it was all just a hallucination brought on by his traumatized mind, Erik gave in and returned to the darkness.

He floated in and out of it. He'd almost make it to the surface, but then the pain would swell, and his entire body would scream in agony. Much like his cat when he'd been caged and tormented by Rasa.

He wondered just how many rounds with the tiger he'd been subjected to. He only recalled the two, but who knew how much damage he'd sustained at Rasa's paws while he'd been vulnerable.

And through it all, his cat was still missing.

Where are you?

Distraught and utterly alone, he let himself slide to the bottom of the well again where nothing could hurt him.

~~~

"How long is he going to be like this?" Bri asked Kaia, looking down at Erik.
~~~

He appeared to just be sleeping, but he wasn't waking up. He moaned in pain once in a while, but then he'd go still again. He'd been like this for over twenty-nine of the scariest hours Bri had ever experienced.

Bri thought the twenty-six he'd been missing had been the longest of her life. But the last day and a half since Kaia and Mac had brought him home had been harder than anything she'd ever had to endure.

She'd been so relieved when they'd called to tell her they'd found him.

That is, until they'd carried him in and put him in the guest room. Bri had almost fainted seeing the extent of his injuries. There wasn't an inch of skin that didn't have some kind of wound marring its once-perfect surface. Scratches, gouges, and bites of all sizes littered his body.

After she'd pushed the initial shock of his condition aside, she'd cleaned the countless lesions carefully, and then made him as comfortable as she could.

That had been so long ago, and yet nothing had changed. He'd not shown any signs of improvement, nor had he woken up.

"Shouldn't he be healing by now?" Bri asked Kaia. "His injuries don't look any better today than they did when you found him."

"I know." Kaia's voice was anxious with worry. "I don't know what's happening to him." Kaia frowned. "But Bri, there's something else."

Bri's stomach plummeted. "What?"

Kaia bit her bottom lip before taking a deep breath. "I can't sense his cougar anymore. I didn't want to say anything before—I was hoping it was just because he's so far under, but I still don't feel him in there."

Bri gasped. *"What?"* Her gaze shot to the man she loved. "How can that be?"

"The only thing I can think of is that Rasa gave him the same drug they use on those girls, the one that puts their tigers out of commission."

Oh God. No! "Will it wear off? Will his cat come back?"

"I don't know. But from what Jayme told us, it doesn't sound like a permanent change, and the shifter side *does* return. But who knows how much of the drug they gave him, or how long it normally lasts?" Kaia sighed. "I hate to say this, but we'll just have to wait and see."

That seemed to be the rule over the next day. Wait and see.

Bri was waiting, but she wasn't seeing much of anything. No healing, no rousing, no Erik. She was so scared. She didn't know what to do.

They'd put off calling his family, hoping he'd regain consciousness soon. But if his comatose state continued for very much longer, it looked like they were going to be making those calls.

Bri crawled into bed with him and gingerly wrapped his limp arm around her. Resting her head on his shoulder, she laid her arm lightly over his chest where she could feel his heart beating strong.

"Erik. Can you hear me?" Bri tilted her head back and looked up at him. "Come on, honey. You need to wake up now." She rubbed her hand over his chest, careful of the barely-scabbed-over lacerations.

"Come back to us. *Please*. You're safe now. Mac and Kaia brought you home. Can you feel me? I'm here, and I need you to open your eyes and see me."

Bri thought she heard a change in his breathing. She rose up onto her elbow and watched his face closely. "Erik, baby, come on. Open your eyes. I'm right here."

Under his closed lids, his eyes moved, rolling in jerky movements. "That's it, you can do it. Follow my voice. I'm here, waiting for you to come back to me. Come on, baby. Let me see those pretty blue eyes."

His mouth moved as he tried to moisten dry lips. Bri reached over him to retrieve the cup and straw. She placed the tip of it on his mouth.

"Here's some water. Take a drink. Slow now."

Miraculously, he did. His lips parted and closed over the end of the straw. She saw the water flowing up the plastic tube as he sucked it into his mouth.

"That's it. Good job."

When he indicated he was finished, she pulled it away.

He licked his lips. "Not pretty. Manly." His voice was barely above a whisper.

Bri grinned. "*That's* what finally woke you up? That I said your eyes were *pretty*? If I'd known you were that sensitive, I would have teased you about it a long time ago."

He cleared his throat. "How bad?"

"Don't worry about that right now. You're back, and you're healing. That's all that matters."

"Bri…" His eyes opened to look up at her. His tone was still soft but it held a hint of stubbornness.

She took a breath and let it out. "Rasa had you for over twenty-four hours. He hurt you badly, but Mac and Kaia found you and brought you home. You just need to rest now and work on getting better."

"My cat."

Bri felt the hit in her gut. "I know. We're assuming he gave you that drug he gives the girls in Laos. We hope once it wears off, he'll be back."

"How long?"

"We don't know how long it will take…"

"How long…have I been asleep?"

"Three days."

"Three…? Why am I still so weak? Why haven't I healed yet?"

"We're not sure, but it could be related to the drug he gave you. Maybe with your cat suppressed, your healing abilities are too."

Erik closed his eyes again. A single tear escaped from the corner and trailed down his temple to soak into his hair. Bri's heart shattered, seeing him in so much pain.

"He was so broken after what Rasa did to him. He kept shocking him with a cattle prod, and then, when my cat was so exhausted he couldn't even respond anymore, he stabbed him with a knife. Shallow cuts, over and over, everywhere."

Silent tears rolled down Bri's own cheeks. She cried for Erik and for the poor animal who'd had to endure so much agony at the hands of a sick, twisted fuck like Rasa.

She wrapped Erik in her arms and held him. "Shhh, rest now. I've got you. I've got you both."

"Min?" His voice was drifting off.

"She's fine. She's safe. Waiting for her Erk to come play with her again."

<p style="text-align:center">~~~</p>

Erik quieted but didn't sleep. The warmth of Bri's body next to his grounded him in the now.

He'd heard her voice calling to him, begging him to come back to her. He'd had to fight harder than ever before to break through the weight holding him under. The pain was still there. Not quite as fierce, but still as all-encompassing as he'd remembered.

Rasa had really done a number on him, leaving no part of his body untouched, and he lay there, feeling all of it. After more than three days of respite from the torture, he wasn't nearly as far along in the healing process as he should have been, still as weak now as a newborn cub. Why wasn't he healing? Under normal circumstances, he would have been almost back to normal by now.

And shouldn't his cougar have returned already?

Was that why he continued to feel so drained and lifeless? Was Bri right? With his feline side suppressed to the point of extinction, had his heightened abilities also been extinguished?

How could he protect Bri, or anyone else for that matter, if he couldn't depend on his speed and strength to back him up? What good was he to the clan if the thing that made him a shifter was also a thing of the past?

His brain started to fog with weariness, all the trauma from the past few days weighing him down again. Erik hated being this pathetic and crippled, but there was nothing he could do about it right now.

Tomorrow would be another day. He'd gather his energy, fight back, and he'd find his cat.

~~~

When he awoke again, it was easier to think. His mind wasn't so sluggish. He opened his eyes to bright sunlight streaming through the window in the spare room at Kaia's house. He'd still been too out of it the day before to notice.

He was alone too, which was a good thing. It gave him a moment to take stock of himself. He threw the blankets aside and then struggled to hoist himself to sit on the edge of the bed.

As he sat there, his gaze tracked over the expanse of his body he could see, which was a lot. He was completely naked.

Both of his legs had rips and gashes running the length of them. Puncture wounds he knew to have come from long fang teeth dotted his calves and thighs. His torso and arms had sustained more of the same.

The fucker had used him like a goddamned chew toy.

Erik inspected some of the rake marks on his body. None of them were fatal obviously, but none were superficial either.
~~~

Rasa had controlled himself, to a point.

Erik knew if Kaia and Mac hadn't gotten there when they did, it might have been a different story. Rasa had been toying with him at first, punishing him for the way he'd shown the leader up. A mere mountain lion had had the audacity to refuse the Lao tigers their prize, and so Erik had paid a hefty price. But it was still far better than it could have been, and he likely owed Kaia and Mac his life.

Erik tried pushing himself up to his feet. But immediately dropped back to the bed. His skin went clammy, and darkness edged into his peripheral vision.

Erik gritted his teeth. He would not pass out just from the simple act of trying to stand, damn it!

Waiting for the wave to pass, Erik tried again. Moving slower this time, he actually made it fully upright.

Wobbling from the effort it took to stay on his feet, Erik looked up when the bedroom door opened. Bri stopped when she saw him.

"What are you doing?" She came in and closed the door behind her.

"I have to take a piss, if that's okay with you." His voice was sharp.

"Yeah, sure. That's a good sign." She started towards him, apparently unconcerned with the bite in his tone. "Come on, I'll give you a hand."

"What are you going to do—hold it for me?" he spat out. He knew he was taking his frustration out on her, but he couldn't stop it.

Ignoring his bad mood, those bright amber eyes looked up at him, glittering with interest. "Can I? I might not have as good an aim as you, but I'll give it a go."

Her optimistic gaze held his until he cracked. He shook his head and smiled down at her. "Why do I actually believe you would really hold my dick while I pee?"

"Because I so *would*." She grinned and then turned away to grab some sweats he hadn't seen on the end of the bed. "Being a girl, I have no idea what that's like. My squat is a thing of beauty, I assure you, but I've always been jealous of how easy men had it."

Bri opened the waist for him to step into. Erik braced his hand on her shoulder and lifted his foot. Once she had them pulled up around him, she leaned in and kissed him before helping him into a t-shirt.

She adjusted herself to his side, taking some of his weight, and guided him towards the hall.

Together they made it to the other side. When he stopped at the bathroom and started to close the door behind him, she almost looked disappointed.

"You are *not* helping me piss."

"Suit yourself." She shrugged with a smirk. "But I'm going to be waiting right here for you to finish."

Erik shut her out and limped his way to the toilet. He tried to stand there and relieve himself, but he just didn't have the strength. He'd never admit it to anyone in his life, but for the first time since he was very young, he sat down to take a leak.

When he was done, he stepped up to the sink to wash his hands and brush his teeth. Feeling somewhat better, he turned the knob, pulled, and, true to her word, Bri was still standing there.

She fit herself under his arm again and took him back to bed. Once he was tucked in, she sat on the edge of the mattress. "Are you hungry? Can I bring you something?"

Erik hadn't noticed he was starving until she'd mentioned it. "Actually, that would be great."

She rubbed a hand over the side of his face. "I'll be right back. I love you."

He frowned. Would she still love him if his cougar never returned? Could she ever respect him if he couldn't protect them as he once had? Their children needed a father who could teach them about shifting, but if he couldn't do that, would she still want him around?

"Erik?" The concern was clear in Bri's question.

He forced a smile. "Sorry. I got lost in thought for a minute." He brought her hand to his lips and kissed it. "I love you too."

Bri studied him for a moment. "It'll get better. I promise."

"I know."

"I'll be right back with some breakfast."

She hadn't been gone long when the door slowly opened again. Erik glanced over, thinking she'd forgotten to tell him something, and saw a tiny girl in the doorway.

"Hey there, sweet girl." Erik pushed himself up until he was seated and leaning against the headboard.

Min cautiously came to the side of the bed. "Erk owie?"

"Yeah. I've got a few owies. I'm okay though," he tried to reassure her.

She tilted her head, considering him. "Erk kitty go bye-bye?"

Her simple question made his gut clench. "Yeah. But just for a little bit. He has owies too, like me. He'll be back when he's feeling better." Erik took a breath to ease the tightness in his chest. "You want to come up here and sit with me? I would really love that."

Min didn't hesitate. She scrambled up to him, causing him some pain, but once she was snuggled in next to him, he knew it had been worth it.

Bri found them a few minutes later.

"Sorry. She's been asking about you." Bri set the tray on the bedside table. "I told her you were in an accident and were sleeping."

Erik looked down at Min. "She's fine. We've been having a nice little chat about who-knows-what." He laughed but then grimaced as pain radiated through his side. "But she was very invested in whatever it was."

Bri took her place again on the edge of the mattress. "Probably the new book we've been reading. It's full of princesses and fairies and castles and has recently become her favorite."

"I can see why if it has all that."

"Min, how about you and I go have something to eat in the kitchen and let Erik have his here?"

"No," Min protested. "Stay wiff Erk."

Erik looked over at Bri. "Why don't you bring your food in here too, and we'll have a picnic?"

"Pinic Momma. Pinic wiff Erk."

Bri laughed. "Well, who can say no to a picnic? I'll only be a minute."

She returned quickly and set up their food on Erik's bed. They ate and talked and kept it light for Min's sake.

Once his belly was full for the first time in days, Erik suddenly grew very tired. When Bri noticed, she hurried Min along and cleaned up the picnic mess.

"We'll go and let you rest." Bri leaned in and kissed him. "I'll be back later to check on you."

15

Sleep took him quickly. And dropped him right into the middle of a nightmare. He was still lying on the cold concrete floor with Rasa standing over him.

"Look how inadequate he is." Rasa turned to the side, and when Erik's gaze followed, Bri was there.

The contempt he saw on her face hurt him worse than anything Rasa could have inflicted.

She sneered at him. "What good is a mountain lion shifter without the mountain lion? You're useless now. You can't protect us. What can you possibly provide for my children? I needed a shifter to teach them and help me raise them. What can you show them now?"

Erik wrenched himself from sleep, bathed in a heavy sweat. He lay trying to push the dream away. He knew Bri's words had only been an echo of his own thoughts from earlier, but hearing it from her lips had cut deeper than tiger claws.

He absently rubbed the area over his heart.

Taking notice of the harsh light coming through the window, Erik realized that half the day had passed. A glance at the clock revealed it was after two in the afternoon.

Feeling a little better than he had even that morning, Erik slid cautiously out of bed. The dizziness was only a momentary annoyance before fading away completely. He was still wearing the clothes Bri had helped him into, so at least he didn't have to struggle with dressing.

He made it to the door with no issues, and after a quick stop at the bathroom, walked out to the dining room.

Bri and Min were sitting at the table coloring.

"Erk!" Min beamed up at him. "I cowoh!"

"I see that." He smiled down at her. "You're doing a great job too. Is Momma going to hang that on the fridge when you're done?"

Bri laughed. "I would, if it wasn't full of her artwork already. We might have to buy another fridge."

"My mom always had stuff on ours too." He settled gingerly into a chair. "With five kids, it could get pretty cut-throat for space. She tried to put something from everyone up there, but of course, we thought it was a competition. We'd count who had the most and whose was the highest on the door. We thought that meant she loved it best."

"That's awful." But Bri chuckled at his story. "It's insight into the life of a parent, so I'll just have to make sure all of our kids are equally represented."

That had Erik questioning the future. If his cougar never returned, would any future child conceived still be a shifter? Or would the baby she currently carried be the last mountain lion he ever produced?

The idea that he may not be able to further the clan's lineage had both fury and hatred rushing through his veins.

Bri must have sensed the change in his mood. "You okay?"

Erik gave himself a mental shake. "Yeah. I'm good." He rose again and headed into the kitchen for some coffee.

He could feel Bri's eyes on him, but he didn't acknowledge it. He watched the brewing machine like it was imperative he not take his attention from it. A silent sigh left him as she finally switched her focus back to Min.

They went back to their crayons and chatting and ignored him. He decided he needed some air. Taking his cup with him,

Erik pulled the sliding door wide. And that was when he saw a pair of patrolmen walking the yard and surveying the property.

Erik swung around to look at Bri, who obviously realized what had caught his attention.

"Mac's guys. They've been standing guard ever since you went missing. He told them I had a stalker that meant to do me harm. It was as close as he could get to the truth while still leaving out the whole shifter thing. He thought it would be a good idea to keep them on until you're healed and back to one hundred percent."

Whenever the fuck that was going to be. It was just another kick to the gut. He obviously couldn't defend anyone, so they'd brought in people who could.

He bit back an oath. "That's probably a good idea. God knows *I'd* be useless if something happened."

Bri pushed out of her chair and came to stand toe-to-toe with him.

"Hey." Her topaz eyes caught and held his gaze, and they blazed with steely determination. "This isn't permanent. You'll regain your strength, and your cougar will most definitely come back. It's just going to take some time. No one knows anything about this drug he gave you. If he shot you with a large dose, that could account for the length of time your cat has been absent."

Her expression softened. She reached up and laid a hand on his chest. "And, for the record, you are nowhere *near* useless. Even in your condition *right now*, I want you at my side over anyone else. Just give it time. Please don't get frustrated."

The sincerity in her eyes gave him a nudge towards hope that she was right, and everything would return to normal. Erik leaned in and kissed her on the forehead and then rested his head against hers. "I'll try."

"That's all I can ask."

"None of you have said, but I'm guessing Rasa wasn't caught."

Bri let out a sigh. "No."

"Did he show up here? He taunted me that he was going to come...hurt you, and take Min, since I wasn't here to protect her."

The way she watched him told Erik that something *had* happened that she hadn't shared. Had Rasa gotten into the house?

"Rasa didn't, no. But his clanmate did. The night you were taken, Feng knocked out a couple of the guards stationed at the back of the house. He came in, but I was ready for him. I waited for him in the hallway, and when he rounded the corner, I shot him. He spooked at the last minute, but I hit him in the shoulder.

"That was the last we saw of either of them, until Mac and Kaia found out where they were holding you. The men who drugged you—local hired thugs as it turns out—were the ones guarding the place you were kept. Mac and Kaia's cat had to fight their way past them to get to you. Rasa must have paid them well, because they didn't go down easy. They've since been arrested."

"Is Kaia okay? I thought she might have been captured when I was. I was so afraid they were doing to her what they were doing to me."

Bri glanced back at Min and pulled Erik a little further outside, out of the little girl's earshot.

"She was shot with a tranquilizer, just like you were. But because she's been hit with one before, she knew right away what had happened. Somehow, she was able to get the dart out, so she didn't get the full dosage. She made it back here and told us what happened. We regrouped, and Mac and Kaia went after you."

Erik nodded, watching the patrolman scan the tree line. "We'd better get back inside."

Bri turned with him and walked back through the doorway.

"You slept through lunch. Would you like something to eat?"

He shook his head. "No, I'm good for now. I think I'll sit in the living room for a while."

Erik was moving a little easier. He made it to the adjoining room with no issues. Before sitting down though, he went to the window and lifted the curtain enough to see out. His eyes searched out the other two guards Mac had put on the house. All of them seemed to be taking this assignment seriously and were staying attentive to the surrounding areas.

Turning from the window, Erik sat on one end of the couch. He picked up the remote and pointed it at the TV, cycling through the channels once before deciding on a show about rebuilding old muscle cars.

He normally liked this kind of stuff, but he couldn't seem to stay focused on it. He constantly searched for his cougar, calling to him inside his head and coaxing him to let Erik know he was okay.

The longer his absence continued, the more hopeless and lost Erik felt. He'd never been without this part of himself. He didn't know what he would do if the unthinkable happened and he never came back.

<p style="text-align:center">~~~</p>

Sometime later, Erik woke. He hadn't realized he'd fallen asleep.

He slowly comprehended what had pulled him from his nap. Voices from the kitchen were talking quietly.

He rose and went to see. As he rounded the corner, he saw Bri, Kaia, and Mac.

"Hey." Kaia came to him and hugged him gently. "How you feeling?"

"Pretty good, I guess."

She didn't have to ask about his cat—she would sense that

he was still missing.

"Have you guys been able to find where Rasa and Yuu went?"

"No." Mac took a swig of the beer he was holding. "They've vanished again."

Erik eyed the brew. "Can I get one of those?"

"Yeah, sure." Mac turned to retrieve another from the fridge. He twisted the cap off and handed it to him.

"Thanks." Erik took a long pull. He felt the cold hit the hot center of his empty stomach. He glanced around the room. "Where's Min?"

"She's already eaten and is currently dreaming little girl dreams." Bri grinned at him.

"And our dinner is just about done," Kaia announced. "How about you guys set the table, and Bri and I will finish it up?"

"Yes, Ma'am," Mac said with a smile and salute.

Erik helped some, but Mac got most of the dishes out and onto the table. They were sitting down about ten minutes later.

Over what Kaia told him was her family's version of goulash, they caught Erik up to speed.

"Rasa obviously found some men and hired them to trap you," Mac said. "The tigers set it up so that you would chase after them, not realizing they were leading you into an ambush until it was too late. They may not have been expecting the second cougar, but they took a shot at her anyway. Unfortunately for them, Kaia was able to escape and race back here. We were on their trail within the hour."

Kaia picked up the story. "I knew where they'd shot us, so we started there. I followed their trail for a while, but then I lost the scent."

Erik could see that this really troubled her. He'd been held and tortured for twenty-six hours. Her guilt over what he'd gone through because she hadn't been able to find him fast enough was etched all over her face.

Some of his anger faded. "Kaia. You did everything within

your power to find me. And you did. I'm fairly certain that had I been with Rasa any longer, I would be dead. He wanted to punish me for beating him down. If his need to see me broken first hadn't been so overwhelming, there would have been nothing for you to find. I'm grateful you came when you did. The rest I can deal with."

"It still kills me to see what he did to you." Kaia's grayish-green eyes swam with tears and her lower lip trembled. "If only I had—"

"You can't think like that." Erik sat forward in his seat and took her hand in his. "I'm here, and I'm alive because of you. That's all that matters."

"But your cat..." Her breath hitched.

"He'll be back as soon as this drug is out of my system." The words burned on his tongue. "You have to believe that."

If only Erik could believe it himself.

Kaia swallowed and nodded. "You're right. He *will* be back." She gathered herself. "Now, how do we track them down?"

They threw some ideas around, and Erik found himself growing tired again. He'd never felt anything like it before in his life. He'd always been strong and healthy, able to push his own boundaries and accomplish almost anything. Now he couldn't sit at a fucking table and eat without nearly falling asleep in his chair.

His wounds were healing, but at a much slower rate than normal. His body was sore, and he felt vulnerable. This new physical fragility was really beginning to piss him off.

Bri must have noticed his increasing fatigue. "We're not going to locate them tonight in any event. Let's table this for now and come back to it again tomorrow."

"Good idea." Mac cast a quick glance at Erik and then rose from the table, gathering dishes. He looked at Kaia. "I'll give you a hand getting this cleaned up."

"I'll take it." Kaia picked up a few more and carried them to the sink.

When he and Bri crawled into bed later, Erik lay quietly, thinking. He couldn't go on like this. He was quick-tempered and curt with the ones he loved most, and it wasn't their fault he was in this predicament. He needed to accept that his life may never return to the way it was before and find a way to move on and deal with it.

To that end, he needed to start building his strength and stamina back up. He'd need that more than ever if his cougar...

He couldn't finish the thought. Instead, he made a plan of another sort.

~~~

Darkness still held the night in its grasp when Bri woke to worried voices. Knowing something was wrong, she jumped out of bed, Erik close behind her when she reached the door. She wrenched it open to see Kaia and Mac in their room across the hall. They were speaking in low tones and rushing around, throwing clothes on.

Bri saw the look of full-blown terror on her best friend's face. Tears were shimmering in her green eyes, and instinctively, she went to her. "Kaia? What's happened?"

"Helen just called." Kaia looked stricken. "The barn is on fire. She's already called the Fire Department, but they won't get there in time." Her breath hitched. "I have to get to the horses."

"You're going to need every hand you can get," Erik said from behind Bri. "We're coming with you."

Bri wanted to say something—*anything*—to keep Erik from going and risking further injury. He was only barely beginning to heal from his ordeal, and his cat was still lost. She was so afraid for him. But she knew better than to say anything.

It wasn't hard to understand he'd been feeling depressed
~~~

and adrift. She'd caught him more than once staring off into the distance, deep in thought. She knew he was scared for his cougar, but he'd never admit to that out loud. Instead, he kept all of those fears and worries locked inside of him.

So, against her better judgement, Bri kept her mouth shut and followed him back into the bedroom to get dressed.

She immediately started pulling clothes from the dresser, hers and Mins. He stopped what he was doing and looked over at her.

"Don't even bother trying to tell me to stay here." He kept his voice low in deference to Min sleeping nearby. "Even if I'm not a shifter anymore, I can still help Kaia save her horses." His tone was sharp and defiant.

Bri buttoned her jeans, taking that moment to calm the hot spike of temper that flared at his accusation. She advanced on him until she was inches from him, pinning him with a hard look and pointing her finger in his face. "Don't fucking *ever* let me hear you say you're not a shifter anymore."

The moment hadn't been long enough. Bri wanted to slap him senseless for his blatant dismissal and callousness. "Don't you dare give up on your cat. Do you hear me? He would *never* give up on *you*."

Bri waited for him to silently nod. "Do I like that you'll be running into a burning building? No, I don't. Do I wish you wouldn't go? Hell yes. But that wish has absolutely *nothing* to do with your cat being absent right now. It has to do with the fact that you're still hurt, Erik. If one of those scared horses bumps you wrong, or God forbid, tramples you, it could cause so much more damage, and you'll be right back where you started, if not worse. But I wasn't going to say any of that until you decided to be a dickhead about it. I know you well enough to know you'd go, no matter what I said, but I wasn't going to stop you, or even try. I also know those innocent animals need every bit of help they can get. Now get your ass dressed so we can go.”

It was clear her words set him back a bit. “I’m sorry.”

Bri spun on her heel and went to wake Min. “You should be.”

While she got her daughter up and out of her jammies, Erik dressed. A few minutes later, they were loading up into two cars and heading out.

When they pulled in, they all got their first look at the burning barn. Flames were licking up one side of the structure. They could hear the horses screaming in fear, loud thumps echoing through the night as they bucked and rammed inside their stalls.

As Bri unbuckled Min and held her close, Kaia ran to where Helen had a hose spraying a feeble stream of water at the blistering inferno.

“Helen, you need to get back inside!”

“We have to get this out!” The elderly lady was sobbing, her thin frame shaking from the wet and from fright.

Instead of letting Kaia wrestle the hose from her brittle hands, Bri called to Helen. “Helen! I need you! Can you please take Min and keep her safe? Let us deal with this.”

Helen relented, passing it to Bri and reaching for Min. “Come on, baby girl. Let’s give these guys some room to work.”

Bri aimed the hose and waved off the others. Kaia, Erik, and Mac bolted towards the barn and into the searing blaze. The plan was for each of them to take charge of a horse and guide it to safety away from the fire before going back in to get another.

As Helen retreated with Min to the porch, Bri looked down at Moose. “Go with them, boy. Keep an eye on them and don’t let anyone near them.”

Moose garbled something at her, turned, and chased after the woman and her child.

Bri kept an eye on them until they were a safe distance away. Keeping them in her sights in case Rasa was waiting for his opportunity, she soaked as much of the barn as she could.

It was a losing battle, but maybe she could hold enough of it back so the horses could be rescued. She prayed the fire trucks would get there soon.

Her eyes were stinging, and the smoke was making her cough, but she didn't stop. It seemed an eternity, but Bri could finally hear sirens in the distance.

Bri counted the horses as they brought them out. When the fifth and final one had cleared the building, she breathed a sigh of relief. Kaia stayed in the pasture with them, trying to soothe their panic as best she could.

She gasped when she saw Erik and Mac run towards the danger again. They were carrying buckets, taking water from the troughs to throw on what they could inside, trying to preserve as much of Kaia's livelihood as they could.

Emergency vehicles finally arrived as tanker trucks, pickups, ambulances, and police cars came speeding up the driveway.

"Oh, thank God."

~~~

Erik was exhausted and his body was screaming in protest. He'd seen the fire department arrive and take over fighting the blaze. Their massive hoses sprayed hundreds of gallons of water on the flames within seconds and started to beat it back.

Thankful for the reprieve, he, Kaia, and Mac went to stand with Bri to watch as the fire was taken in hand.

It took about an hour to douse it completely. After that, the crew picked through the barn methodically to search for any pockets of hot embers that could possibly flare up again.

Satisfied there was no longer any danger, the emergency workers packed up their gear and headed out. Erik, Bri, Kaia, and Mac stayed behind to survey the destruction.

One entire side wall had been engulfed and destroyed, the flames eating through the old, dry wood with ease. The stalls
~~~

on that side had sustained substantial damage and were no longer usable.

It would take months before Kaia could work out of it again.

"How did it start?" Kaia asked the group. "I'm always so careful."

Erik shook his head, already knowing the answer. "I'll give you one guess."

Bri spun to him. "You think Rasa did this?"

"Don't you? The timing of it is just too perfect." Erik gestured to what was left of the barn. "He's throwing a temper tantrum, because you found me before he could kill me. He blames Kaia, so Kaia had to pay."

Kaia's eyes sparked dangerously. "By endangering the horses in my care?"

Erik faced her fully. "He doesn't give a flying fuck about your horses or anything else. The only thing he cares about is himself and what he came here to do. You and I have thwarted every one of his attempts to get what he wants most—Min. So, we're the ones with the targets on our backs."

"I'll take that target and shove it right up his ass the next time I get my claws on him." Kaia almost vibrated with rage.

"This can't go on." Bri's voice shook. "He's taking too much from us. He's causing us more damage than we are to him, and he has to be stopped. This has got to end before he kills one of us, or anyone else who gets in his way."

She swung around to look at Mac. "There has to be a way to find these motherfuckers and get them out of here."

"We're doing everything we can to locate them. Anaconda is a big city, and there are any number of places they could hole up."

"I don't care how goddamned big it is! You have to find them!"

"Bri," Kaia took Bri's hands in hers. "We all want them found. And they will be. You just have to give Mac some room to work."

"They're getting too close," Bri argued. "I brought them here. If something happens to any one of you because of me…"

The pain in her voice struck Erik right in the heart.

Before he could move to comfort her, Kaia pulled her into her arms. "Hey. None of this is your fault. You didn't bring these assholes here. This is all on them."

Bri's words came out through broken sobs. "If I hadn't…"

Kaia leaned back to look directly into Bri's eyes. "If you hadn't what? Let me post those pictures online? It's okay to be so proud of your little girl that you want to show her off every now and then. Look at Facebook—it's just one massive collage of everyone's children. You saved that baby. You gave her the best mom and the best family in the world. And you have just as much right as the next parent to take all the pictures you want of that gorgeous, happy, smiling face. *You* did that for her. Until you came along, she had no one. What do you think her chances were of being adopted from that place? What are the chances for any of those kids?"

"But she would have remained hidden from the clan if I hadn't flaunted pictures of her on the fucking internet."

"How can you know that? Huh?" Kaia demanded. "What makes you think they weren't already tracking her down? She would have ended up right back in the same place her birth mother risked her life to get her away from. And say, by some miracle, someone else *did* adopt her. Could *they* have protected her from the Lao tigers?"

Kaia shook her head so vehemently her long hair swirled. "No. A normal family would have been decimated right from the start. That baby is exactly where she was always meant to be. With us. And we'll defend her from anything that tries to threaten her. So, stop with the blame game and let's get these assholes."

Erik couldn't have said it better himself. When Kaia released Bri, he brought her in close to him and cupped the side of her face in his hand. "Yeah. What *she* said," and leaned down to kiss her.

16

The next morning, despite his continued disquiet about his cat's return, Erik put his new plan into motion. Everything Kaia had said the night before had been true. They were the best protection for Min. And that meant he had to regain his strength, especially if that was *all* he had to work with.

He pulled some gym shorts on and stretched out on the living room floor. He started with push-ups. He'd only reached fifty-five when his arms felt like they'd give out.

Rolling over, he began counting off sit-ups. The still-healing wounds on his stomach and back pulled and stung, but he ignored them, breathing through the pain. When he hit sixty, he knew that was all he could do.

This is just fucking sad. Before meeting Rasa Chai, he'd been able to beat every member on the squad at both.

In the afternoon, he pushed to do more. And over the following days, drove himself even harder.

A week to the day after his rescue, Erik was nearly back to normal. The injuries Rasa's tiger had inflicted were inconvenient now more than debilitating. His muscle tone and stamina were coming along, and he got better every day.

The only thing that tore at him was his cougar. He'd still not sensed him at all.

The longer it went on, the shorter Erik's temper became. He was tired of waiting. He was irritated with everyone telling him not to rush it. He was so frustrated, and he tried his best to hide it, but he was failing. Miserably.

Just that morning, he'd snapped at Bri over nothing. He'd seen the flash of hurt in her eyes before she'd turned on her heel and left him where he stood. He hated that he was causing those around him heartache, but his life was fucking falling apart, and he didn't know how to put it back together.

What the hell was he going to do if his cat never came back?

Bri, Kaia, and even Mac had tried to offer their comfort, but nothing they said or did could make this shit even the slightest bit bearable. His goddamned cougar was fucking *gone*. There was no way for them to understand what missing a major part of yourself felt like.

He was still sitting on the floor after completing his last round of sit-ups when he saw Min peeking around the corner of the wall.

Great. He was so fucking mean, he was scaring little kids now. He made an effort to get himself in check before saying anything.

Erik smiled at her as he sat up cross-legged on the floor. "Hey, sweetie. Whatcha' doing?"

Min came to him, but she was tentative. "Momma cwy."

Aw, shit. He knew he'd upset Bri, but hearing it from a three-year-old made him feel like a real sorry son of a bitch. "I know, baby. I've been in kind of a bad mood lately. I didn't mean to make your momma cry. I'll make it better. I promise I will." Erik looked down at his hands resting in his lap. He took a breath and let it out.

She wouldn't understand, but maybe that was for the better. Maybe he could tell her what he'd been too afraid to tell everyone else. "I'm having a hard time with something."

Her voice echoed his sadness. "Kitty."

Smart beyond her years. "Yeah, sweetie. He's still resting, and I'm really worried about him. I'm afraid he'll never wake up."

She studied him for a long minute and then stepped in closer to him, reaching up to put her small hands on either side of his face. Her expression was so serious, her gaze so intense, it seemed mismatched to the tiny little body in front of him.

She looked deep into his eyes. "Iss okay, kitty. Min wuv kitty. Come pway."

Erik's eyes burned and a lump formed in his throat. If he hadn't realized before how much he loved this little girl, and she loved him, he knew in this moment. He cleared his throat and blinked back the emotion, trying to figure out a way to explain that even asking so very sweetly may not work.

But to his utter astonishment, he felt something stir deep inside of him.

His heart leapt as hope burst through the fog of depression that had been clouding his mind and breaking his spirit. He stared in awe and bewilderment into the deep, dark eyes of his itsy-bitsy savior.

He clung and held tight to that simple stirring like a lifeline and took Min's hands into his own. "Keep talking, baby. He can hear you, and I think he's starting to wake up."

As Min spoke about playing and rides and hugs, Erik sensed his cougar slinking ever closer. He was tentative and leery, but he was coming.

And then Erik grew concerned. Would his cougar still be the same? Would he be damaged in some way? He'd suffered a great deal at the cruel hands of Rasa Chai—maybe even more than Erik had. Would that change him in some fundamental way and make him mean or unpredictable? Could he be trusted not to strike out at anyone around him?

Would he hurt Min, even though he didn't mean to?

"Bri!" Erik called. "Can you come here, please?"

Even upset with him, she responded to the urgency in his voice. She rushed into the room. Her eyes were red but dry.

"What is it? What's wrong?"

"Can you please take Min? Somehow, unbelievably, my cat is responding to her. She was able to coax him back."

"Oh my God, Erik. That's incredible!" Her worry changed to elation as she picked Min up into her arms.

"I'm not too sure," he warned her with a grimace, rising to his knees. "He was hurt severely. He was all but broken, Bri. I don't know what he'll be like when he reemerges. He might... not be the same."

His gaze flicked to Min, and he saw the corners of Bri's eyes tense. She understood.

Erik could feel his cougar pushing at his mind now. He was fully present, and after such a long absence, he wanted *out*. Erik tried to get a read on him. He felt different, but Erik didn't know in what way.

What they'd gone through was bound to change them on a cellular level. His cat had been wrecked when Rasa banished him. Had he been able to heal during his forced sabbatical, or was he still damaged? Physically or mentally?

"If he tries anything..." Erik swallowed hard, "it might not be a bad idea to have your gun handy."

She gasped. "Erik. No."

"Please. I just want to keep the two of you safe." Erik fought to hold him back.

"Should you do this outside? In the woods?"

Erik shook his head. "If he goes on a rampage, I'd rather him not have access to a forest full of people. You and Min need to lock yourselves in the bedroom with your gun and your phone. If anything happens, call for help."

He pleaded with her when she didn't move right away. "Now. I can't keep him contained much longer."

Bri nodded and left with Min. He heard the door close.

"All right, buddy. Let's do this." Erik stripped out of his clothes and knelt down. "You have no idea how glad I am that you're back, but please don't make Bri shoot you. Keep it together, and we'll work through it. And then that motherfucker is going to *die* for what he did to us."

Erik let the change take him. The transformation made all of his cuts and bites scream, but he was more than happy to endure it. It meant he was able to shift again.

When his cat was fully emerged, he screamed out in fury. Hissing, fighting now when he couldn't fight then.

Erik delved deeper into his cat's mind. He was able to get a better handle on his emotions with the cat fully in charge. It was like opening a window directly into his brain. Erik breathed a sigh of relief. Other than being one extremely pissed off feline, his cougar seemed like he was okay and in control as he prowled around the living room.

Erik got a mental image of Min from his cougar.

"I had her mom take her away until I could see if you were all right. I didn't want either of them to get hurt."

The male sent back what could only be interpreted as a scoff.

"Be that as it may, you went through a lot because of that bastard. Can you blame me for wanting to take it slow when it comes to the girls I love?"

Erik received another image, but this one was of Min riding the mountain lion's back. Then one of the day in the meadow when he'd rubbed his face over Bri's belly.

"I know you love them too. But I had to know for sure. Are you okay? I am so sorry I couldn't do anything to spare you. If I could have shifted and saved you from that, I would have."

The cougar slammed Erik with hatred and rage again. And then a picture of Erik on the floor, covered in blood.

That explosive anger was more than he had ever felt from his cat before. Erik was pissed off too, but he worried that this new volatile temper would be a part of his cougar forever. He'd have to be very careful.

"He'll pay. I promise you—that asshole is going to fucking

pay with his life."

The cat showed Erik his desire for Min again.

"Okay, bud. But before that, can I just say how much I've missed you? I swear I'll never take you for granted again. This time without you has been the worst of my life."

Min again.

Erik laughed. *"Yeah. All right, hold on. I'll get her, but you're going to have to let me take over again, so I can call them out here."*

The cougar huffed but receded.

Erik shook his head and grabbed a blanket from the end of the couch to throw around his waist. "Bri, it's okay. You can bring Min back out."

They slowly emerged from the hall. "He's all right?"

He considered. "Mostly. I sense a lot of anger in him, but it's only directed at Rasa. But he really wants to see Min. I think she's become a sort of talisman to him. She represents pure love and kindness, and I think he needs that after what he's been through."

"If you're sure he's okay." Bri was hesitant, and he didn't blame her. He saw she had her pistol tucked into the waistband of her jeans.

"You won't need that." He indicated the weapon. "But if it makes you feel more secure, I don't have a problem with it. Yours and Min's safety is always most important."

Bri watched him for a moment and then nodded. She still held tight to Min's hand as she waited for his male to make his appearance.

"Nice and easy, bud."

Erik shifted. The cat immediately lay down on his side.

Bri held Min back as the little girl tugged on her hand. "Momma, pway wiff kitty."

Reluctantly, Bri released her.

Min flew at the cougar, squealing with delight. And Erik felt nothing but contentment from his cat as he began to purr in earnest.

They played and wrestled on the living room floor, and Erik felt whole again. When Bri called a halt for lunch, Erik resurfaced and dressed.

He went into the kitchen and walked up behind Bri at the counter. He wrapped his arms around her middle and pressed his forehead to the back of her head.

"I'm sorry I've been such a miserable jerk." He pitched his voice low. "I didn't know how to cope with my cat's absence, and I'm sorry I hurt you in the process."

"Yes, you did." Her tone was whisper soft too.

"You were so patient with me, and even then, I knew you were only trying to help me. I was lost in a world of self-pity, and I couldn't see past my own pain at losing my cat. I couldn't accept the love from you and Min, because I didn't think I deserved it anymore."

She spun around in his arms. "Erik, you have to know how wrong that thinking was."

"In my heart, I do…and I did. But there was a voice in my head telling me that I would never be good enough for you or our family without my animal side. How was I supposed to protect you both? How was I going to help you raise two shifter children if I wasn't one myself? I'd be nothing and of no use to you."

Her eyes heated with anger. "You thought so little of me? That I'd just shun you for not having a cougar anymore? You being a shifter had nothing whatsoever to do with my falling in love with you. It's the *man* that you are, Erik. It's the *father* you will be to our children. I've told you this before, and I'll say it again now. I want you by my side, every day, with or without that cougar inside of you."

Erik pulled her into him. "I love you so much."

"You're damned right you do," Bri huffed out.

Erik laughed. "I have no idea how I got so lucky."

For the first time in what felt like forever, everything was finally right with his world again.

17

With Erik back to feeling like himself again, they redoubled their efforts to find the two Lao men. But, try as they might, the sneaky little shits had somehow managed to fall off the map after the incident at Kaia's barn.

There'd been no sign of them since then, and they were all starting to get a little uneasy about what the foreigners could be up to. The waiting only worsened the dread of what was coming. It was out of the question to think they'd given up and gone home, which could only mean they were holed up somewhere, planning their next attack.

The two men Rasa had hired were in jail, but they could offer no new information beyond what they already had.

According to Mac, the men had been contracted and paid but knew nothing of those who'd hired them. Money had been transferred directly into their accounts, and they'd always met in public places, so they didn't know anything about their whereabouts.

While they'd be cooling their jets in the jail cell for the foreseeable future, Rasa and Yuu were still out there somewhere, free to do as they pleased.

And for that reason, Bri had put Min on lockdown.

Seeing what they'd done to Erik and his cat were proof enough of their brutality, and they weren't getting anywhere near Min. To ensure that, Bri kept her inside and under guard.

No less than two people were with her at any given time, and at least one of them was a shifter.

Kaia and Mac were watching over her while Bri and Erik went to her twelve-week prenatal appointment that morning. Bri hated when Min was out of her sight for even a second, but she trusted Kaia and Mac to keep her safe while she was gone.

Erik glanced at her from the driver's seat. "So, what will he be checking at this appointment?"

"He'll measure the baby and the size of the placenta to make sure it's growing like it should, take all my vitals, check for high blood pressure, and anything else that might endanger the pregnancy." She grinned at him. "And we'll probably get to hear the heartbeat."

His face lit up. "Seriously?"

This was the part Bri was most looking forward to. She couldn't wait to hear the baby's heartbeat again, and for Erik to experience it for the first time.

"Yup. It's amazing how fast it is."

"You've gotten to hear it already?"

Bri nodded. "Yeah. We did an ultrasound to determine the due date. It was early in the pregnancy, about seven weeks, but it was there, just fluttering away."

"Do you want to find out the gender beforehand?"

"If you don't mind, I think I'd rather be surprised."

Erik smiled. "I don't mind at all. I like that idea."

Her doctor's office was in Anaconda, about a twenty-minute drive from Kaia's. They pulled into the parking lot, and Erik chose a spot nearest the building. He came around and helped her out of the car.

They walked hand-in-hand to the office door, Erik stopping to pull it open and hold it for her.

"You're quite the gentlemen," she teased.

He grinned. "Hey, my mom drilled it into all of us boys' heads. I wouldn't dream of embarrassing her."

They were both laughing as they approached the front counter.

"Bri Calladega. I have a nine-a.m. appointment."

"Yes, I see you right here," the receptionist said. "We'll get you signed in, and we should be calling you back shortly."

"Thank you." Bri turned back to wait in the chairs arranged in two rows facing each other.

Erik grasped her hand and brought it to his lips to kiss the back of her hand. "I'm kind of excited. It still all seems so unreal to believe there's a baby in there." He reached over and laid his hand over her barely-rounded stomach.

"I feel the same way." Bri put her hand over his and then grimaced. "Other than when I'm sick. Then I believe it wholeheartedly."

Erik's face wore a mask of concern. "Should you ask the doctor about that? I've read it can get pretty bad."

Bri laughed. "He assured me the last time that my morning sickness is the garden-variety kind. It usually goes away on its own after the first trimester."

The nurse stepped into the doorway. "Miss Calladega?"

She and Erik rose and followed the hushed steps of soft-soled shoes. She guided them to a small office where Bri took a seat next to the desk.

"I'll just get your vitals, and then we'll be ready for the fun part next." The nurse took Bri's temperature, slipped the wide cuff up her arm and recorded her blood pressure in the computer, and had her step on the scale before keying her weight into the field on the screen.

After some quick subtraction, Bri judged she'd gained eight pounds.

"Everything's looking great so far. If you'll follow me, the sonographer is ready to see you now."

Bri and Erik followed the perky nurse down the hallway and into a small room on the right. Inside, there was an ultrasound machine with a stool in front of it, and a bed a couple of feet off the wall.

"Just lay back on the bed and tuck your shirt up into your bra, and then roll the waistband of your pants down. The technician will be with you shortly." The nurse walked out and closed the door behind her.

Bri reclined back in the bed and did as the nurse instructed. Pointing to the monitor in front of her mounted to the ceiling, Bri explained, "Everything the sonographer does on this machine will show up on that screen."

Erik looked from the TV to Bri and back again. "This is a little more high-tech than what I was expecting."

Bri laughed. "Just wait. It gets better." A thought suddenly occurred to her. She lowered her voice to a whisper. "Are shifter babies different than other babies? I mean, they don't like, have a tail or paws or anything, do they?"

Erik's jaw clenched as if he were gritting his teeth. But the humor in his eyes said he was desperately trying not to laugh.

"Um…no. It's just a regular baby. No tails, no pointed ears, no fur."

Bri narrowed her eyes at him. "You're making fun of me?"

Erik cleared his throat. "Not at all. I would never do that."

"Yeah, right."

A soft knock on the door announced the sonographer's arrival, and in walked an equally energetic brunette in blue scrubs.

"Good morning. My name is Stephanie. How are we feeling today?"

Bri couldn't help but grin. "Doing well. Still suffering from some morning sickness, but other than that, I feel fine for the rest of the day."

Stephanie sat down on the swivel stool and clicked a few keys on her keyboard before turning to face them. "That's still considered normal for this stage of your pregnancy, but hopefully that starts to clear out soon. How about we see what's going on in there?"

She leaned in to adjust Bri's shirt and pulled her waistband down just a little further. Taking a bottle off the edge of her desk, she hovered it over Bri's bare belly. She gave her an apologetic smile.

"Fair warning, this might be a little cold." And with that, she flipped the cap and squeezed.

Bri let out a small gasp as the cool gel oozed onto her stomach and into her belly button. She laughed and gazed up at Erik. "Yeah, I'd say that's cold."

Stephanie pulled out a wand and dipped it into the puddle of gel, spreading it out over the small expanse of her tummy.

An image came to life on the screen above Bri's head, and she grabbed Erik's hand. "Look! There it is!"

Erik squinted his eyes at the monitor and tilted his head. "Um, what exactly am I supposed to be seeing?"

In truth, Bri couldn't discern any of the shadows and blurred images any better than he could. She looked over at the sonographer to see she was studying the images intently, methodically moving the wand over her belly, pushing and probing before pausing briefly here and there to click a few keys on the mouse.

Bri began to feel a bit concerned, but then Stephanie's face broke into a small, secret smile.

"Oh, what do we have here?"

Bri held her hand up. "Wait! Don't tell us! We want to wait until delivery to find out what the baby's sex is."

The technician laughed. "That's not what I was going to tell you."

Erik was apparently as anxious as she was. "What? What do you see?" Both of their eyes were glued to the woman and her Cheshire-cat grin.

Stephanie moved the wand one more time, pressed a little

further into Bri's abdomen, and then made a couple of quick clicks on the mouse. She typed briefly and then turned back to them, her radiant smile threatening to crack her face.

"See for yourself," and pointed to the screen.

Bri and Erik collectively focused on the monitor, the breath catching in Bri's throat. On the TV was a wide black circle, accompanied by shadows. But that wasn't what caught her attention. The words she saw there had her heart stuttering and tears filling her eyes.

Baby A and *Baby B.*

Her gaze flew to Erik's, and in disbelief, they turned back to Stephanie.

"Congratulations! You're having twins!"

"What?" Erik gulped. "There's..." His words trailed off.

"Two!" the sonographer supplied happily.

Stephanie zoomed in on a spot on the screen, dragged a line across a lighter gray area, and clicked again. "That," she said, moving her mouse over the line, "is Baby A. The head is right there, and those are the little hands. The feet are just here." She repeated the process with Baby B, taking measurements and pointing out the miniature anatomy. "Since they share the same placenta, these two will be identical."

Bri and Erik looked at each other.

"Holy shit," Bri said, at the same time Erik said, "Oh my God."

Bri watched Erik's face as he studied the screen. It was alight with fascination and wonder, and when he looked back at her, his face was glowing with joy and pride. Her eyes brimmed over as they both turned to marvel at the tiny humans they had made.

Stephanie continued the pattern of move-and-click as she documented the babies from every possible angle. Seemingly done, she turned back to them and beamed. "Are you ready to hear their heartbeats now?"

At their enthusiastic sounds of affirmation, she flipped a switch.

And then the sound filled the room. The swoosh, swoosh, swoosh of fluttering hearts, beating strong and steady and fast.

She grinned over at Erik, and there was a look of awe on his face. "Is that...?"

"Heartbeats. Isn't it amazing?"

"Oh, man." Erik held her gaze. "Those are our kids in there."

Stephanie hit a little button to the side of her keyboard, and a long string of paper started spilling from the small device underneath. Reaching down, the pulled the strip free and handed it over to them. "Babies' first pictures."

Bri held them aloft, and they leaned in closer to the images, *oohing* and *aahing* over the miniscule features. Stephanie wadded up a handful of paper towels and began wiping the goo from Bri's belly.

"Your doctor is ready to see you now, and you can pick up a DVD of your ultrasound at the desk before you leave."

Erik nearly stuttered. "A DVD? Of our babies from this visit?"

Stephanie laughed kindly at the floundering new father. "Yes, sir. It's standard practice in our office during an ultrasound. Given that you guys are expecting multiples, you'll have another one every two weeks for the remainder of your pregnancy. Well, until your last trimester, that is. At that point, your ultrasounds will be scheduled weekly."

~~~

The door had only just latched when there was a light knock, and in walked Dr. Howard.

He was tall for a man in his late sixties, with short brown- and gray-flecked hair, wire-rimmed glasses, and a well- maintained salt-and-pepper beard. He'd told her once he ran
~~~

every morning to keep in shape, so he was lean and toned and looked every bit the picture of health. His voice when he spoke was just a bit gravelly but friendly.

"Good morning, Bri. How are you today?"

"I'm good," Bri acknowledged with a smile. "A little shocked by the news, but otherwise no issues to speak of."

"I heard. Congratulations!" Dr. Howard looked down and consulted his iPad. "And by the looks of things, everything is coming along nicely." He turned to Erik. "And who is this fine young man?"

Erik rose with an outstretched hand. "Erik Reid, sir. The father."

The doctor gave it a shake and nodded. "I'm so glad you're going to be a part of these babies' lives."

"If I have my say, I plan to be a permanent fixture."

Dr. Howard grinned. "That's good to hear." He turned back to Bri. "Now, let's see how Momma and babies are doing. Lie back, please."

Mimicking what she'd done in the sonographer's office Bri reclined and hiked her blouse up under her breasts. Then she undid her pants and pushed them down to just below her hips, exposing all of her tummy.

The doctor brought his hands to her lower abdomen and felt around, palpating into the soft flesh here and there, feeling the boundaries of her womb. "Any discomfort?

Bri shook her head as he continued his prodding, and a moment later, he pulled her shirt down and returned to his iPad.

"Well, Bri. Everything seems to be progressing beautifully. Your scans are all normal, and everything looks and feels just as it should. Are you still experiencing morning sickness?"

Her hands automatically went to rest over her belly. "Unfortunately, yes. Any idea how much longer that will last?"

Dr. Howard nodded. "It usually clears up around the end

of the first trimester, which is where you are. However, with multiples, we tend to see that it can sometimes extend past that. As long as you continue to steadily gain weight and can still keep your meals down, there's nothing to be concerned about."

He finished making notes in his tablet and then looked back up. "Bri, we'll want to see you back in another two weeks. Until then, do either of you have any other questions or concerns?"

She looked to Erik who shook his head, so she turned back to the doctor. "No, I think we're good for now."

"Okay, then. It was great to see the both of you. The receptionist will schedule your next appointment on your way out and give you your disc. Call if you need anything."

They were still in shock ten minutes later when they sat in the car after leaving the office.

Erik had yet to start it.

For Bri, the numbness was beginning to wear off and the excitement was moving in. Twins. She couldn't believe it. *Two babies*. And identical too! They were going to have two little boys or two little girls.

Holy shit, she thought again. Bri glanced over at Erik. "Are you okay? You look a little shell-shocked."

"Yeah," he said distractedly. "Yeah, I'm good. Still trying to wrap my brain around it." He turned to her, and there was the slightest bit of a smirk lifting his lips. "We're having twins."

"I heard that somewhere, yeah. How do you feel about that?"

"That I could have two blonde-haired girls with topaz eyes?" Erik reached over and pulled her into him across the center console of the car and kissed her deeply. "Incredible."

"It could just as easily be two boys with surfer-dude good looks and blue eyes."

"I still vote for girls."

"Really?" She drew back. "I figured you would want sons."

"Truthfully, I want anything with you as long as they're

healthy and happy. But I would love to see two more of you running around."

Bri laughed and rolled her eyes. "Whatever. You'd be completely outnumbered. And what are you going to do when all of your girls are old enough to date?"

The grin melted off Erik's face and he shook his head. "Nope. None of them will ever be old enough to date. I've had plenty of practice at driving boys away from Jayme. Those horny sons-of-bitches aren't getting anywhere *near* my daughters."

Bri laughed. "Boys *or* girls—can you imagine?" She rubbed her hands over her stomach.

"I can't. Not yet. But I have a feeling it'll be all too real very soon." Erik chuckled. "Oh man, my parents are going to *flip*."

"We should probably get back, so we can tell Kaia and Mac too."

Erik turned to her, and she could see a plan forming behind his sparkling blue eyes. "I think we need to celebrate first. It's not every day you find out you're having twins."

Bri laughed. "Count me in! What did you have in mind?"

"I want to buy something for the babies."

That surprised her. "Really? Like what?"

"Let's get their coming-home-from-the-hospital outfits."

"We don't know whether to buy pink or blue."

Erik snickered. "We weren't going to know anyway. So, we'll buy four. Two in case of girls and two for boys. Or we can go with neutral colors. But I want to get *something*. I want to have something in my hand that represents them, so I can see it every day until they get here."

His words had Bri getting emotional again. "That's so sweet."

Seeing her tears, Erik sobered. "I didn't mean to make you cry."

"Ignore them, they'll go away. It's just hormones."

Erik gave her a sidelong glance, unsure. "Okay."

He consulted his phone for a moment and then started the

car and drove out of the lot. Less than five minutes later, he was parking outside of a chain baby store.

They walked in and, after some wandering, found the preemie section. The doctor had warned them on their way out that with multiples, the chances of delivering early were high and the babies' birth weights would be less than a singleton.

They couldn't get over how small the outfits were. Erik held up a tiny dress.

"Look at this. It's the size of my hand."

Bri touched the hem of the skirt that looked more like a doll's clothes than that of an actual newborn. "It doesn't even seem possible a baby could be that small."

Some of the doubt she'd carried all her life snuck back into her mind. Her hand started to shake. She looked up at Erik.

"Can we really do this? I was scared when I adopted Min, but she was a fully formed toddler. She didn't need the same kind of care and attention that babies require. I don't know anything about caring for infants, and we're going to have *two* of them. They're both going to be that size." She indicated towards the dress.

Erik put it back and took her hands in his. "You are an amazing mother to Min. Just like you will be to these two. We're going to make mistakes. What parent doesn't? But we'll learn from them and do the best we can. And if we need help, I happen to know a whole bunch of people who'll be banging down our door to step in with anything we need." He cupped her chin in his strong hands. "And guess what? They don't stay that size forever. They'll be Min's size before we know it. And then I think we'll all be in trouble."

The fear gripping her faded, and she was able to laugh. "You're probably right. From what I've read, parents don't really lose their minds until their kids are two and three."

He pulled her in and kissed her gently. "We'll have each other's backs, because those two in there are going to be a force to reckon with, I'm sure."

Bri curled herself into Erik's warmth and held him close until she was steady and sure again. She leaned back and smiled up at him. "Momentary panic. I'm better now."

"Good." He gave her a quick peck. "Remember this when it's my turn to freak out. Because I'm going to at some point, just to let you know."

Bri sank into his body, relaxed and content. "I will, I promise."

"You still feel like shopping?"

She sent him an incredulous look.

"Sorry." Erik grimaced. "Stupid question."

They spent the next hour looking at all the selections the store had to offer. They ended up with two tiny white knit rompers with knit hats and blankets to match. As an accent on each piece, one set was embroidered with a little yellow bear, while the other set had a green bear.

Bri had fallen in love as soon as she'd seen them. When she'd shown them to Erik, he'd smiled and agreed.

"Perfect."

Walking out hand-in-hand, Bri felt lighter and happier than she had in weeks. The burden of having to be on guard every moment had been suffocating her, and she'd almost forgotten what it felt like to live a normal life. It had been a day of discovery, a day to unwind and reset.

She'd been off-balance and had needed this time—with Erik—to find her center and recharge.

As they climbed into the car and started on their way home, Bri felt ready to battle whatever came at her next, with Erik by her side and a big family on the horizon.

18

Mac and Min were playing a board game on the living room floor when Bri and Erik finally made it back. Moose was in his usual position at Min's side. The massive dog dwarfed her, but Bri knew he would protect her just as fiercely as everyone else in this house.

"Who's winning?" Bri bent and ran her hand over Min's silky black hair.

"She is," Mac groused teasingly.

Bri laughed and saw Kaia step out from the hall. "So? How'd it go?"

Bri looked up at Erik and grinned. She opened the bag in her hand and grasped the two hangers at once. She slowly slid both outfits out of the bag, careful not to give away its contents too soon.

Erik took the shopping bag from her, and she held out a romper in each hand.

It took a second for realization to strike. But then Kaia gasped and raised a hand to her mouth. "No way," she said from behind her palm.

Bri nodded. "Way! Twins!"

Kaia squealed, grabbed Bri, and hugged her hard. Bri indulged her best friend and held on just as tight.

When Kaia released her, she was talking fast. "Oh my God, Bri. I can't believe it. This is so freaking awesome. Holy crap."

"Yup. Holy crap seems to cover it." Bri glanced down at the matching outfits in her hands and felt a nervous jump in her belly.

Dinner was lively and festive, full of laughter and easy chatter. By silent agreement, everyone kept to topics that were light and fun. Nothing dark or evil would bring down the celebratory mood after finding out the news.

Once Bri had put Min to bed, they spent the remainder of the evening making plans for happier times, and as the hour grew late, they decided to call it a night. Erik held Bri back as Mac and Kaia headed off down the hall.

"Did you think of something else?" Bri asked.

"No." He took a breath, and Bri started to get nervous. "You're not going to like it, but I need to let my cat out to run tonight. It's time."

Bri had known this moment was coming. She knew the cats needed their freedom just as much as their human counterparts did. But she had hoped both of them would be back to one hundred percent before the time came to venture out again.

While Erik's healing had improved by leaps and bounds since the return of his cougar, he wasn't quite there yet. She sighed, resigned.

"I know you both need this. Just promise me you'll be careful. They could be out there waiting."

"I promise." He leaned down and kissed her. "I'm so glad you understand."

She smiled. "I've been friends with Kaia a long time. You don't grow up with a shifter and not know how all of this works, especially after what your cat has been through. He needs his time as much as you did."

"I'll be back by dawn. I love you."

Bri caressed his cheek. "I love you."

She watched him step outside and walk down the stairs. He became a shadow in the night as he crossed the yard to the trees. By the time he entered the woods, she'd lost track of him in the darkness.

She sent up a silent prayer that he'd be safe and turned to go to bed. She lay in the moonlit room, staring at the ceiling, and eventually drifted off.

At some point, she fell into dreams.

She was in the hospital, and both of her beautiful babies were there. She held one in each arm and gazed lovingly down into their angelic faces. Blonde hair and bright blue eyes stared back up at her.

Erik had gotten his wish. They had two girls.

The door to her room was thrown open loudly and Rasa Chai strode in.

"What the hell are you doing here?" Bri demanded.

"I've come for the children." He drew closer to the bed, and Bri hugged her babies tighter to her chest.

"You aren't taking them anywhere. They're not even tigers, you fucking moron. They're mountain lions and no use to you."

Rasa tilted his head and dropped his feral gaze to the infants. "Aren't they?"

Bri's eyes shot down and she gasped. The wispy soft blonde fluff and their father's blue eyes were gone. Now the babies had short, spiky black hair and dark-brown eyes. Asian features took the place of Caucasian.

"That's not possible. These are *my* children. Mine and Erik's. Where is he?" She looked up at Rasa again. "What have you done with Erik?"

Rasa laughed and turned to gesture to the still-open door.

Out in the hall, Bri could see Erik bound and beaten. His was on his knees, and his hands were tied behind his back. His chin rested on his chest, and he wouldn't look up at her.

"Erik? What's happened?"

It was then her attention was drawn to Rasa's clanmate. Yuu held Min's hand tightly in his. She stood motionless and crying, giant tears raining down her small face as her eyes pleaded with Bri to save her.

Bri's awareness was wrenched back to Rasa as he reached out to tear one of the babies from her arms.

She fought to hold on to her child. "No, you bastard! You can't have them! They're mine!"

"My clan needs all the female shifters it can get. In a few years, these three will produce offspring that will build our numbers." He put the newborn in a plastic pet carrier and snatched the other from her to join its sister.

Bri cried out for her babies, but she couldn't move from the bed. Something was holding her in place, and she could do nothing to save any of her children. The twins and Min would be taken back to Laos to be raised as chattel and mated like rabbits. Their lives would be hell on earth, and Bri was helpless to stop it.

She screamed over and over as Rasa walked imperiously out of her room, taking what she loved most with him.

Bri jerked herself out of the dream. She didn't realize she was crying until she felt the wet tracks snaking down her face and into her hair.

She rolled to the side of the bed and sat on the edge, trying to breathe away the remnants of her nightmare. Her eyes darted to the far corner where Min slept peacefully, her dark hair against the light pillowcase easily seen in the dimness.

"She's fine." Bri placed her hands over her twins. "We're all fine."

A quick glance at the clock showed it was just before five in the morning. She should really try to get more sleep, but she suddenly needed Erik, the warmth and comfort of his arms around her.

Bri went to the closet and pulled out a long, open-front sweater. She wrapped it around herself, the bottom falling to nearly her knees to cover the bare skin of her legs. After checking on Min, she stepped out into the hall. Kaia and Mac's room was directly across from hers. She went to the door and tapped her fingernails lightly on the surface, knowing Kaia would hear.

Within seconds, her best friend was opening it.

"Hey. Is something wrong?" Kaia's voice was raspy from sleep, her wild tawny hair a nest around her head.

"I knew you were going to be up soon to go for your run anyway, and I need a huge favor."

"Anything. Name it."

"Can you watch Min for a while? I want to go out and meet Erik as he comes in."

Kaia studied her. "Are you okay?"

"Yeah. I had a bad dream, but it really hit me hard. I just need some time with him."

"Of course you do. I understand completely. Go. Min will be fine."

Bri hugged her. "Thank you. I love you."

"I love you too. Now go get your man."

Bri grinned. "I will."

She turned and, after a quick stop in the living room for a blanket, made her way to the sliding door. Brisk morning air greeted her as it slid wide.

The wood decking was damp with dew and cool on her bare feet. The grass was soft and tickled her tender soles. Walking more carefully, she crossed the tree line and entered into another world.

Having never been into the forest at this hour, Bri was amazed how completely different it was. The sounds were unlike anything she heard during the day. The darkness seemed heavier under the canopy of trees, the dense foliage above blocking out all of the ambient moonlight.

As she made her way deeper into the thicket of woods, she watched her surroundings carefully. She knew Erik's cat would spot her long before she was aware of his presence. He probably had her in his sights already.

She came across a small flat area that would be perfect for what she had in mind. Choosing the best spot, she laid out the blanket and settled onto it.

Only a few minutes had passed before she sensed she was no longer alone. Tracking her eyes around her, she saw him. The large male mountain lion.

"Good morning." She smiled at him. "Are you going to join me?"

He stalked into the clearing, straight for her, his blue eyes never leaving her.

Bri's breath caught. She could count on one hand the number of times she'd been alone with the cougar. Everything about him amazed her. His size. His coordination. His speed. His beauty.

The hulking feline didn't stop until he was inches from her. Bri reached up with both hands and ran her fingers through the fur on either side of his face and down his neck. He leaned in farther and rested his forehead against her chest.

Bri let her hands wander over the muscled beast. He seemed content to let her continue.

"I take it you had a good night?"

A heavy purr vibrated the bulk beneath her palms.

He put more pressure on her chest, nudging her back until she stretched out over the blanket. His massive head went to her baby bump and sniffed, his cheek rubbing lightly against it.

Bri laughed.

The cougar walked around to her bare feet and drew in the scent of her skin. His whiskers tickled, and she jumped.

"Watch it, buddy," she warned. "That's dangerous territory there."

Bri relaxed again, staring up at the sky. Suddenly, the cold nose was gone, and warm hands wrapped around her ankles. Wet, open-mouthed kisses trailed slowly up her legs.

She hummed deep in her throat, much as the cat had done only moments before.

"Hey, you," she breathed out.

"Don't you know the forest is a dangerous place at night?" he growled, continuing to devour her sensitive flesh.

He explored every inch of her shins, calves, and knees, raising each leg to kiss and lick his way upward.

"It's a good thing I have my very own predator to protect me then." She gasped when his teeth took a bite out of her inner thigh just above her knee.

"This predator is going to eat you up himself."

"Promise?" He nibbled higher and she sucked in a breath. "Oh, god."

He slid the hem of her t-shirt up and out of his way, finding nothing to bar his progress.

"I can't believe you came out here like this," Erik said against the skin of her upper thigh. "There's no telling what you could have run into."

"Then I'm thankful you found me first." Bri closed her eyes as his warm breath washed over her center. "No more talking."

He chuckled. "As you wish, my love."

His hot mouth found her, and stars erupted behind her lids. Her hands automatically went to tangle in his hair, pulling him closer as he rhythmically sucked and licked on her pleasure nub.

Her orgasm ripped through her before she even knew it was coming. This man was incredible, and she knew he wasn't done with her yet.

Heated naked skin slid over hers as he continued his assault up her body, the thin cotton tee riding higher as he did. Those talented and tormenting lips reached the curve of her breasts, and he gave each of them his total attention before finally narrowing in on first one taut nipple and then the other.

Bri was writhing underneath him. He was destroying her—mind and soul.

As he worked her puckered nipples, his fingers curled into her searching channel.

She growled low and undulated her hips, demanding more. She needed him inside her, filling and stretching her.

"Fuck, Erik. I need you." Her words were a prayer, spoken through pants of air.

He ignored her plea and instead, pressed a thumb to her clit. She shattered instantly, the spasms more violent and intense than before.

Her body was still thrumming, the aftershocks still pulsing, and already he was driving her up again. Surely, she'd never survive this night. She'd perish among these trees and be happy to do it.

And then he was hanging over her, blocking out all thought. Every nerve-ending she possessed was like a live electrical wire, and when she felt him pushing his full length into her, she cried out. Her sex was so swollen and sensitive, it barely admitted him. But he took his time, rocking his hips back and forth, entering her inch by glorious inch.

Once he was seated all the way inside her, she let out a sigh of contented pleasure. This. *This* was what she wanted—what she craved. All of him filling her to bursting as he cherished her.

Bri loved how they fit. She was made for him, and he for her.

Erik drew back his hips and thrust forward in a long, torturous glide, her body so aroused and ready for him, it coated him with slickness.

"God baby, you feel amazing." Erik withdrew and slid back in. "I can feel every muscle inside you, pulling at me and squeezing so tight."

He rode her languorously until she thought she'd go crazy

with desire. Another orgasm was hovering just out of reach, but she needed harder, deeper thrusts to get her there.

"Harder, Erik. Faster. Please. Oh God, baby, deeper." Her hips were raising and lowering, trying to coerce him into moving how she wanted. How her body demanded.

Erik rose up above her, taking his weight on his hands and pressing his pelvis into hers. He ground his hips around once and then pulled back until only the head of his cock was still in place.

When he slammed back into her, Bri screamed. He set a brutal pace, but she met every drive.

"Yes. Yes. Yes." Bri was lost in another realm, one where only Erik existed. A pack of wolves could have stormed the clearing, and she wouldn't have cared. In this time and space, the only thing that mattered was him and what he was doing to her.

Her breathing grew sharp and with each exhale, she moaned. Her head thrashed back and forth on the blanket underneath her. She was wild, clawing at Erik's back with her nails, her feet digging into the ground at his sides, so she could meet each of his powerful thrusts.

Suddenly her world exploded. Her channel convulsed around him, and Bri's vision went black. She swore she lost consciousness as pleasure so strong, so all-consuming, slammed into her.

Erik thrust twice more and found his own release. He buried himself deep inside of her and growled, a sound so primal it rivaled that of his cat's.

She loved it.

He collapsed on top of her, both drenched in sweat and breathing heavily. Deep draughts of air sawed in and out of lungs worked to the point of exhaustion.

They lay sprawled, wrapped in each other's arms, watching as the sky began to change from dark blue to gray to opal pink as the sun rose.

"We should probably get back to the house." Erik said the words, but his body didn't move. Instead, he snuggled into her more.

"In a minute," Bri agreed with a contented sigh.

"I love that you surprised me this morning. But why were you up so early?"

Bri hesitated.

Erik leaned up to look down into her face. "Bri. Hon. What is it?"

"I had a dream. It started out really nice, but then it took an awful turn."

"Tell me."

This was why she'd come out here. She'd needed to share it with him. He would understand her fear and see why it upset her so much.

"I was in the hospital. I'd had the babies—girls with blonde hair and blue eyes like yours. As I was staring at them and talking to them, he came in."

"Who did?"

"Rasa. He came into my hospital room and took them, and he had Min too. The babies changed." She swallowed. "When the dream started, they looked like you, but when Rasa got there, they were Asian with black hair and dark eyes."

He held her close. "I'm so sorry I wasn't there when you woke up." He planted a gentle kiss to her temple. "You're dealing with so much."

Her breath hitched. "He put them in a pet crate like they were animals."

Erik's large shape rose above her. "Hey. Look at me."

He waited until she did.

"No one is going to take our children." His eyes were hard, filled with a conviction he tried to pass on to her. "I won't let that happen. The babies are safe and sound inside of you, and

I'll kill that fucker before he ever gets close to Min."

Erik lay down next to her again, pulling her in and rubbing her back.

"It was only a dream, and it's over now. You're safe, and so are Min and our twins." He slid his hand around and settled it over the slight mound of her stomach. "Rasa Chai will be long gone before these little ones ever make their entrance into the world."

"I know. But you can't control your dreams, and it shook me to the core. I needed you."

"I'm sorry this is causing you so much distress. I dream of finding them and ripping their heads off with my bare hands."

"I'll hold your coat."

Erik chuckled a little. "I know you would, baby. That's why I love you."

"I love you too."

They eventually made it back to the house. Mac, Kaia, and Min were all seated at the table.

Mac looked up and grinned at them. Bri was wrapped in her sweater again, and Erik had the blanket tied around him toga-style.

"Have a nice morning?"

Erik sent Bri a hooded look. "I did, actually."

Mac grew serious. "Did you see anything out there last night?"

Bri interrupted by touching Erik's arm. When he glanced down at her, she asked, "Coffee?"

"Yes, please." He took a seat and addressed Mac's question. "No. I kept an eye out for anything out of place, but it was all quiet and normal in the park."

Bri made Erik's coffee and brewed a mug of tea for herself. She turned with both and carried them over to the table. She set Erik's in front of him and slid into the chair next to him.

She leaned over to Min and whispered, "Good morning."

Min smiled at her with a mouthful of yogurt and blueberries.

Knowing her daughter was happy and occupied, she turned her attention to the conversation.

Mac was giving them an update on the search. "We're combing the streets and asking around, but as of last night, there was still no sign. I do have some good news though. We finally tracked down their plane. It's sitting at a small airstrip about thirty miles away. I've got men in place watching it. Sooner or later, they'll make a move and we'll know it."

Bri dearly hoped for sooner, the dream from the night before still haunting her. She wanted to settle into her life and not worry about anyone coming for her children.

Her brow furrowed, and she thought again of Min's birth mother and the other victims who were trapped and abused. Something needed to be done to help them and put a stop to this clan that thought they could destroy the lives of anyone they wanted.

Erik had explained the responsibilities of the ruling clans. Bri wondered if those in power could actually be trusted to take care of what was happening in Laos.

When there was a pause in the conversation, she looked over at Erik. "You said before that the ruling clan deals with major issues going on within the smaller groups. Are the leaders going to listen to us, being that we're outsiders?"

"It's rare, but it's not unheard of, for an unrelated clan to get involved in another shifter species matter." Erik's eyes became fierce. "It wasn't an idle threat. I fully intend to let them know what's been happening, and I'll make damned sure they listen. By the time I'm finished, either they'll put an end to it, or my clan will—a point that will be made abundantly clear. But Rasa and his friend need to be dealt with first. I'm not leaving here until the threat to my family has been eliminated."

Bri nodded and felt hope bloom in her heart, that soon, those young girls, women, and mothers would find an end to their torment.

19

The next morning, Erik ran out to pick up a surprise for Min. Since Bri was keeping her under house arrest, Erik wanted to give her a little something fun. To that end, he'd gotten up early and left the house. Kaia and Mac were both still there to guard over his girls, and this errand wouldn't take long.

He pulled into the bakery parking lot and got out. As soon as he stepped inside, the scent of sweet fried dough met his senses.

"Oh, man. That smells amazing."

The lady behind the counter grinned. "Fresh out of the fryer. What can I get you?"

"I'll take a dozen. Mix them up, but make sure there are a couple with sprinkles. I've got a little girl at home who deserves something as sweet as she is."

"You got it."

Erik watched as she pulled from this shelf and that one. Long donuts, square ones, jelly-filled, frosted, powdered sugar, chocolate, and as requested, two with pink icing and colorful confetti.

She rang him up, and Erik returned to his car. He slid behind the wheel and carefully set the box on the passenger seat. The interior instantly filled with the aroma of sugary goodness.

Checking his mirrors, Erik glanced over his shoulder to see behind him and caught sight of something.

"What the hell?"

There was a row of empty buildings two blocks from where he sat, which was now an abandoned strip mall. Past that stood a single structure, also deserted.

And he could have sworn he'd just seen a dark-haired man dart around the corner of the building that looked suspiciously like Rasa's lackey.

Curious now, and with a sense of certainty growing deep in his gut, Erik pulled out of the donut shop lot and turned in that direction. He parked at the end of the little plaza, farthest from where he'd seen what he thought to be one of the Lao men.

Had they been hiding out in empty buildings around town? It would keep them near the area while hiding them from the public and authoritative eye.

Erik got out of his car and, using the mall as cover, made his way closer. If they were in there, he'd be walking into a confrontation outnumbered. He should probably call Mac or Kaia—someone to provide him with some backup. But by the time anyone got there, they could be gone into the wind again, and in case he was wrong altogether, he didn't want to leave Bri and Min unprotected.

He had to check it out on his own.

And if he turned out to be right, he'd make damned sure that whatever happened here didn't fall back on Mac. A dead body, especially that of a tiger, would raise a lot of questions for Lost Creek's sheriff, so Erik would just have to tidy up when he was done.

Hell, he was probably just jumping at ghosts anyway. What were the chances he'd actually stumbled upon their hideout by accident while out buying fucking donuts?

But still, he had to know. Erik edged closer.

It was a single-story office complex. A quick peek around the corner revealed a set of double glass doors leading into the front. The glass was tinted to keep the sun out, so there was no way to know what the setup was or how many offices were inside. The whole front of the building was made of the glass panels, so there'd be no way of knowing if he were being watched from inside until he gained entrance. And by then it would be too late. They'd either be long gone or get the jump on him instead.

Thinking the rear might net him a better way in, he circled around to the back and found a single entry. On this side, only the top half of the walls were made of glass, the bottom portion consisting of solid concrete. He could remain hidden from view from anyone inside.

Edging as close to the door as he could, he tried to turn the knob.

Locked. *Shit.*

He may have to risk trying the front door after all. He needed inside this building—he had to know if the Lao men were in there.

He started to make his way back around to the other side, when something told him to try the door again. Instead of attempting to twist it though, he simply pulled lightly. Erik was shocked when the door actually opened an inch.

Arrogant assholes. They were so sure they wouldn't be found, they didn't even bother making sure the door had latched after locking it. That, or they were just plain careless.

Pulling it slowly, Erik waited for any sound that would announce his arrival. Thankfully, only small groans emitted from the hinges. Nothing that would draw any notice from deeper inside the building.

He slipped through and let it close softly behind him, careful not to let it latch all the way. He took a moment for his eyes to adjust to the dim interior. He was in what looked to be the employee break room.

Immediately to his left was the counter with sink, dishwasher, and refrigerator. On his right were three round tables with chairs. Straight ahead were double bi-fold doors to what was probably a closet. To the right of those was a closed door that may lead into the front office area.

As he moved forward, Erik saw that there was another door on the left. He hadn't seen it, because it was blocked by the fridge. It too was shut tight, with no hint as to what lay on the other side.

He moved to it and, putting his ear to the wood panel, listened for anyone in the adjacent room.

He heard nothing.

Grasping the lever handle, he pushed down and pulled the door towards him. He peeked through and saw a short hallway. This was another, separate office area with its own smaller kitchen area. Sink, counter, and mini refrigerator were on the left, and directly across from that was a bathroom. He slowly made his way through, alert to any sound or movement coming from within.

At the first corner, he darted his head out for a quick look.

There were three offices in a row. He cleared each one and could see through a large pane of glass that the conference room was empty. The rest of the space was open, with no indication of anyone having been there in some time. The dust and debris on the floor hadn't been disturbed.

Going out the way he'd come in, Erik crossed the breakroom to the other door.

That one too opened without protest. He glanced in and saw restrooms right in front of him and a hall that led to cubical areas in both directions.

He was about to go right and begin his search when he heard something from the left side.

Erik silently crept down the hall, eyes scanning, always moving.

Where are you, you cocksucker?

Erik noiselessly stalked his prey. As he neared the end of

the hall, his ears zeroed in on where the sound had come from. There were several cubicles grouped together, and his target was somewhere in the middle of them.

Senses concentrated on his quarry, Erik moved closer. When he was in position, he stepped into the opening and surprised Yuu Feng. He was laid out on the floor, apparently resting and watching some kind of video on his phone.

"Hey, fuckhead."

Dark eyes shot up to Erik and went feral. The man sprang up and attacked, hitting Erik in the stomach with his shoulder and knocking him back. The air left Erik's lungs in a grunt. But Erik had been ready for him, so it hadn't taken him down.

Taking advantage of his assailant's bent position, Erik wrapped his arm around the guy's neck and held him in a chokehold. With his free hand, he plowed blows into the smaller man's ribs.

The scrawny little bastard was somehow able to slip free of Erik's grip to spin and kick out with a foot aimed at Erik's face. Erik pivoted away, but it still caught him with a grazing blow, stunning him momentarily.

They fought, each man knowing they'd reached the end of the line. Only one of them would be leaving the abandoned building.

They fought, hard and dirty, landing blows to any body part they could reach, and wearing themselves out until both were sweating and panting.

Erik finally had him just where he wanted him. But sensing what was about to happen, his opponent struck out wildly. The hit caught Erik on the chin, forcing his head up and back and loosening his grip just enough for the smaller man to slip away and run.

Giving chase, Erik came upon a trail of ripped and shredded clothing. In his hurry to shift, Yuu hadn't even bothered to discard his clothes before transforming. He must have changed midstride and let the ruined material fall away from him.

Erik followed, shedding his own quickly as he went. His own clothes had to remain intact, as he had every intention of walking out of there alive.

"So, this is how it's going to be then? Fine by me, you fucking coward!"

Erik let his cat out to play, who screamed his promise of revenge.

He's giving you the opening you wanted. It's all on you now. Take that motherfucker down.

He could feel his cougar seething as he prowled through the office area on silent feet, all his senses alert and looking for the hidden tiger.

It roared out of one of the side offices and slammed full body into the mountain lion's side. They rolled and tumbled a few feet before each found their footing.

Not wasting a moment, the cougar pounced, teeth snapping and claws flying. The four-hundred-pound tiger outweighed his cat by double, but the cougar had a score to settle.

He tore into the tiger with every bit of rage and vengeance he had, spitting and hissing his fury as teeth ripped away flesh, and claws shredded through fur and tissue and muscle. It was a nasty, bloody battle, and both man and beast reveled in the glory of retribution.

When the tiger finally lay still in a motionless heap on the floor, the mountain lion stood over it and roared his triumph.

Erik made the shift back, and the next hour passed in a haze of activity. There could be no sign of what had happened here. Or at least, no body to raise any questions. Fortunately for him, the elite team he belonged to had taught him how to do just that.

He was almost tempted to stick around and ambush Rasa when he showed up. But as much as he would have liked to put an end to all of it, right now, right here, he didn't think his cat could take another round just yet.

Rasa would have to wait.

~~~

With the side trip, everyone was awake by the time he got to the house. Erik had left a note saying he'd be right back, but he'd obviously been gone a lot longer than intended.

He'd cleaned himself up as best he could with napkins from his car, and the healing process had already begun. But the battle had been fierce, and there were still a few wounds that hadn't closed up yet. He'd need a few butterfly bandages to help things along.

He didn't want to walk in and scare everyone—least of all, Min—so Erik pulled out his phone and typed out a text to Bri.

Hey, love. I'm in the driveway. Can you please come out here? Bring the first-aid kit. And before you freak out, I'm fine.

Within moments, Bri was rushing out the front door, white plastic box clutched in her hand.

Erik grabbed the donut box and got out, grimacing when a claw mark on his side pulled. He set the box on top of his car.

Bri caught the moment of pain. "What happened?"

"Just help me get cleaned up, so I can go inside without scaring Min."

He lifted his shirt and Bri gasped. "Erik..."

"Really, I'm okay. I promise. I'll explain in a minute, but everyone needs to hear it."

She did what she could in the driveway with bandages and sterile pads. When she'd stuck the last dressing, Erik dropped his shirt back down. He carefully took the treats in hand and, smiling at Bri, walked into the house.

"Who wants donuts?" he sang out. He was actually feeling pretty damned good, despite the wounds. He'd lessened the threat to his girls.
~~~

One down, one to go.

Min loved the sweets, and his surprise was a big hit. Mac and Kaia watched him curiously but said nothing.

When breakfast was over, Bri took Min to clean up all the stickiness and settle her in the bedroom with some toys. As soon as she returned, her face was impatiently expectant.

"Okay, spill it, Reid. What the hell happened?" Her topaz eyes glittered as she took her seat again.

"Yuu Feng is dead."

Gasps echoed around the table before everyone erupted at once.

"What the hell do you mean he's dead?" Mac's stony gaze pinned Erik.

"How?" Kaia asked. "When?"

Bri stared at him, almost as if unsure she'd heard him correctly.

Erik retraced his steps. "I'd wanted to do something fun for Min, since she hasn't been able to get out of the house much lately. I thought donuts would do the trick. But as I was leaving the bakery, I caught a glimpse of him going into an empty building a few blocks away. Dumb luck. I just happened to be in the right place at the right time."

He didn't leave anything out, and when he was finished, Mac had a few more questions.

"You're sure there won't be anything to find there? No evidence that can possibly lead back to you? Or to us?"

Erik wasn't going into detail, but there was nothing left of the tiger to find. "None. I know what I'm doing. We're in the clear, and down one douchebag."

He hated that they'd given him no other option, but their refusal to leave had signed their own death warrants. Rabid animals deserved to be put down, and if the choice was between that tiger and his girls, his girls won, paws down.

And it gave him a certain grim satisfaction that Rasa was

now on his own. Erik only wished he could have been there when the alpha discovered his beta was no more.

20

Bri would have thought they'd see a swift and brutal retaliation for what had been done to Rasa's partner. Surely, the tyrant had to know by now that his sidekick was dead and gone. And most likely, at the hands of Erik.

It had been three days, and there'd still been no sign of him.

She hated this—sitting on pins and needles, waiting for something to happen. Bri didn't figure Rasa's payback would stem from sorrow at the loss of his friend and companion. If anything, it would be a matter of pride, because once again, they'd gotten the better of him.

They'd taken something away from him and set him back another step. Just as Erik had said a few weeks before, Rasa was a spoiled child. A dangerous one, but a spoiled child nonetheless.

There was no telling what he'd do. He'd tried to burn down Kaia's barn, endangering her animals and dealing a blow to her business in the process. He'd hired men to ambush Erik and Kaia, imprisoning him, so that they could torture him mercilessly. And there was nothing stopping him from doing it again, or sending an army of men to storm the house.

The possibilities were swimming around in Bri's mind, making her crazy.

Her thoughts were broken when her phone buzzed in her pocket. Sliding it free, she saw that it was Kaia.

Bri swiped her thumb across the screen. "Hey, Kai," she greeted.

Silence met her ear.

"Kaia? Are you there? Can you hear me?"

A scream pierced her eardrum, and then a man's voice came on the line. "If you want to see your friend again, you will come to the barn. *Alone*."

Bri's heart stopped and then beat again in hard, pounding thumps. "Rasa. Where's Kaia? What have you done to her?"

"Nothing she won't heal from. Yet." His voice dripped menace. "Come now or she dies."

There was another agony-filled cry, and the line went dead.

Her mind raced. She could barely think.

He was going to kill Kaia, and Bri knew the threat was real. Rasa had proven time and time again just how brutal and vicious he could be. Not only would he kill her if Bri didn't comply, but it would be slow and agonizing, and she couldn't doom her best friend to that fate.

But how could she go without Erik demanding to join her? She had to come up with a reason to leave that wouldn't draw Erik's suspicion.

She wrung her hands as she fought the fear and panic to make her mind work. As she paced the floor of her bedroom, her gaze landed on a box of diapers. An idea formed and she went to find Erik.

He was at the dining room table working on the computer.

"I need to run to the store for diapers." Bri tried to steady her voice. Any waver and he'd know something was wrong. "Would you stay here with Min? I won't be gone long."

Blue eyes slowly rose to meet hers. She could tell by the steely set of his jaw that this was about to be a fight.

"I don't think that's a good idea, Bri. I don't like you out there alone. Why don't we all go?"

"There's no need for all of us to trek to the store. I'll run out and be back in twenty minutes—half an hour at the latest." She had to slow her words down. Slow her breathing. "I'll be fine. He's not after me. You, Kaia, and Min are tops on his list. And I'd feel better if she stayed here with you."

Erik drew in a breath and let it out, rubbing his hands over his face. "Text me when you get to the store and when you leave there. I want to know where you are at all times."

Bri nodded, silently saying a prayer of thanks that he'd agreed. "Can do." She leaned down to kiss him. "Want anything from the store?"

"Just you."

Bri forced a laugh. "See you in a bit."

She got into her car and cranked it on.

Pulling out of the driveway, she turned left instead of right that would take her into Anaconda.

The farm was only a few miles away and wouldn't take her long to get there.

All went well until she was about three-quarters of the way there. Out of nowhere, a car came from the side and slammed into her broadside, right at the driver's door.

Bri's head swam from the force of the impact. She must've blacked out, because the next thing she knew, she was being dragged from the passenger side of her wrecked car.

She knew there was some reason she needed to keep her purse close. Thoughts fuzzed and cleared and blurred again so quickly, she couldn't remember why.

But she did it. She made a swipe at the strap of her purse and managed to grab hold. She gripped it tightly in her hand, hoping she'd recall why she needed it.

Consciousness came and went. She surfaced once to realize she was being dragged over rough ground. But everything went black again before she could clear her brain enough to think.

The next time cognizance came, Bri was lying on dirt. There were trees overhead, and standing above her was Rasa.

He wore an evil glare and was unfastening his pants. "He took something from me, and now I'm going to take something from him." His grin turned even more wicked and crazed. "But first, I'm going to have a little fun."

Oh God. He was going to rape her before he killed her to get revenge on Erik.

She struggled to regain her wits. To make her body move. To get away.

Her brain was sluggish, and the commands to her limbs were slow. Much too slow to allow her to fight him off.

His pants were hanging open when he reached for her. She kicked out at him, trying to connect with his obvious erection, but the effort was too weak. He caught her foot and jerked her closer to him.

Fear did what she hadn't been able to do on her own. It brought a clarity that had been missing since he'd smashed into her car.

Her purse. Where was her purse?

She became aware of the long leather strap wrapped around her hand and wrist. Bri fought, twisting her body around, pivoting at the point he held her ankle. She made it to her stomach and frantically pulled her purse closer. She wrenched the zipper open and drove her hand into her bag. When the butt of her pistol met her palm and her fingers encircled it, a wave of calm came over her.

Rasa took hold of her other leg and tried to use them to lever her onto her back again. And this time, she let him. As she flipped, her hand slid free. At the same time, she brought it up in front of her and leveled the gun at him.

Undaunted, he dove at her.

She hadn't been ready for that. His fingers found and tightened around hers on the grip as he landed on top of her. Bri knew if she lost her hold on the only weapon she had, she wouldn't make it through this encounter.

They grappled for control of the gun for several tense moments, each flailing and struggling to wrench it from the other.

Suddenly, a loud report echoed through the woods.

Bri expected to feel the burn and pain of being shot. But it never came. Rasa hauled himself off of her to stand a few feet away.

Not sure of what he was planning next, she brought her aim up to center mass. That's when she saw the blood on his arm. He'd been the one to get shot, but not badly enough to end this nightmare. And before she could pull the trigger again, he took off into the trees.

"Fuck!" Bri yelled, which made her head throb with pain. She probably had a concussion. *Asshole!*

Bri searched frantically for her phone to call for help, but it was nowhere to be found. Maybe it had fallen out of her purse in the crash. She stumbled to her feet and started off in the direction she thought the road was. As she drew near the edge of the woods, she saw her mangled car. She hoped it was in there somewhere.

The driver's side was completely destroyed, so Bri had to crawl in through the passenger door. Between her throbbing head and her trembling hands, it took way too damned long to find it, but finally she saw it. It was in that dead-zone of space between the center console and the seat. Carefully, she snaked her fingers underneath and was able to push it out.

Snatching it up and fumbling with the screens, she called Erik.

He picked up on the first ring. "Bri?"

"Help me. He has Kaia."

"What? Tell me where you are."

"On the road to the farm. Rasa has Kaia, Erik. He's going to kill her. I had to come."

"I'm on my way. Don't move."

Only a few minutes later, she watched as a car screech to a halt behind her own car.

"Bri!" Erik's shout reached her.

"I'm here!" She stumbled out of the car, headed in his direction.

As soon as he saw her, he broke into a run.

"Kaia. He's going to—"

"Kaia is fine. She and Mac are together. She's perfectly safe."

Bri couldn't wrap her mind around it. "Wait. What? Are you sure? He called me from her phone. He said he was going to kill her if I didn't meet him at the barn alone. I heard her scream."

"Then it wasn't her. She and Mac are getting ready to head back to the house. After I got off the phone with you, I called Mac first thing. He's been at the barn with Kaia all day, helping to clear out the debris left over from the fire. When I told them what you'd said, they got worried and decided to call it quits for the day. Once they're finished wrapping up, they're headed this way."

The panic in Bri's heart lessened at Erik's assurances. But how could Rasa have called from Kaia's number?

Erik looked at her from head to toe. "What happened to you? Are you hurt?" He pulled at her shirt, trying to raise it up.

That's when she saw the blood on her blouse.

"It's not mine. It's Rasa's. I shot him, but only in the arm."

Her brain must have still been a little woozy, because it took her too long to ask about her daughter.

"Where's Min?"

"She's in the car with Moose." Erik gave her the once-over. "Are you sure you're not hurt?"

Bri brought a hand up to her aching head. "I said I wasn't shot. I didn't say I wasn't hurt. The bastard rammed into my car." She glanced back at her vehicle. The driver's side was caved in to about the middle of the car. "I must have hit my head. It hurts like a bitch, and I'm still a bit loopy."

He opened his mouth to speak, but she cut him off.

"Can the rest please wait until we get home? I need something for my head. And I want Min under cover again."

"No, we cannot." Erik's face was set and hard. "We're going to drop Min and Moose off with Mac and Kaia, and then I'm taking you to the hospital to get checked out. By the looks of that car, you took a really hard hit, and I need to make sure you and our babies are okay."

She was about to respond, but Erik held up a hand.

"Bri. Get in the damned car, so we can go see a doctor."

Bri huffed out a breath but didn't argue about going. "What about my car?"

Erik nodded. "We'll have to leave it here. I'll call Mac back. He can have someone tow it to a body shop. You get into mine, and I'll get what you need out of yours."

Bri nodded and settled into the passenger seat, turning to grin at Min.

"Hey, baby girl."

"Moose go fo' wide." Min beamed up at the dog, whose head was touching the roof of the car.

"I see that. It looks like he's having fun."

Erik, carrying the few personal items from her car, popped the latch on the trunk and dropped them onto the floor. Slamming it closed hard enough to make her ears ring, he pulled the front door open to slide behind the wheel.

Bri reached over to take his hand in hers.

It took him a moment to look over at her. His blue eyes were shadowed with worry and vengeance.

"I'm okay. He tried to hurt me worse, but he didn't. I didn't give him a chance."

He continued to hold on to her hand, but he didn't say anything.

<div align="center">~~~</div>

The health of the babies and a slight concussion confirmed, they arrived back at the house a few hours later. Bri went to check on Min to find her and her ever-faithful guard dog settled in watching her favorite movie.

As Bri came out of the hall, she threw a wish-me-luck glance at Kaia and Mac in the living room as she went to find Erik. They had a few things to work out.

He was waiting for her in the kitchen. He stood at the sink looking out over the back yard. There was a bottle of beer in his hand. She watched as he took a long drink and then set the bottle down.

She went to him and pressed into his back, wrapping her arms around his waist. She laid her cheek on the expanse of his shoulder.

His large hands covered hers and squeezed.

Bri felt him take a deep breath and let it out.

Bri hugged him tighter. "I'm okay. It was a close call, but nothing happened."

Erik turned around quickly. "Damn it, Bri."

She leaned up and kissed him. He didn't respond at first, but she wouldn't let him hold back on her.

Erik grabbed her around the waist and pulled her closer to him. His long, strong arms banded around her. He ended the kiss and just held her, his head tucked into the curve of her neck and shoulder.

"I can't lose you," he whispered.

"You're not going to."

When they were both settled a little more, they went to join Kaia and Mac, so they could hash out the details.

"I still can't believe what happened." Kaia's eyes were heated. "The call came from *my* phone? This phone?" She held up her own cell.

"Yes."

"I bet he spoofed Kaia's number," Mac said, as though

everyone should know what that meant.

But Bri was confused. "What?"

"It's a scam that robocallers and con-artists are using now. It's called neighbor spoofing. It's where they can modify what phone number appears on a caller ID. All Rasa, or anyone else, would have to do is use Kaia's number when he called you."

Kaia looked at him. "I didn't even know that was possible." She shuddered. "It's kind of scary, actually, especially given what's happened."

Mac shifted his gaze back to Bri. "Speaking of which, what exactly *did* happen?"

Bri recounted the accident and the incident in the woods, and when she finished, she looked up at Erik.

He'd not said anything through her explanation and remained silent, his jaw flexing with tension as his eyes glittered savagely. And Bri knew his thoughts would be just as lethal. She was right.

Erik bit out through gritted teeth, "When the time comes, Rasa is fucking *mine*."

~~~

As Rasa sulked somewhere over his wound, more and more days passed.

And it was getting harder and harder for Min to stay sequestered. She just didn't understand why she couldn't go outside or over to Kaia's barn. She'd asked every day to go help Aunt Kaia or to go to the park, but Bri had had to tell her no. She would have liked that herself. Just being outdoors enjoying the nice weather and sunshine would have gone a long way towards settling their minds. But it just wasn't an option. Not now. Not until Rasa was stopped once and for all.

That morning in particular had been the worst so far. Min had been irritable from the moment she'd woken up. She'd
~~~

asked to go see the horses, and Bri had had to disappoint her once again. And ever since, Min had been whiny, and nothing had made her happy.

Not even Moose. So, in an effort to spare the dog's sensitive ears, Bri had told Mac just to go ahead and take him home to play with Duncan for the day.

When she saw her daughter come into the living room dragging her baby along behind her, Bri took a fortifying breath.

"Hey, my love," she greeted in a soothing voice.

"Wanna pway ouside. 'Orsies wide," Min demanded, tears shimmering on her long black lashes.

Bri closed her eyes briefly, asking for strength. When she opened them, Min was on the verge of a full-blown meltdown.

"I'm sorry, sweetie. But we can't today."

The apology had barely passed her lips when Min let loose. Huge, heartbroken sobs racked her little body, and it broke Bri's heart to see her daughter so distraught.

Erik came hurriedly into the room. "Hey, what's going on?" His gazed traveled from Min to Bri.

Bri felt like crying too. She rubbed her hand over her face. "She's upset that she can't go ride Rayna today."

Min was hiccupping now, she was crying so hard. Bri was afraid she was going to make herself sick if this continued.

Erik's phone rang in the middle of the temperamental toddler storm. He looked at the screen and then at Bri. "I'm sorry, it's Mac."

"Go." She waved him off. "Take it. You just might want to find someplace quiet, so you can actually hear him."

Erik nodded, turned, mand headed out through the dining room. Bri heard the sliding door open and close behind him.

She went back to her daughter and knelt down in front of her. "How about Momma gets you some juice? And then, you know what?" Bri made her voice more cheerful. "How about we play with some Play-Doh? Would you like that? We can make a statue for Aunt Kaia and give it to her when she gets home tonight."

With tears still streaming, Min nodded.

"Okay." Bri wiped at the wetness. "You wait here while Momma gets your drink. Then we'll play and have lots of fun."

Min drew in a hitched breath, but she seemed to be a little calmer now. The moldable goo was Kryptonite for Min, and Bri held it in reserve for special occasions. And emergencies. If this didn't qualify, she didn't know what did.

She kissed Min on the forehead, rose, and walked into the kitchen. She was momentarily distracted when she saw Erik out on the deck. He stood tall and handsome in the bright noonday sun, his cell phone up to his ear as he listened to whatever Mac was telling him. His posture seemed stiff. Was Mac imparting some bad news? It had to be about Rasa.

Bri got the juice for Min but didn't go immediately back to the living room. Seeing that Erik was disconnecting the call, she waited for him to come back in, so she could find out what Mac had said.

"What is it?"

"Mac wanted me to know that his men still haven't had any luck tracking the tiger down. We were hoping we'd have found him by now, but he's obviously holed up somewhere. Mac's guys continue to watch the airstrip where the plane is, but there's been no movement, in or out."

"Do you think he'll come here?"

"I would have hoped our warnings had gotten through by now, but I'm not betting on it. He still wants Min, but this isn't about her anymore. This is a pride thing now, and Rasa Chai isn't going to give up until he wins." Erik grinned ruthlessly. "Or dies."

He pulled her into his arms. "Until then, we're going to keep Min safe and wait him out."

"I know." Bri leaned into him. "I'm glad you're here with us."

He smiled down at her. "Me too."

Erik took her mouth in a soft, sweet kiss.

"I'd better get this juice to Min. I'm surprised she hasn't come looking for it yet."

They walked hand in hand back to the living room. But they didn't find Min.

What they saw was the open front door.

The cup fell from Bri's nerveless fingers and juice splashed all over the carpet. "No, no, no!" She ran outside with Erik right behind her. "Min! Min!" she screamed. "Where are you?"

"Go check by the cars," Erik commanded. "I'll go out to the road."

Bri took off running, circling first around her car and then Erik's. She bent down to look underneath them, and even scanned the interior of each vehicle to make sure Min hadn't somehow gotten inside.

"Min!" Bri yelled again.

Erik came jogging back. "I don't see her anywhere."

"Why would she leave the house? She's never done that before. I didn't think she even knew how to open the door."

Bri couldn't control the dread spiking through her system. Where was her daughter?

"Kids see and learn so much more than we think." Erik tried to offer her comfort, but Bri couldn't get past the terror of losing her child. "She probably saw us do it. She's been upset about not getting to go to the barn. Do you think that's where she thought she was going?"

"I don't know." Nothing was making sense. She couldn't think. "Maybe. But she wouldn't know how to get there. Where could she have gone?"

Bri's world was collapsing. She turned in slow circles, searching. Suddenly, she stopped. "We have to call Mac and get everyone out here to help look for her. We have to find her,

Erik. We have to find her before Rasa does.”

“I'll make the call.” He pulled his phone from his pocket.

This can't be real. It has to be a nightmare. Bri cried silently as she made another frantic lap around the house, weaving in and out of the parked cars, just hoping and praying Min had merely been overlooked and was innocently sitting under a shade tree playing in the dirt. Returning to the front of the house, Bri ran her hands through her hair, gripping and pulling it. The reality that her daughter was missing all became too much, and she screamed.

“No!” The hysterical lament poured out of her, dragging all the air from her lungs.

Erik caught her before she made it to her knees. She felt like she would fly into a million pieces, and it was only the strength of this man that was holding her together.

“We have to get out there—we have to look for her.”

“I called Kaia. She's going to shift and cover the woods between the farm and here. I'll do the same from this side. We'll find her, Bri. Mac said he's scouring the traffic cameras nearby to see what he can find. He's also going to need a picture of her for the search and rescue team, and something that she's worn for the dogs. Can you do that?”

Bri nodded. “Yeah. I'll get what he needs. You go. Now. Find her. Bring our baby home.”

Erik kissed her and then he was gone, and Bri was alone.

She stood there unmoving, just staring out, looking for any sign of her daughter. She wanted to run. Run in every direction at once to find her child. But she couldn't seem to move.

Erik was out there looking. If anyone could track Min, it was him and Kaia. Their cats would find her.

She had to hold on to that.

Bri turned and raced for the house. She went straight for the bedroom and found the most recent picture of Min. Going to her little bed, Bri picked up the pillow and stripped the case from it.

She mechanically put each in a zipper-top bag and returned to the driveway. She was still standing there when Mac's cruiser pulled in. She was at his door before he even stopped.

"Did you see anything? Did you find her on the cameras?"

"Where's Erik?" Mac's gaze tracked behind her to the house.

"He and Kaia are still out looking. They're searching the area between here and the farm in case Min tried to find her way there."

Just then, Erik came running back into the yard, followed by Kaia's cougar. Erik came straight to Bri and wrapped his arm around her.

"We didn't find any sign of her. She wasn't out there."

"I think I know where she is." Mac drew all of their attention.

"Where?" Bri cried. "Let's go get her!"

Mac looked down at Kaia. "Let's take this inside. Kaia can shift and dress, and I'll tell you what I found."

The next few moments were excruciatingly long. But soon they were gathered around the table.

"The nearest traffic cam is about a mile from here. It captured an image of the rental car the Lao men have been driving. Rasa could be seen clearly in the front seat." He paused a beat. "According to my calculations, it was shortly after Min went missing, and he was traveling at a high rate of speed."

Bri gasped. "Oh god, no." She turned to Erik. "He has my baby."

"He must have been watching the house." He pulled her into his arms and held her tight as she fell apart at the seams. "When she went outside alone, he saw his chance and took it." Erik's hands rubbed up and down her back and arms. He spoke to Mac over her sobs. "Which way was he going?"

"Next camera to pick him up was to the east. After that, we lost him."

"East is the opposite direction from the airport," Erik noted.

"What the hell is he doing?"

"It doesn't matter." Kaia stood. "We know where he's heading. We have to get there and stop him before he leaves the country with her."

"Just wait." Mac laid a hand on her arm. "The plane is being watched. If it moves, I'll know. But the fact that he's going east makes me wonder. What if the plane we've been watching all this time is just a decoy? What if he has another way to get her back to Laos?"

"Shit," Erik swore.

"Yeah," Mac agreed. "We've been so sure we were a step ahead of him, when all along, he may have had another way out."

Bri's stomach pitched. She felt like she was going to be sick. "What do we do now? How do we get her back?"

Erik placed a finger beneath her chin and lifted her tear-stained face, so she had to look at him. "No matter where she goes, I will bring Min home." He hugged her and whispered into her ear, his vow for her alone. "And then I'll kill him like I did his friend."

As long as this bastard remained alive, he would always be a threat to Min. And everyone else they loved. She pulled out of his arms, held his gaze, and nodded.

"So, how do we track him?" Kaia asked Mac.

"There's a BOLO on the vehicle. And an Amber Alert on Min," Mac said. "Someone will spot them. And when they do, that motherfucker is going *down*."

21

Bri thought the wait would kill her. Sitting here, doing nothing, was going to drive her out of her mind. While Mac paced and talked on his phone, Kaia prowled.

Bri knew her well enough to know that her cat was pushing to be released. When Kaia was upset and agitated, that transferred to the animal side of her. The lioness's answer to that was action. Bri knew all too well how that felt.

Erik continued to hold her, his roped muscles corded around her protectively. She knew he had to be fighting the same urge as Kaia to shift and hunt, but he showed no sign. He stayed right there with her and helped to keep her sane.

She suddenly became aware of a difference in the atmosphere of the room. Behind her, Erik had gone on alert. She looked over her shoulder at him, but he was staring at Mac.

When Bri looked up, Kaia was also watching him intently.

"What is it? What's happened?" Bri's heart set a quick, hard pace.

"We got a lead." Mac slid his phone into his pocket and was already on the move. "We need to go. A woman called the tip line that she thought she'd seen the car parked off 273, near where it runs into I-90. If we leave now, they won't get too far ahead of us."

Erik set Bri on her feet and got to his own. Kai swung around and followed Mac. All conversation paused until they were in Mac's cruiser and flying down the road, lights and sirens blasting.

"She *thought* she saw?" Erik picked up on something Bri had apparently missed in the rush to leave.

"Yeah." Mac glanced at Erik in the rearview mirror then concentrated on the blacktop in front of him. "She said the man matched the description on the Amber Alert, but there was no little girl."

Bri's head spun. *What had he done with Min?*

"Instead," Mac went on, "she said he had some kind of animal with him. She was a little reluctant to say what it was at first, but then she swore it was a baby tiger."

Bri gasped and her hand flew to her mouth. Her eyes went wide, and she looked to Erik in alarm. "What? How is that possible? She's only three."

"Remember what Jayme said?" Erik, beside her in the back seat, tried to soothe her. "Sometimes, when there's danger, the animal side of a shifter will take over. She must have sensed Min's fear and came out to protect her."

"Oh, Erik." Tears flowed freely down Bri's cheeks. "She must be so scared. They're both just babies still."

"Yes." A gleam lit Erik's eye. "But this may be the break we needed, in more ways than one. Hauling a tiger cub around in public is a lot harder to do than a small child. It draws a lot more attention, and people are more apt to report the sighting of a tiger, even if they're not aware a child is missing."

"What if he has more of that drug?" Bri couldn't stand the thought of Min going through the same thing Erik had. "What if he takes her tiger from her like he did your cougar?"

Erik grasped her face and made her look at him. "He could. But, even if he does, we'll get through it. We'll help her through it. Who better to help her than me? I've already been there and came out whole."

He was right. They would get through this. And they would

do whatever Min needed to recover from what was happening to her at Rasa's hands.

Bri leaned into his strength. Taking a deep breath, she drew his resolve deep into her soul and used it to bolster herself up, giving her the power she'd need to finish this. Min needed her.

When she sat up, she nodded at him, ready to do whatever it took to save her baby girl.

Kaia, in the front passenger seat, was busy on her phone—typing and tapping. "If he takes I-90 and continues northwest, he'll have any number of airports he could leave from—smaller, ranch airports to Missoula International."

"Missoula would be too big." Mac shook his head, thinking. "Too much security, especially now that he has an endangered animal with him. The ranch airstrips may be possible, but they're usually privately owned and require permission before you can land there." He glanced over at Kaia. "What else is out that way? We're looking for something mid-sized."

She enlarged and moved the map around. "The only one I see is Seeley Lake."

Mac was nodding before he spoke. "That could be it. Seeley is publicly owned, but it doesn't have a control tower. It's pretty isolated, and just has a couple of runways. It could be just what he needs."

Bri sat silently as Mac made some phone calls.

Kaia turned and reached around the seat to take Bri's hands in hers. "How you holding up, sweetie?"

"I'm not sure," Bri told her honestly. "I'm so terrified, I can't think. I keep wondering what she's going through right now—the trauma she must have suffered for her tiger to emerge two full years early."

She turned teary eyes to her best friend. "If he hurts her in any way..."

"He'll pay for it." Bri saw a bit of the cat in Kaia's green gaze. "He'll pay for everything he's done. To all of us."

Mac hung up. "I was able to get ahold of the manager of Seeley. He told me a small Cessna flew in carrying three men about a few weeks ago, and the plane is still there. Since we haven't seen hide nor hair of the third man, I'm guessing he's the pilot and sticking close to the plane. The manager said they asked about motels nearby. But the most interesting part is that one of them showed up today and asked about gassing it up."

"How long will it take to get there?" Erik checked his watch. "He's got a good jump on us."

Kaia consulted her phone again. "It's two and a half hours. If he has a wild tiger he's dealing with, it could slow him down. We may end up catching him before he gets to the airstrip."

The world outside passed in a blur for Bri. She'd always been one to keep her head through a crisis, but now, having it be her daughter, she was at a loss.

"Hey." Erik's voice was gentle as he turned in his seat and took her chin in his hand. "You have to pull yourself together. Min is going to need you."

Bri knew he was right. Her earlier resolve had faded with the news of the airport, her determination replaced with a heightened fear that Rasa might really get his way this time. But she swallowed it down and beat it back. She had to be strong for her child.

She nodded at him and sat straighter. "I'm all right." Bri took a breath and steeled herself. "What do I need to expect when we find her? I'm assuming she'll still be a tiger. How do I deal with that?"

Erik cupped her face and leaned in to kiss her. "In exactly the same way you would Min—you love her and comfort her. The cub knows you, and she'll know your scent. Even as young as the cub will be, she'll know that you mean safety."

The next two hours were excruciatingly long. Bri didn't think they'd ever pull off the highway to reach their destination.

The sudden silence when Mac cut the sirens had Bri sitting up, taking notice of where they were. She wasn't familiar with the area, so she didn't have any idea of how far out they still were.

Mac saw her come to attention. "We're getting close. I just don't want to give them any warning we're coming."

They'd pored over the satellite images of the area and had made a tentative plan. Mac would stop so Erik and Kaia could get out and approach on foot, or paw, from the cover of a nearby wooded area. Mac would drive in as near as he could and hide the car behind one of the outer buildings. He'd search for Min while the other two took care of Rasa and the pilot.

Bri hated it, but she was to wait with the car for Mac to bring her baby back.

Pedal still to the floor, Mac drove for another half-hour before he flipped the switch to turn off the flashing lights. He slowed and turned onto another road.

Bri could see metal buildings in the distance. A few planes sat parked. *Was Min already boarded on one?*

Mac slowed even further and stopped. He took a pair of binoculars from the glovebox in front of Kaia.

He studied the small airport.

"He's here. I don't see any sign of him or Min, but they're here somewhere." Mac lowered the field-glasses and looked at Kaia and Erik.

"You ready?"

Kaia leaned in to kiss Mac. At the same time, they both said, "Be careful."

As Kaia turned to open her door, Erik drew Bri into his warmth and kissed her. "It ends here. Rasa will no longer be a threat to our family after today." He caught a stray tear on his knuckle.

Bri took a shuddering breath and let it out. "I love you."

"I love you." He lowered his lips to hers again for a short, powerful kiss.

And then he was gone, and Bri was left alone with Mac.

They drove on in silence. Once he'd parked, he turned to where she sat in the back seat.

"We talked about this. I want you to *stay here*. Kaia and Erik will take care of Rasa and the pilot. I'm going to have a look around. I'll locate Min and bring her to you."

Bri nodded her agreement. But as soon as Mac had walked out of sight, she opened the door. She couldn't stay in the cramped confines of the vehicle, so she paced next to the truck and worried.

Were they too late? The car was here, but that didn't mean they still were. Had they taken off with her daughter already? Were they whisking her half a world away as she stood here and did nothing?

Bri was fairly familiar with most of the different kinds of aircraft. She'd flown with her parents numerous times in smaller planes, and she'd done her own fair amount of travel since then. She'd know a Cessna when she saw it.

Edging closer to the corner of the metal wall, her gaze searched the surrounding area. And found what she was looking for sitting off to the right of a hangar not too far away.

Her body started forward before her mind even became aware of the movement. But the emergence of a man out of that hangar drew her to a stop. He was of similar size to Rasa and his clanmate, and his hair was pitch black. Was this the pilot?

She crouched low and watched him.

He seemed to be loading supplies into the plane. Duffels, boxes, a suitcase. This had to be them, and it looked like they were prepping to leave. Within minutes, her daughter could be airborne.

Bri looked around frantically, but she didn't see Erik, Kaia, or Mac. Where were they? The pilot was right there, which meant Rasa had to be nearby too.

The man went back inside. Bri tried to see into the interior of the plane, but the light didn't reach inside. The next time he came out, he carried a mid-sized plastic pet carrier.

Oh, God. Min.

For one terrible second, the sight had her flashing back to the nightmare she'd had not that long ago. The sight of her daughter in a crate had anger boiling to the surface and hatred coursing through her veins.

She'd sworn she wouldn't put herself in danger. She'd promised to let Erik and the others handle this.

But she saw no one.

And her child was locked in a *fucking cage*.

When the man disappeared back into the building a third time, Bri made her move.

Staying concealed as best she could, Bri edged closer.

The guy came out again, carrying more duffle bags. He threw them up into the plane before turning back to the structure.

As soon as the hangar door closed behind him, Bri dashed to the open cockpit. She launched herself into the cramped interior and ducked down.

The little tigress growled and hissed. "Shhh, baby. You have to be quiet. Momma's here, and I'm going to get you out of there, but you have to stay so quiet for me."

Bri pinched the lock to release it. As soon as the wire door was free, the little orange and black striped body came shooting out into her arms. She took a moment to check her over and give her a kiss on the side of her furry face.

Never in her life had Bri held such an animal. To know that it was a part of her daughter was almost unbelievable. But she couldn't deny it—she was absolutely stunning.

"Okay, honey. We have to go now. Can you be still for me? Momma will keep you safe, but you can't make any noise."

Bri adjusted her bundle for a better grip. She didn't know much about tiger cubs, so she couldn't judge how old she might be, but Bri would guess she still weighed a good thirty to forty pounds. Running with an animal that size wasn't going to be easy, but it had to be done. She had to get her baby to safety.

Scooping the cub up into her arms like she would a newborn, Bri slid to the doorway and peeked out. Seeing no one, she dropped to the ground and ran as hard as she could. She was nearing the side of the building when something hit her like a truck from behind.

She flew forward, but ever conscious of her child, she twisted her body, so she'd hit the ground first. The air was knocked from her lungs when she collided with the ground, and she couldn't draw any oxygen—partly due to the fall, and partly because there was a great weight pressing down on her.

She was lying on her side with Min wrapped securely in her arms. When she felt the hot, rancid breath on her cheek and heard the low growls, she knew what had struck her.

One of the large male tigers. She had no idea whether it was Rasa or the pilot.

Not that it mattered. It still meant to kill her. Horribly.

Cautiously, bringing her gaze around, Bri came face to face with huge white fangs. Beyond those were two of the blackest, most deadly eyes she had ever seen. Before she could draw breath to scream, he swiped his razor-sharp claws down the right side of her back. From shoulder to hip, he scored material, flesh, and muscle.

Bri shrieked long and loud as the pain ripped through her. The world dimmed as consciousness waned, only fighting the blackness off through sheer force of will.

Oh, God. She couldn't lay here and get mauled. She had to move. She had to save Min.

But, in shock, her body refused to listen to her brain's command.

He was going to kill her and take Min back to that terrible place if she didn't think of something.

She tucked Min in close to her chest, whispering into her ear. "You have to run, baby. Find Erik or Aunt Kaia. They'll take care of you. Now. Go."

If she could hold the tiger's attention long enough, maybe Min could escape and find safety. She knew Erik, Kaia, and Mac would care for her and raise her.

Bri loosened her grip on her daughter and rolled to her back. She beat at the full-grown cat with all she had, digging her fingers into its throat or any other vulnerable place she could find. If she could reach his eyes, she'd claw them out with her bare hands.

She shouted and cried and begged whatever God was listening to let her child live. To let the babies she carried be kept safe and secure. Her children had to survive and have a good life. That's all that mattered.

Suddenly the big cat was gone. It took Bri a moment to realize her attacker was no longer pinning her to the ground. She looked around and saw the tiger gripped in a life or death battle with a cougar she recognized instantly.

Erik.

Bri scrambled to her feet, gasping as the wounds on her back burned like the hottest fire. She bent double, then dropped to one knee as the pain nearly overwhelmed her. Blood flowed from the gashes, soaking her pants to stream down her leg. As she tried to gain her breath back, she heard a faint chuffing sound. She turned to find her cub cowering a few feet away.

"Come here, baby girl. Momma's got you."

The little cat came running, and Bri scooped her up.

She held her close to her body, shielding her view of the ferocious cats locked in combat.

When all sound ceased behind her, Bri was almost afraid to turn around. Would Erik be lying dead on the ground?

Holding her breath and chancing a quick glance over her shoulder, she saw her valiant protector standing victorious over the body of a very large, very dead tiger. The blood pouring from the cat's neck revealed its throat had been ripped open.

Erik's mountain lion screamed out its rage. Panting heavily from the exertion of the encounter, it turned to where Bri and Min were huddled next to the building. He padded over to them and looked up at her with concern.

"We're good. We're okay. Go help Mac and Kaia. I don't know where they are."

But he didn't leave, and soon Bri became aware of Mac, with Kaia's cougar by his side, making their way towards them.

"Is it over?" Bri split her gaze between the three of them. "Completely over?"

"Yeah." Mac answered, the only one with a mouth to speak. His hand rested on the butt of his pistol. "They're dead."

"Oh, thank God." Bri buried her face in the cub's soft fur.

She lifted her head when she felt Erik's cougar sniffing at her back. He gave a low growl and looked up at Mac.

He got the message and came to her immediately. He gently pulled the shredded fabric away from her wound. She gasped as it tore free where it was stuck to her raw skin.

He leaned back and looked her in the eye. "This is bad, Bri. It needs tended to. Right now."

Bri remembered the searing pain of the nails scoring down her side and back. It throbbed with such force now, it threatened to make her sick. The wetness of her clothes sticking to her only added to the nausea, and she swallowed repeatedly, trying to fight it back. If she thought it hurt now, she could only imagine how bad it would be if she wretched.

"I know. And it will be. But first, you guys need to deal with what's here. You can't just call in the cavalry on this one. I'm assuming there are two dead tigers lying out there, and something needs to be done with them first. I'll be okay for a few more minutes." At least, she hoped she would. "I'll go sit in the truck while you get this straightened out." Mac took some of her weight when she tried to stand. Bri gripped his arm as her head went light.

"Just try not to take too long. I don't want Min here any longer than necessary. I need to get her home."

Mac held her steady until she thought she could walk.

She swayed and nearly blacked out but fought it off. Slowly, she began the arduous trek back to Mac's truck.

Erik followed along behind her until she was safely in the back seat with a squirming Min on her lap. He put his front paws on the door jamb, rose up, and leaned in. He nuzzled her face with his and then did the same to Min's tiny cub.

"Go," Bri told him. "Help Mac. We'll be all right."

He gave her a small hiss.

Bri could guess what he was mad about. "I know. We can discuss my running into danger later."

If a cougar was capable of scowling, that was the look he was giving her. He watched her broodingly, not going anywhere.

Bri leaned her head back against the seat. "If you're not going to leave, then at least go find your clothes and come back to us, so we can talk."

The cougar finally moved off.

Her back was throbbing with every beat of her heart, making her woozy. But she had her child in her arms again, so all was right with the world. She buried her nose in the scruff just behind the perfect pointed ear.

"I love you so much, my Min. Momma is here, and those bad men will never come near you again. Erik..." Bri stopped herself. "No, sweet girl. He's your Daddy in every way that could possibly matter. He loves you so much, do you know that?" Bri stroked her hand over the soft fur. "Daddy, Aunt Kaia, and Uncle Mac made the mean people go away. You won't ever have to worry about them coming near us again."

The tiger cub looked up at her, and Bri saw Min's dark eyes staring back, even down to the birthmark. They held each other's gazes for several moments until the body in her arms shifted and changed. As the tiger cub receded, Min settled into her lap.

"Momma?" Her voice was whisper soft and filled with fear.

Bri held her tighter. "I'm right here, sweetie. I am so proud of you. You were so brave."

"Min kitty."

"Yes," Bri gave a short laugh. "Min's kitty woke up and protected you. She is a very courageous and smart kitty."

Just then, Erik returned. He grinned at Min. "Hey there, short stuff. How ya doing?" He removed the shirt he'd just put on to cover her, smoothing her hair back away from her face. "You had quite the adventure, didn't you?"

"Min kitty," she repeated for Erik.

"I know, I saw her. She's very strong and smart. Just like you."

"Daddy fight bad men?"

Erik drew in a sharp breath. Bri knew it was the first time Min had called him that. The sudden emotion swirling in his blue eyes told her just how much that meant to him.

"Yeah." His voice was choked up. "Daddy fought the bad guys. And for you and your momma, I always will."

Bri was shocked when the air went alive with the sound of sirens. "What the hell?"

They both watched in confused horror as emergency vehicles of all kinds came roaring into the airstrip.

"Why are they here? Who called them?" Bri looked at Erik in panic.

"I don't know." Erik turned to follow the progress of the firetrucks, police cars, and ambulances.

They were still staring in alarm when Mac came striding towards them with EMT's at his side.

"This woman's been injured. She has severe claw marks down her back from the escaped tigers."

Escaped tigers? Bri sent Mac a questioning look, and he nodded at her to play along.

"Is the child injured?" one asked her.

"Um, no. She's just scared." Bri gazed down at Min.

"Can you give her to someone else to hold, so we can check you out, please?" the same medic requested.

Erik reached in and took Min out of her hands.

The first responder assisted her out of the vehicle and guided her to sit on the gurney they'd rolled close to Mac's truck. As they assessed her, Mac filled the First Responders in on what had happened.

But Bri knew it was for hers and Erik's benefit as well.

He spun a story about two tigers having escaped from some private collector in the area. Once she'd advised the paramedics of her pregnancy, Bri stopped listening, enjoying the relief the anesthesia brought with it.

Her respite was cut short though when the medic informed them she'd need to be transported to the nearest hospital for further evaluation and treatment. She'd been tackled to the ground quite severely by the heavy cat, and she'd experienced major blood loss. The gashes in her back were going to require several stitches, and she needed an ultrasound to make sure the babies hadn't suffered any trauma from everything their momma had gone through.

She didn't fuss at all about going. She could handle the rest, as long as she knew her babies were okay.

And leaving the site of so much carnage would go a long way towards relieving Bri's mind. She needed some separation and distance from the horrors of the day, and she was finally starting to breathe easier knowing that Mac's account had been recorded and the bodies of the tigers taken away.

Feeling no pain, Bri dozed for most of the ride, and the next few hours passed in kind a blur of sterile white lights, beeping equipment, and the haze of painkillers. But by the time she was released to go home, Bri knew that her babies were healthy and secure in her womb, and Min was unhurt physically. Any mental trauma would have to be watched for and dealt with if it arose.

But overall, everyone was whole and happy to be going home, so they could finally begin their lives together.

22

A few weeks later, they were on their way to Asia.

Bri had chartered a large jet to hold the contingent of mountain lion shifters that were making the journey with them. Erik pulled his thoughts away from what was to come to glance around the plane at the people assembled.

Bri and Min were seated next to him, and Mac and Kaia were across the aisle. Erik's Uncle Phillip, the leader of their clan, and his second in command, Thomas, were sitting behind him, speaking quietly. And scattered throughout the remaining seats were men and women from his squad—Hank, Paul, Theo, Garrick, Meg, Danielle, and Cutler.

They were on their way to Lanzhou, China to meet with the members of the leading clan that oversaw all of the tiger clans in Asia. There, they would sit down and discuss the situation with the Laos clan. It hadn't taken much talking to convince those here to come. They'd all been horrified to discover what had gone down in Montana and what was continuing to happen in Laos.

Uncle Phillip had immediately requested a meeting. It seemed to take forever to get a response, but eventually it had come.

And now, here they were, winging a half a world away.

Bri and Mac would have to stay back at the hotel with Min when the others went to attend the meeting. Being a shifter matter, only shifters were allowed entrance. Bri wasn't happy—she wanted to add her argument for action against the others—but she understood. She knew Erik wouldn't stop until something was done about the Lao tigers and their practices.

"Daddy, wook! Cwouds!" Min's excited voice drew him out of his thoughts. She was up on her knees, face plastered to the window.

Erik grinned at her and remembered the first time she'd called him that. It had been right after he'd killed Rasa Chai. It had taken his breath and left him reeling. His heart had fallen at her dirty little feet, smoothing out the hard edges the fight had left him with.

The sound of it still made his heart stammer and swell with love.

"I see, baby girl. Aren't they pretty?"

"Pwetty cwouds."

Min kept them entertained for the first several hours of the flight. About hour six, she fell asleep in Bri's arms. Erik helped her to lay Min across a couple of seats and took the blanket Bri had packed to cover her with it.

Once she was settled, they returned to their seats. "You doing okay?" Erik pulled Bri close into his side and wrapped his arm around her shoulders.

"Yeah." She nuzzled his neck, and when she gazed up at him, he kissed her.

He loved her eyes. They were an amber the exact same color as his cougar's coat. He secretly hoped the babies she carried would have her eyes.

"How's your back?"

"It's good. Itches mostly, which is annoying as hell. But no pain at all." She laughed lightly. "Top that with not having morning sickness anymore, and I'm a happy camper."

He kissed her again. "Do you know this area we're going to?"

"Some, but not well."

"You're sure this place you have us staying has enough room for all of us?"

She smiled up at him. "Plenty. I reserved the two penthouse floors. There are two suites per floor—one with two bedrooms, and one with four."

His thoughts turned again to the reason for their visit.

"Thank you for understanding about the meeting. I wish you could be there to add your account to ours, but that's just not how it's done."

"It's fine, Erik, really. Of course I wish I could be there too, but I get it." Her expression turned pensive. "You don't think they'll say anything about us raising Min, do you?"

"I don't care if they like it or not. She's ours, and she's *staying* ours."

"I know. But I just want to be ready if we're going to have another fight on our hands."

"Uncle Phillip didn't mention them being concerned when he talked to them, so I guess we'll just have to wait and see what they say."

Bri nodded and dropped the subject.

The rest of the trip continued uneventfully. After spending more than half a day in the air and being severely jetlagged, they went straight to the hotel and checked in. Since their meeting was set for the following morning, they decided to stay in and rest up.

Gathering in the larger four-bedroom suite, they ordered authentic Chinese food, marveling at the differences between the real thing and the food served back home.

The tone was light and the atmosphere relaxed, but Erik could tell Bri was still nervous—worried for her child, and concerned for the girls that had been so wrongly imprisoned for who knew how long.

He would have felt better if she could have joined him, as he knew it would ease her own peace of mind. He just hoped when he returned, he had good news for everyone involved.

The next morning brought with it clouds and the threat of rain. Bri hoped it wasn't a foreboding of what was to come from their meeting. She hoped the leading clan of tiger shifters would listen and take care of what was happening within the smaller Indochinese Tiger clan. Those girls and women were desperate and needed someone to step in and help them.

Rasa's mother needed to be put down and a new Alpha appointed in her place. One who would have the best interests of the entire clan in mind when figuring out how best to bring their numbers back. Someone who would be more open-minded and respectful of human life.

That was their goal today. To find solutions, as well as salvations.

Bri, Erik, Min, Kaia, and Mac shared one of the two-bedroom suites. They gathered around the table for breakfast before Kaia and Erik had to leave with the others.

"How long do you think it'll take?" Kaia asked.

"A while I'd guess, but it's hard to say," Erik told her. "I've never been involved with anything like this. As leader of our clan, Uncle Phillip will do most of the talking. The rest of us will be there to give evidence and represent our intent—that if they don't do something to resolve this, we will."

"Let's just hope they listen, and it doesn't come to that." That's all Bri could ask for.

All too soon, there was a knock on the door, and it was time to go. Erik hugged Min first and kissed her until she giggled to be put down.

Bri walked into his arms and wrapped hers around his middle. She was anxious. They were walking into a literal tiger's den. "I'm expecting a full account when you get back."

"You'll get it. I promise."

"I love you." She rose up on her toes to kiss him. "Please be careful."

"I will. I love you too."

The door closed behind them and they were gone. Bri didn't know what to do with herself. How was she going to occupy the coming hours until they returned with news?

"What do you say," Mac interrupted her worry, "we take Min out for a walk? Maybe we can find a park or something? We can't stay cooped up in here all day, or we'll both go crazy. Plus, this will give me some practice for when my little one gets here."

He was right. She needed something to distract her from dwelling on the meeting all day. She smiled. "I think that's a perfect idea. And knock yourself out."

The next half hour was spent getting everything they'd need ready. Small snacks and drinks from the minibar were loaded into Min's diaper bag. Then both girl and bag were strapped into the stroller, and off they went.

The weather was fair for being overcast. Not too chilly or too hot.

They stopped at the concierge desk to ask about a nearby park and were told there was one about five blocks away.

The three of them exited the hotel and turned in the direction of the park, finding it with no problems. Children ran and played and had a good time. Min was becoming quite the social butterfly and made friends easily.

Bri and Mac sat on a nearby bench and watched her play. If either of them were watching the time, neither said anything. They talked and chatted about different things, getting to really know each other for the first time. Though they'd gone to school together, Bri had held everyone except Kaia at arm's length for all those years.

She discovered, surprisingly, that she and Mac had a lot in

common. Their taste in music leaned more towards classic rock than pop. Both had an interest in baseball and coincidentally liked the same team. They talked sports for quite a while, debating the value of the bullpen and who needed to go.

They had a good time, and while they talked easily and kept the topics light, she knew in the back of their minds, they were still counting down the minutes and wondering how the meeting was going.

They'd been at the park for about three hours when Mac and Bri's phones went off. Bri pulled hers from her pocket and looked at the screen.

On our way back, was all it said.

She looked at Mac. He showed her his screen. Kaia's note hadn't given any more details either.

"That didn't take as long as I expected. Do you think that means good news, or bad news?" Bri looked up into Mac's face, trying to read his expression.

Mac shrugged. "I could see it going either way, so I really don't have any idea."

They pulled Min from the slide and buckled her back into her stroller. She'd played so hard and for so long, she didn't put up much of a fight. And about halfway back to the hotel, she fell asleep.

Bri and Mac beat the others back naturally, so she spent some time tucking Min into her little cot and closed the door to the bedroom.

Mac had made them something to drink while they waited for the others to arrive.

It was another thirty minutes before the door opened and Erik and Kaia walked in. They both had smiles on their faces.

"Well?" Bri demanded.

"They're stepping in," Erik announced. "They were appalled when Uncle Phillip told them the extent of what the Lao clan was doing. They're going to send someone out to deal with Mrs.

Chai and her cronies right away."

Erik came to her and drew her in. "They apologized for all the trouble we've had with the miscreant clan and confirmed Min's adoption is both valid and legal. They wished us well with our family and a long and happy life together with Min. She's ours."

Bri was almost in shock. "They didn't have any objections specifically to cougars raising a tiger?" That had been her biggest fear all along—that they would expect her to give Min back to the clan, because she needed to be with her own kind.

"Only that we make sure she knows of her heritage. And one day, they hope she'll come back to visit."

Bri felt lightheaded from so much weight suddenly being lifted from her shoulders. "Oh, god. I can't believe this. It's over. It's finally over."

"It sure is." At Kaia's words, Bri looked back over her shoulder to find her best friend standing in the circle of Mac's arms, beaming. "I say we throw a party to celebrate. A big ass BBQ."

"Better yet..." Erik drew her attention back. He had a sparkle in his eye. "What do you say to a wedding?"

He reached into his pocket. As his hand slid free of it, he dropped to one knee. He gazed up into her eyes, and in him, she saw love and happiness and trust. Commitment and home. Family.

"Abrianna Elizabetta Calladega, we haven't known each other long, and we've gone about things kind of out of sequence, but I cannot see a future without you in it. You are the other half to my soul that I didn't know was missing. You are the first person I want to see when I wake up and the last when I close my eyes at night."

There was a slight hitch to his breathing, but he went on. "You not only made my life amazing by just coming into it, but you've brought with you a little girl that I fell in love with almost before I did you."

Bri gave a short laugh, because it was true. And she was okay with that.

"And now we have these two new babies to add to our family." He laid a gentle hand on her belly. "I want to spend the rest of my days with you and this wild and crazy brood we're making. Will you do me the honor of marrying me?"

"Yes, yes, yes!" Bri laughed as the happiest tears she'd ever cried rolled down her face. Her daughter was safe, they were expanding their family in just a few short months, and she was going to marry the most amazing man and father she ever could have hoped or wished for.

Life truly couldn't get any better than this.

~~~

They ended up holding off on the wedding for another two weeks, and in the meantime returned back to the States. That gave his family time to make arrangements for travel and accommodations. And for Bri and Kaia to shop and plan.

The night before the big day, Erik had been banished to the hotel where his entire family was staying. He was not to see Bri until she walked down the aisle.

Lying in bed as the sun came up, he missed the feeling of Bri's body next to his. He missed resting his hands on her growing belly and his babies moving and rolling around underneath them. He couldn't wait to see them.

He'd met her parents for the first time the day before. They'd flown in from some foreign country they'd been visiting and had descended on them.

After having heard how she'd grown up, Erik had been ready to dislike them. But after just the first five minutes, his prejudice had fallen away. They weren't bad people. It was like Bri had said—they just hadn't known any better when it came
~~~

to raising a child.

Thankfully, Bri was the opposite of them. Erik knew that she would have a very large, very positive presence in their children's lives, just as he would. They wouldn't grow up feeling afraid or unsure. When monsters in the dark needed hunting, Erik and Bri would be there to slay them. Together.

And as Min and the twins grew, they would give them the tools they needed to slay the monsters themselves. He had no doubt their kids would be strong, independent, and know how to face their problems head-on.

A knock on his door roused him from his thoughts. Erik rolled to the side of the bed and threw his sweats on.

He'd no sooner turned the doorknob than the door was pushed wide. All three of his brothers shoved in.

Zane, the oldest at thirty-seven and the ring leader, cuffed him up side of the head. "Ready for today, runt?"

Erik hated the nickname he'd been given at birth. Zane had been ten years old when he'd come along. He'd taken one look at Erik's six-pound baby body and christened him *runt*. It didn't matter that he'd outgrown nearly all of them. The name had just stuck.

Rubbing his assaulted head, he glared at Zane. "Who invited *you* in here?"

"Don't need an invite." Zane grinned, unrepentant.

Liam, thirty-one and next in line, made himself at home on Erik's bed, stretching out and commandeering his pillow.

Erik scowled at him and slapped his feet. "Comfy?"

"Yes, actually. These two idiots woke me up way too early. I'm tired."

Liam had always been the laziest of the bunch—always skirting out on the chores their parents had given them and bargaining with his brothers to do them instead while he lounged somewhere daydreaming.

Josh was the middle child. Twenty-nine and the only one

fully settled. He'd married his high school sweetheart soon after they'd graduated, and in the last ten years, had given their parents four grandchildren. The next generation of Reid shifters.

Erik looked at them all. They may drive him nuts most days, but they were family and he loved them. And he was glad they were here.

With his brothers to keep him busy, the morning flew by and before he knew it, Erik was standing alone in front of a full-length mirror in a black tuxedo.

When the door to his room opened again, he thought his brothers had come back to rib him one final time. Instead, he turned to see his mom in the doorway. There were tears in her eyes.

"My sweet baby boy." She came the rest of the way in, brushed non-existent lint from his lapel, and straightened his tie that was already straight.

Moisture shimmered on her dark lashes when she finally raised her gaze. She was so tall, she nearly looked him in the eye. His mom, Simone Reid, was five feet ten like Jayme. She was a strong woman and shifter. She'd had to be to ride herd on five stubborn, active kids and turn them into confident, independent adults.

"Mom." Erik reached up and caught a tear that had fallen from her lash. "Why are you crying?"

She sniffled. "I think I'm entitled. You're getting married today." She checked him over head to toe. "And you look so handsome." Long, thin fingers ran through his hair and smoothed it down. "A lot like your daddy did on our wedding day. So tall and proud and ready for anything."

"Little did he know, huh?" Erik teased her. It was a long-running joke in their family that his dad hadn't really known what he was getting into when he'd stepped up to the altar that day.

"So, I kept my more…head-strong tendencies to myself for a while." Simone grinned at the memory. "He learned to love me in spite of it."

Erik laughed. "He didn't really have a choice though, did he?"

"No, but that was ages ago. He's forgiven me for the lapse."

"I'm just glad I know all there is to know about Bri. And she knows all about me."

His mother looked at him piteously and patted his cheek. "Oh honey, it's so sweet that you think so. I hate to break it to you, but you will *never* know all there is to know about women. Let alone, your wife. She will surprise you on a daily basis for the rest of your life."

Erik thought about it and decided he was actually looking forward to that.

"I just hope Bri and I have the same kind of relationship you and Dad have."

"Communication and compromise are the secrets to a happy marriage. Remember that, and you'll be fine."

She reached for the square box she'd set on the table when she'd come in. It looked to be about eight inches long by eight inches wide.

"I wanted a moment alone with you to give you something." She paused and gazed down at the gift in her hands. "I gave Josh his on the day he married, and I'll do it for each of you as you find your mates. Just before each of you were born, I searched for and found something special that was meant just for you. Just for the baby I carried. And then, when you were born, I wrote a letter to the adult I hoped you'd become. I took both of those and set them aside for the right time."

She handed it to him. "Please wait to open it until tonight when you and your beautiful new wife are alone."

Simone leaned in and kissed him on the cheek, lingering to hold him close for a moment. "I love you, my baby boy."

Tightness almost clogged his throat. "I love you too, Mom."

She kissed him again and then turned and left.

Erik stared at the gift his mother had given him. It was such a special thing she had done for her children. Something they all would treasure for the rest of their lives. He wanted to continue that with his own children. He'd start with Min, the daughter of his heart. He hadn't been there when she'd been conceived or born, but he would be there for her for the rest of his life.

As soon as it was possible, he'd sit down and write his feelings out and then go find something meaningful that he would be able to give her on her wedding day.

He set his own gift aside to finish getting ready to marry the woman of his dreams.

23

Across town, Bri stood before her own mirror. She stared at her reflection, still amazed that the day was finally here. She was getting married.

The dress she'd found on a shopping trip with Kaia was perfect. Simple, yet elegant.

A strapless, long white silk sheath hugged her expanding curves and just brushed the ground. Hand-sewn flowers had been stitched intricately around the hem, and the white thread was barely visible on the delicate fabric, but when noticed it was exquisite. The moment she'd seen it, it had reminded her of the field where she, Min, and Erik had had their first picnic.

Her long blonde hair was upswept with soft tendrils escaping to float gently against the sides of her face. Secured to the back of her head by a hair-comb borrowed from Kaia, was a mid-length veil that had the same floral design at its edges.

"Oh, Abrianna. You look so beautiful." Amanda Huxley-Calladega stepped into the room to see her daughter.

Bri turned and smiled at her. "Hi, Mom."

Amanda came to her, lovingly touched her growing baby bump, and then her cheek. "Where did all the years go?" She adjusted the way her veil draped over her shoulder.

"Are you sure you wouldn't have rather done this more formally? Or invited more of our friends? There are so many who would have loved to see—"

Bri grinned to herself. Her mother would never change. Always had to be *on*. Had to be a Huxley-Calladega.

Bri stopped her before she could finish. "I am so sure, Mom. This is exactly right for me."

Amanda drew in a breath and let it out. "It is, isn't it? You only ever tolerated our lifestyle, didn't you? I could never understand why, but I love you dearly."

"I know." Bri smiled softly. "I love you too."

"Don't tell him I told you," her mom leaned in and lowered her voice, "but your dad is having a hard time with you getting married. It's killing him that his baby girl has another man in her life now."

Tears sprung to Bri's eyes. "He'll always be my first love. I'll make sure he knows that."

They shared a sentimental moment, and then blinked furiously so as not to ruin their makeup.

"Now, where is that granddaughter of mine?" Amanda demanded.

Bri chuckled. "She's with Kaia and Jayme. They're getting dressed in the other room."

"I think I'll go see how it's going."

Before leaving, Amanda pulled Bri into her arms and hugged her tight. "I love you, sweetheart. My wish for you is that you be so very happy."

"I am, Momma. I am."

Her mother drew a tissue from somewhere and blotted gently at her eyes and nose. "So beautiful."

Bri faced the mirror again for one last inspection. It was all perfect. She was ready. When she walked out of her bedroom, her parents, Kaia, and Min were there waiting.

"You look amazing," Kaia gushed. "You were right. It's perfect."

"Yours too. I really do love that color on you, Kai."

On their shopping expedition to find dresses, they'd seen a

gown that closely resembled Bri's. The lines and design were very similar. The color, though, was a deep burnished amber that accentuated her creamy skin and tawny hair.

Bri gazed down at her daughter and bent to her height. "And don't you look very pretty. Do you like your dress too?"

Min twirled in a circle to make the long white skirt float around her. Everyone laughed at her innocence and joy.

It was a knee-length white sleeveless smocked dress. Bri had fallen instantly in love with it. She'd matched it with little white sandals, and Min's hair was held back away from her face by white barrettes on either side.

"We getting mawwied."

Bri's heart swelled. "We sure are, baby girl. How about we leave, so we can go get our guy?"

"Daddy!" Min bounced on her toes.

Bri picked Min up into her arms, held aloft on her hip. "Let's go."

Bri's dad drove them to the clearing. Cars filled the lot nearby.

Bri thought she'd be nervous, but there was nothing except happiness and anticipation. She was calm and confident, having found that one man in a million who would love her and stand by her side through life. He'd be the most amazing father to however many children they had.

A white lace runner had been laid on the ground to mark the path she'd take to the man she loved.

With one last kiss, her mom went to find her seat. When the music began, Jayme, Kaia, and then Min walked out ahead of her.

Her dad, Bertram—never Bert—Calladega, grasped her arm and turned her to face him.

"Are you happy, Abrianna?" His face was set and serious.

"I am, Dad. He makes me so very happy. He loves me, and he loves Min." Bri remembered what her mom had said. She leaned up to give her dad a kiss on the cheek. "But he'll never replace you."

He eyed her carefully. "Your mom said something, didn't she?"

"Yeah," Bri reluctantly admitted with a grin. "But it's the truth. You'll forever be the first man I ever loved."

He kissed her softly on the forehead.

Bri took a deep breath and let it out. On her father's arm, she started down the aisle.

Her gaze found Erik's across the meadow. She saw his eyes go wide at the sight of her, and a slow smile spread across his face.

When she finally reached his side, he mouthed to her, "You look so beautiful."

They'd opted to keep the ceremony traditional and short. They exchanged "I do's" and rings before everyone they loved. When the Priest said to kiss the bride, cheers rose.

The rest of the day flew by, but Bri took it all in, recording every moment into her memory. She wanted to remember this day for the rest of her life.

~~~

He carried her over the threshold of their hotel suite.

Erik was happier than he ever thought possible. He'd found the woman of his dreams, a daughter he adored to the deepest places in his heart, and two beautiful babies on the way. His life was the best it could possibly be.

When he'd seen Bri walking down the aisle towards him, his heart had stopped. She was so stunning it had taken his breath away. And in front of everyone he loved, he'd said his vows to her and bound his life to hers for the rest of eternity.

Closing the door with his foot, Erik carried her to the middle of the room and set her down.
~~~

"Wait right here," he told her and then crossed the room to the sound system.

Finding the right music, he returned to her and took her hand in his.

"Will you dance with me, Mrs. Reid?"

"Of course, Mr. Reid." She flowed into his arms, and to the soft sounds of John Legend's All of Me, they swayed and gazed into each other's eyes.

"Have I told you I love you?" Erik couldn't hold the words back. What he felt for her just swelled and exploded out of him.

"Not in the last fifteen minutes. I thought you'd changed your mind," she teased him.

"Never in this lifetime." He leaned in and kissed her deeply.

Passion took hold of both of them. Erik found the long zipper at the back of her dress and slowly lowered it. As it loosened from around her torso, it slid down her body to puddle at their feet. Finding the warm skin of her back, he spread his fingers wide to take in as much of her as he could.

Still slowly dancing together, he reached up and pulled the pins from her hair that held her veil in place. It too fell to the floor. She wore nothing now but white panties and heels. Her long blonde hair had tumbled down around her shoulders, and she looked exquisite.

With her breasts pressed tightly against his chest, Erik kissed along her neck and across her shoulder. He loved the feel of her silky-smooth skin. He wanted to touch and taste all of her at once. Running his hands down and over her hips, he dragged the last scrap of material out of the way.

He danced her closer to the bed, never losing contact with her. When they stood beside it, he laid her back on top of the duvet. While she lay ready for him, Erik stripped out of his tux with sure and efficient movements.

Her gaze followed every move his hands made. Each bit of his body he revealed drew her rapt attention. She licked those gloriously full lips of hers like she couldn't wait to taste him either. Erik's erection was hard and throbbing. Released from the confines of his pants, it sprang forward.

Bri came up to her knees facing him. She edged closer to the end of the bed and took him in hand, squeezing firmly.

Fuck. Her hands on him felt amazing.

Sliding his own hand down her rounded stomach, he found her wet channel. Dipping his fingers in and out, she moaned in time with his rhythm.

"I want you inside me so badly," Bri breathed.

Who was he to refuse his gorgeous wife?

Wife.

This incredible woman in his arms was his *wife.* The other half of himself. His soulmate, his heart, his life.

Erik crawled onto the bed and took her underneath him. Her legs opened automatically, making room to fit him. With one smooth, powerful thrust, he filled her. She cried out and her hot, slick sheath bore down on him like a vice.

Making love to her was beyond anything he'd ever experienced. Ever since that first night, he'd been lost to this woman. The feel of her, the scent of her, the taste of her, all had settled deep inside of him and made him crave her every minute of every day.

He pulled slowly out of her tight body, letting the walls of her sex pull and drag at his length, fighting his withdrawal and sucking him back to her. He pushed into her again and felt the constriction of her body around his. Out to the very tip of his shaft. And then all the way back home.

She was burning him alive. From top to bottom, her core was scorching and bathing him in her own sweet nectar.

The slow tempo was taking her higher, and her body wouldn't remain still under his. Her hips were undulating, a silent plea for more. Blonde hair spread across the pillows to tangle under her thrashing head.

"Erik. Please. Please. Faster. Harder." She groaned with every thrust, the sound tantalizing and spurring his own desire for her.

He wanted to work her and hold her on that precipice for even longer, but his own body was giving him signs of impending eruption.

Soon, he couldn't ignore the need to take her. He drew back his hips and pounded into her once, twice, and on the third, she shattered. Calling out, Bri rode the wave of orgasm. Over and over her inner walls clamped down around him, squeezing him almost to the point of pain. Heaven or hell, he didn't want it to stop.

He continued to thrust into her until he exploded into her, her lingering aftershocks fueling his own.

After, they both lay quiet and sated.

Erik, contented for the moment, looked forward to many, many days, months, and years of making love to his incredible wife.

"Happy honeymoon, wife."

Bri giggled. "Happy honeymoon, husband."

~~~

The next morning, Erik remembered the gift his mother had given him. He rose early to retrieve it from where he'd stowed it in his overnight bag.

"Where are you going?" Bri's sleepy voice asked from the rumpled sheets.

"Just to grab this." Box in hand, Erik returned to the warm cocoon of his marriage bed.

Bri sat up next to him. "What is that?"

He repeated the story of what his mom had told him.

"That is so sweet and thoughtful."

Erik broke the tape holding the box closed. He removed the
~~~

lid and pushed it back out of the way. Sitting right on top was a folded sheet of paper—the letter his mom had written. He lifted it and set it aside to read in a minute. Balancing the box on his lap, he began to dig through the tissue paper filling the interior.

His hand brushed something hard. Sorting through the folds of wrapping, he found what must be the edge of the item inside.

Pulling it free, he saw that it was an intricate wooden carving of a mountain lion. As inch by inch was revealed, he gasped at the detail that had gone into the piece. Once the base cleared the cardboard, Bri took the empty container and set it aside.

"It's beautiful," she whispered.

It truly was. Erik tipped the statue this way and that to admire the complexity of such fine craftsmanship. It was about seven inches tall. The big male was perched, standing on a tree stump, looking out into the distance. His eyes were fierce and ready for battle. For at the base of the tree was a female with cubs.

Cougars were solitary creatures, so this scene would never occur in the wild. But as a shifter, Erik's mother had known that someday he would have a family, and he would protect them and stand as their guard against all the evils of the world.

Erik handed the statue to Bri and picked up the letter. Unfolding it, he began to silently read.

My dearest son,

As I write this, you are sleeping a few feet away. To see you now, to see how small and vulnerable you are, it's hard to believe that in a few short years, you will be a grown man.

From the moment of your birth, I've sensed a strong will in you. As I have one of my own, I imagine you and I will clash a time or two.

I know that strength of character will mold you into the man you will become. You will be loyal and brave, and stand for those you love, just as the mountain lion does in the carving. As soon as I saw it, I knew it had to be yours. I see in him what I see in you—a devoted mate and father. One who will place the wellbeing of those in his care over that of his own.

As you begin to stir in your cradle, the life I wish for you is one free of heartache and strife. I know that's a lot to hope for, but no parent wants to see their child hurting. I dream for you a life filled with many years of love and laughter and happiness.

I can't wait to see the man you will become someday (as long as we both make it through your teenaged years).

I love you, my sweet boy. Be well, be safe, be happy. That's all I can ask.

You will forever be in my heart.

Love, Mom

Erik gave an emotion-filled chuckle, because there *had* been a few years where it was touch-and-go.

He refolded the letter slowly and then turned to Bri. She'd sat quietly as he'd read his mother's words.

"Are you okay?" she asked him. There was no mistaking the moisture in his eyes.

"Yeah, I'm good." He held the paper out to her. "Would you like to read it?"

Bri shook her head as she leaned into his side and held him. "No, baby. That's between you and your mom, and I can see it means a lot to you."

"It does. She had me nailed, even though I was an infant when she wrote this."

"That doesn't surprise me. Moms are pretty good at knowing their kids."

Erik looked down at the woman in his arms and back to the carving now lying nestled in the folds of the comforter. He thought of Min and the children he would share with Bri, and emotion surged hard once again.

His mother's dream for him had come true.

~~~

A few weeks later, married and freshly moved into their new home, Bri threw the last empty cardboard box in the pile with all the others. Her husband...her thoughts skidded to a stop. Wow, it was still weird to believe she was married, Bri thought with a laugh.

Bri Reid.

It had a good ring to it. And soon Min would become Min Reid, as Erik had plans of adopting her. His name would be forever on her birth certificate. He would be her father and it would be official. They would be a family.

A family in a home they loved. Bri looked around.

It was big enough to hold their growing brood. It backed up to the Lost Creek State Park, and they'd fallen in love with the airy, open layout—perfect for rambunctious cats to rough-house and play.

It had so many windows, it was almost as if there were no barrier to the beautiful view beyond. The warm September sun beamed through and lit every corner.

As she stood in the middle of the living room soaking up the bright rays, she ran her hands over the bump of her stomach. She was four months along now and could feel the babies kicking and bumping and jockeying for position.

Finding out there were two in there had come as a huge shock, to say the least. But once the news had sunk in, Bri couldn't have been happier. Erik, on the other hand, had taken a little longer to adjust. She laughed to herself, remembering. There had been a few sleepless nights on his part until he'd finally come to terms with having three kids under four years old.

He was all in now and talking baby names with her each
~~~

night.

Through the large glass panels, Bri could see him and Min out in the yard. They ran and tumbled and played in the late summer sun. She could hear Min's riotous giggles ringing in the air.

Their daughter had come out the other side of her abduction with no lasting effects. Her tigress hadn't made another appearance. Erik, in talking with his mom, had come to the conclusion that she'd gone back to sleep until it was time for her to emerge for good when Min was five.

Min was happy and healthy and loving life.

And so was her Momma.

Bri laughed out loud as Erik swooped Min up and ran for the house with her. They came barreling in, both panting and sweaty.

"Since you got her all dirty," Bri pointed in the general direction of Min's room, "you can give her a bath while I take my shower. We have to leave soon to make Jayme's graduation."

Forty-five minutes later, they were ready to go. The drive passed quickly, and when they pulled into the parking lot, Bri recognized quite a few cars. The clan had come back to Montana in droves to congratulate Jayme on accomplishing her life-long dream. And of course, to celebrate.

The ceremony was taking place outside, and there were chairs lined up for all the guests. Parents, cousins, aunts, and uncles were spread out over the green lawns, some sitting, some standing. Bri and Erik made their way over to them and saw that Kaia and Mac had already found their seats.

Once off her feet, Bri looked around at the faces in the crowd, to those she now called family. She never would have thought her life would turn out this way. She had a man she loved, she was a mother, and she was a part-time photojournalist with a showing of her work scheduled for two months from now.

Having a home and family and a man she adored more every

day had never been on her radar. But life had unexpectedly gifted her all the things she never knew she wanted.

~~~

Bri was in labor.

And had been for the last few hours but hadn't said anything to Erik. The contractions had started that morning but hadn't been very consistent. The time between ranged from five minutes to fifteen or twenty. She figured until they were coming at an even rate, she may as well stay at home where she was comfortable.

She was early. The doctor had warned them that twins rarely went full-term. Her due date was still a few weeks away, but the babies were healthy. Her last appointment had verified that, so while she was scared of what was to come, she wasn't worried about the babies making their entrance a little sooner than expected.

It was late January and snowy and cold outside. The longer she could hold off going out there, the better. To keep her mind off of what was happening inside her body, she'd putter around the house nesting, and when her contractions became too much, she'd tell Erik and they'd head to the hospital.

Easy, peezy.

Only it wasn't. As Bri took care of Min throughout the day, the waves of tightness in her abdomen became stronger, some even taking her breath away for a moment. Once, she had to brace herself on the counter and breathe through it. Swaying her hips seemed to help, so she did that, a slow dance to the music of her laboring body.

She thought the time was coming to go, but then her body settled, and she didn't have another for fifteen minutes.

A few more hours passed. The pains became more and more regular, and Bri knew. It was finally time. She went to find
~~~

Erik in his office.

"Hon. It's time to go to the hospital. The babies are coming. My contractions are eight minutes apart."

His gaze shot up from his computer. "What? You're sure?"

Bri nodded and breathed. "Yup. We need to go. Now."

And then he caught up with exactly what she'd said. "Wait. Eight minutes? Isn't that fast? Doc said first babies can take hours."

"It *has* been hours." Bri shrugged at his confused look. "I've been in labor most of the day."

"Why the hell didn't you say anything?"

Another wave hit. "Can we discuss this later? I'd like to leave now. Unless you want to deliver the babies *here*."

"Right. Right." Erik jumped up and busily started collecting the things they'd need. He grabbed her hospital bag from the hall closet. Hustled Min into her coat and hat. Checked to make sure he had his phone and keys, and got everyone out the door.

They made a quick detour to drop Min at Helen's, and they were on their way.

Three torturous contractions later, he pulled into the Emergency entrance. He helped her out of the car and walked her into the hospital. Nurses were right there with a wheelchair to whisk her away, Erik hot on their heels.

They were taken straight up to Labor and Delivery and checked in. Within a short time, Bri was in a bed and hooked up to monitors. Some took her vitals, and some tracked the babies.

Through it all, Erik was right there, holding her hand and coaching her through it.

"You need to call Kaia." Bri panted out as the muscles of her uterus squeezed tight. As it passed, she continued. "Jayme. Mac. Parents."

"I did." Erik brushed her hair back and wiped the sweat from her forehead. "Group text took care of all of them."

She nodded. "Good. Good. Oooohhhhh," She moaned as another came. She clamped down on Erik's hand with hers.

Bri didn't know how much more she could take. Each contraction tore through her with an intensity stronger than the last one. She'd watched the videos and read the books, but she'd had no idea it would hurt this bad. In truth, she'd kind of thought all the other mothers were just wimps. But now she knew better. It felt like her hips and pelvis were being pulled in opposite directions.

Kaia arrived to offer her support.

"Hi, Momma." Kaia held her hand. "I won't ask how you're doing. That's a silly question."

Bri stared up at her best friend and shook her head. "I don't think I can do this."

"Yes, you can. Remember what you're doing it *for*. Concentrate on those babies. Soon, you'll have them both in your arms."

Bri nodded, fighting past the pain and keeping her mind on the ultimate prize. Her babies.

She was focusing on her breathing when Jayme flew in. Bri took a deep, cleansing breath and let it out.

"Hey. How ya doing?" Jayme approached the side of her bed.

Bri pasted on a smile. "I won't lie—it's rough. It hurts like a bitch, actually. But, when this is finally over, I'll have my two babies to show for it."

With the next wave, a stronger, pressure-filled pain took her. Bri felt it deep inside and her body took over. "Ooohhh, I need to push."

Bri looked up at Erik and saw his eyes go round in panic. He turned and caught Jayme's gaze. "Can you go tell the nurse?"

"Yeah." Jayme was already moving towards the door. "I'm on it."

She escaped the room as Bri cried out as the next pain swelled.

Bri lost track of time then. She got the sense of people

rushing in and doing things around her, but she was busy concentrating on bringing her babies into the world.

Suddenly, the deep voice of her doctor was there.

"Okay, Bri. Let's do this. On the next contraction, I want you to bear down. Erik, you hold her leg up and back. The nurse will take care of the other."

Bri felt her belly hardening again.

"All right. Here we go. Bri, take a deep breath and push for a count of ten. Release it and do it again. Dad, help her count."

Bri did as she was told and pushed through the pressure. When Erik got to ten, she blew air out, gathered it back in, and bore down again.

"Good job. The head is moving down. Great pushes. Okay. Rest for a minute and we'll do it again."

For the next half hour, Bri pushed and breathed and rested. And pushed and breathed and rested. All of her lady-bits were throbbing and burning as they stretched to allow her child to be born.

On a final push and scream, the first of her twins made its debut. And immediately cried out in protest, none too happy about its arrival.

But Bri laughed and cried hearing those wails. She looked up at Erik, and tears shimmered in his blue eyes as well.

"You did it." He kissed her gently.

She leaned into him to gather some of his strength for the next round.

Bri turned her attention to the doctor between her legs. "What is it?"

He stood and laid the baby on her stomach. "It's a boy! Congratulations, Mom and Dad!"

Bri pulled him close and kissed his tiny head. Erik bent to see his first son.

"He's beautiful. Just like his momma."

Before she was ready, Bri had to give up her son to the nurse to prepare for his twin. Contractions began again in earnest.

"Let's get this second one born and reunite these boys." The doctor smiled at Bri. "One more, Bri. You got this."

She nodded, bore down, and five minutes later, had her second son on her chest.

24

Just like the scene straight out of Bri's dream, she was sitting in her hospital bed, holding both of her babies.

But this time, they were boys instead of girls. And she wasn't alone. Erik, Kaia, and Jayme were all there with her. At least, Jayme *had* been there. Bri briefly wondered what had happened to her. But then her attention was drawn back to the infants in her arms and all other thoughts floated away.

She gazed down at her sons and felt a wave of love wash over her. Identical, they both had barely-there blond peach fuzz on their heads. At just over five pounds apiece, both had two arms, two legs, ten fingers, ten toes. And a cougar, sleeping now, that would be their companion for a lifetime.

Erik reached down to take one of the babies. He sat on the edge of her bed and leaned in to kiss her. He'd been doing that a lot.

Bri grinned up at him.

Just then the door opened, and Jayme and Mac walked in.

Kaia rose from the chair she'd been sitting in and went to Mac.

"You got here."

"Yeah, just as things were heating up. I figured I'd wait in the hall with Jayme."

Kaia kissed him and beamed up at him. "They're beautiful."

Jayme came over to see her nephews. "Wow. Look at you

guys. One for each of you." She took her phone out and snapped a couple of pictures.

"So..." She slid her phone back into her pocket. "Dying here. What do we have?"

"Two identical boys," Erik said proudly.

"Congratulations, guys. Do you have names picked out yet?" Erik smiled down at Bri.

They'd talked about this for months. Finding the right names had been important to her. One she'd known right from the beginning, and Erik had agreed. If the babies were boys, one would be named for Kaia's brother.

Bri felt tears sting her eyes. She looked to Kaia and her still-big baby bump, and then to the baby in Erik's arms. "This is Andrew, after Jace."

A small sob caught Kaia's breath, and her eyes filled. "Oh, Bri. That's so wonderful. I love it. Thank you."

"I was hoping you'd say that." She smiled at her best friend and then finished the introductions. "And this is Mason."

"Any special meaning behind that name?" Jayme asked.

Bri and Erik laughed. "No. Just the only other name we could agree on."

Watery chuckles went around the room.

Bri looked at each person in turn. Each and every one of them had become a member of her family, and she theirs. Even though she didn't possess an inner cougar, she was just as much a part of the clan as any who did.

Never again would she have to suffer alone.

She and Kaia, sisters of the heart for so long, now shared a bond like no others. They'd love and raise their shifter children together with the mates they adored.

Bri had always heard the saying, "Good things come to those who wait." Bri hadn't known she'd been waiting, but good things had definitely come her way. More than she ever could have dreamed of.

She glanced up at Erik and saw the light in his blue eyes as he stared lovingly down at her.

This was the man who would walk the floor with her at night when their child was fussy. The man who would be by her side to teach and train a new generation of shifters to be strong, independent adults. This was the man with whom she'd share every adventure life had to give, and this was the man she would grow old with.

And she couldn't wait.

Misha McKenzie has been an avid reader since learning how at four years old. Countless books later, she still loves to immerse herself into the lives of the people within those pages. After graduating high school, she went on to earn a degree in Business Administration, married her high school sweetheart, and had two beautiful boys. At thirty years old, while working as an office manager for a construction company, a family of witches began to brew, and The Magic of the Heart Series was born.

9 781942 318538